To everyone who wants to escape the life they've found themselves in; to the people wondering if there's a better way to do things.

Have faith in yourself and you'll find out who you really are and what you're looking for.

And don't let anything or anyone stop you.

In the end, it was Miriam and Paul who showed me the way.

Anne Grange, May 2014

Thanks to Christopher Crewe for his tireless editing, Rachael Dixon for the beautiful cover artwork, Susie Morley for the Ramraid Press Logo, Kirsty Chamberlain for putting up with this novel in its many incarnations since 1995, Bill Grange for assistance with graphic design, my mum, David Harmer and the Writing MA at Sheffield Hallam University, Sheffield Novelists Writers' Group, everyone at Bearded Theory festival, Oxfam Festival Stewarding and the whole Oxfamily!

To contact Anne, email: **outsideinsidenovel@gmail.com**

Twitter: anne_grange

Facebook Page: Outside Inside

Professional writing, editing, and teaching: wildrosemarywritingservices.wordpress.com

OUTSIDE
INSIDE

ANNE GRANGE

CHAPTER ONE
DERBY CITY CENTRE, FRIDAY 5TH MAY 2000

As Miriam started to type, a cartoon paperclip with disembodied eyes appeared on the screen and bounced along the bottom of the monitor. An animated light bulb popped out of it. Miriam pitied its pathetic existence, doomed to give useless computer advice forever. A message appeared inside its speech bubble: 'It looks like you're writing a letter.'

'No, I'm bungee jumping off the Eiffel Tower,' Miriam said, out loud.

Clare Price stopped tapping her peach-coloured fake nails on her keyboard and stared at Miriam. They had worked at neighbouring desks for almost two years. When Miriam wrote memos on the back of her hand, or drew surreal doodles during a boring phone call, Clare stared. If Miriam accidentally borrowed one of Clare's pens and chewed the end of it, Clare threw the pen in the bin as if it were carrying the plague.

'Talking to yourself is the first sign of madness,' Clare said. She trundled out stock phrases in response to everything that Miriam did.

'I'm talking to the paperclip.'

Clare sprayed a cloud of perfume around her desk for the second time that morning, as if she was trying to create a scented barrier between their desks. Miriam's eyes watered as she fought the urge to cough. Clare claimed that the perfume was expensive but Miriam reckoned it smelled like the air-freshener in the toilets.

The clock in the corner of the computer screen was crawling this morning. Miriam wished she was walking along the narrow cobbled lane towards the Flying Horse Café. She felt normal among the rainbow murals and the colourful posters but lunch was still a long time away.

She tried to get rid of the paperclip but it refused to budge from the screen. The computer groaned with the effort of processing information. Miriam knew how it felt. She stared at her notebook, trying to decipher the meeting notes she'd written earlier. Miriam hadn't been able to concentrate – she couldn't stop thinking about that stupid argument with her mum. That bereavement group were brain-washing her. Miriam had gone there once, out of curiosity, but Mum went to the meetings twice a week. The people there weren't religious maniacs, just lonely people clinging together because it was too hard to accept reality. But, last night, Mum had come home saying that Ruth had died because she was immoral. Mum hadn't listened to sense, she was so wrapped up in her warped little world.

Miriam remembered lying awake, waiting for Ruth to come back from her date with Mike. Ruth had normally come back on time – her midweek curfew was eleven o'clock – a freedom that Miriam could only dream of. When she heard the noisy engine of Mike's old Mini coming up the hill, it was her cue to close her book and switch off the light. When she heard Ruth's murmured goodbye and the rattle of her key in the front door, she drifted into a contended sleep, imagining being seventeen and in love.

☆

The doorbell woke Miriam from her uneasy dreams.

'She'd better have a bloody good explanation. That Mike's going to get a nasty shock if he thinks…'

Miriam had never heard her father sound so angry, not even when she was little and she'd scribbled on his steam train books. He walked heavily across the hall and thumped down the stairs. The glowing green numbers on Miriam's alarm clock said 03:15. Maybe Ruth had been at a wild party. On a Tuesday night?

She twitched open her curtains. There was a police car on the drive, instead of Mike's Mini. Had Ruth been arrested? Her heart gave an alarming lurch. Miriam switched on her bedside lamp and listened. They spoke too quietly for Miriam to make out what was being said. She sat so still, she could feel her veins throbbing.

Mum ran across the landing and downstairs. She started screaming. Miriam got out of bed and followed her.

The police were in the hall: a man with a woman who had a blonde perm spiralling from underneath her cap. Dad looked vulnerable in his threadbare towelling dressing gown. His arms were awkwardly wrapped around Mum. She was trying to struggle out of his grasp, her face red and crumpled. Dad held his position like a shop dummy.

He moved his eyes to look at Miriam. Mum didn't seem to notice she was there. The police officers curled up the edges of their closed mouths, staring at the Laura Ashley wallpaper. No one spoke. Miriam hugged herself, trying not to shiver. The front door was still wide open, light from the hall escaping into the garden. She could smell hyacinths in the cold, still air. The other houses were dark and silent.

Dad reached out and put his hand on her shoulder. It felt heavy and lifeless.

'They were driving back from the pub. A four-wheel-drive crashed into them – head-on. Someone called an ambulance but…'

His words echoed in the hallway.

Miriam grabbed dad's hand for balance. It felt like a trapdoor had opened up where the floor should be. She stared at her parents' wedding photo, wanting to scream at the happy young people from twenty years ago, warn them that something terrible was going to happen.

The policeman looked at Miriam.

'We're very sorry,' he said.

Mum's knees buckled and she started to fall. Dad gripped her tightly, an automatic reaction. His face was blank.

'You should sit down. I'll make a cup of tea,' the policewoman suggested. She put her arm gently across Dad's back.

Miriam ran upstairs. She sat on the landing, listening to the voices in the living room. She pulled her nightdress over her knees, the one with tiny pink hearts that Ruth had given her. She stared at the hearts until her tears stopped her from seeing them.

☆

'You look like you need to get something off your chest,' Bella said.

Miriam looked up. Her cheekbones were aching from leaning her head on her hands. Bella stared at her from behind the counter. She must have looked strange – staring at the table, ignoring her lunch. Miriam's head felt heavy, as if it would crash onto the table if she didn't hold it up.

'It's alright. I'm fine,' Miriam snapped. She pushed away her almost uneaten vegetable pasty. The other customers were staring at her now.

'You'll feel better after you've told me all about it.'

Bella sat down opposite Miriam, giving her a fresh mug of tea. The wooden chair creaked as she sat down. There was flour on her striped apron and her round, freckled arms. Her husband Alan silently rolled his eyes at another outbreak of impromptu counselling while there was still a queue of customers at the counter.

There was no escape.

'Okay, then,' Miriam sighed. 'My mum says that God punished Ruth and Mike because they'd been having sex before marriage. How can she even think that?'

Bella was the only person she could talk to like this but today Miriam couldn't handle the stress. She wished she'd bought a sandwich and an NME and listened to Ruth's Walkman in the park.

Bella shrugged. 'Ignore her.'

'If I try to talk about Ruth, it's like I'm trying to dig up her grave – and she hasn't even got one.' Miriam remembered the ugly crematorium with its cheap carpet and worn-out hymn books. The thought of all those grieving relatives holding them had made her feel queasy. Why had Ruth had an old lady's funeral? The coffin had slid behind the pleated curtain with a wheezy organ playing in the background. They should have asked Miriam what music Ruth would have wanted.

Miriam sipped her tea. 'But it's all Mum talks about. It's all she thinks about! It was six years ago...'

'Grief's a process. It can take a long time. When I...'

'Why can't she accept that it was just an accident? It was unfair, that's all. Ruth wanted to live abroad and do so much stuff.'

'I know it's miserable for you.' Bella's voice was low and soothing. The smooth curve of apron over her bust reminded Miriam of a pigeon. 'But she's still hurt.'

'She's so scared of something bad happening that she won't let me go anywhere, do anything. I should be at college, instead of this stupid…' Miriam caught sight of her watch. It was nearly two. She pushed her chair back, put her jacket on and grabbed her bag from under the table.

She glared enviously at a bunch of girls, students, chatting in the corner of the café. They often hung out here, talking about boys and music, books and nights out. Miriam sometimes listened to their conversations, pretending to read one of the alternative magazines that Bella kept on the windowsill. Sometimes, Miriam felt that they were laughing at her. The truth was they probably didn't notice her.

'Don't go back to work.' Bella took her hand. 'Stay here and talk.'

'You don't understand what Mr Brown's like…' Miriam felt dangerously raw.

'Forget Mr Brown. I could do with someone to get my accounts in order. Only part time but you could go to college as well.'

'Nice idea but Mum would never let me. She thinks the Mercia Building Society is wonderful. Just because she works there…'

'Take your pasty at least. I'll warm it up in the microwave.'

'I've got no time.'

She took Miriam's plate back into the kitchen.

Miriam waited helplessly. To avoid eye contact with anyone, she stared at an advert on the notice board: *"Female housemate wanted for feminist residence. Must like cats. Non-smoking vegetarian preferred."* There was a hand-drawn picture of a sleeping cat in one corner and the feminist circle and cross symbol in the other corner, to deter cat-hating men from answering.

Bella brought her pasty back in a paper bag, its sides shiny with grease.

'I'm serious about the job,' Bella called, as Miriam rushed

out of the door. She slipped the hot pasty into the inside pocket of her denim jacket.

Miriam hurried back to work. She forced herself up the stairs into the open-plan office. She raced down the aisle of patterned carpet, slung her ID card around her neck, threw her jacket on the back of her chair and sat down in front of her computer, trying to remember what she had been doing before lunch.

Clare Price pointed at Miriam.

'Ugh - what's that?' she shrieked. Miriam thought it was one of her bitchy comments but she followed Clare's peach talon and stared at her chest. There was a large stain on her pale blue polyester blouse. The grease made the material transparent; she could see the pink lace of her bra.

'Shit.' The whole office stared as she ran to the toilets, covering her chest with her hands.

Miriam frantically scrubbed at her blouse with a soapy wad of toilet paper. It disintegrated in her hand. She leaned over the sink and splashed water on the material until it was soaking. Her breathing grew ragged and shallow. She hoped she wasn't about to start crying. She hadn't wanted the stupid pasty anyway. She stretched her blouse underneath the hand dryer, trying to get her breathing under control.

Her blouse no longer clung to her skin but it was creased and dirty. Miriam automatically tucked it into her knee-length navy skirt and smoothed it with her hands. She caught sight of herself doing it. She looked like her mother, obsessed with being neat and tidy, pushing everything under the surface. Grabbing handfuls of material, she pulled the blouse out of her skirt again. Her skin prickled.

Miriam inspected herself in the mirror. She wanted to change everything: the limp, mousy hair pushed behind her ears, her insipid indoor skin and unsmiling lips, the skirt and blouse that were always uncomfortable. Her mother bought her middle-aged clothes with elasticated waists and dull colours. Mum wouldn't have been seen dead in them a few years ago, let alone forcing Miriam to wear them.

Miriam had found some great retro stuff in charity shops but when she came downstairs in a short skirt or a tight top, her mum started the guilt-trip straight away. She said she'd let Ruth get away with too much and look at what had happened. That bereavement group must have twisted her mind. Miriam couldn't make her see it. It had got to a stage where defying Mum wasn't worth the stress it caused.

On the night she died, Ruth had smiled at her reflection. She'd been so confident at sixth-form college, pleased with the style she'd created for herself: the red miniskirt, the ripped black lacy vest, fishnet tights and Doc Martens. Tough, quirky images of rock stars stared down from her bedroom walls. Miriam had stared at their tattoos and smeared lipstick as Ruth had applied her eye-liner.

'Are you alright?' The new Mortgage Advisor stared at her. Miriam wished she'd used the disabled toilet, where she could have hidden for hours. Miriam nodded, biting her lip. She walked back to her desk.

Clare's chair was empty. She'd probably invented an excuse to go and chat to her boyfriend in Human Resources. Miriam sat down and opened the spreadsheet she'd been working on. The computer screen gave her a headache, like she'd been eating too much ice cream. She should have listened to Bella and stayed in the café. Miriam couldn't stop thinking about Ruth now. She remembered the feel of Ruth's hair in her hands as she'd brushed it and tied it into a high ponytail.

Miriam calculated the total for a column of figures but they didn't add up to the right number. She would have to check every cell individually. That would serve her right for not concentrating. The sun shone on her monitor, making her squint. The old guy who'd worked there for years would give her a dirty look if she tried adjusting the blinds.

Clare returned. Miriam tried to ignore her. Then she felt the sudden pressure of a man's hand on her shoulder.

'Miriam!'

She shuddered, hating the way Mr Brown always crept up on her before he spoke. He said her name too slowly, chewing it like toffee.

'Come into my office. I want you to write a letter.' *Write your own letter*, she wanted to say. She grabbed her pen and notebook. Clare looked so smug that Miriam wanted to stab her with her Biro.

Mr Brown's hair was slicked down with Brylcreem but it had turned into a comb-over, not quite concealing the shiny patch at the back of his head. He looked pathetic, even though he acted like a big-shot. That office gossip about his wife running off was probably true.

Everyone called his office the goldfish bowl. It was partitioned from the rest of the room with a glass wall. The blinds were drawn tight against the bright sunlight. He flicked his hand to indicate that Miriam should sit down. She perched on a fake leather chair. Mr Brown sat with his back to her, checking his e-mails. Miriam stuck her tongue out at him.

She chewed her pen and stared at a framed poster of a running polar bear with the slogan "Motivation Comes From Within" over Mr Brown's desk.

Mr Brown spun his chair around and wheeled himself far too close to Miriam.

'Dear Mr Trebor,' he said. She started writing immediately,

to avoid another lecture about school-leavers with no common sense. 'At the Mercia Building Society, we pride ourselves on our individual approach to business banking. I would be delighted to approve your loan application, pending further details.'

He leaned towards Miriam. She could smell his sour coffee breath as he pulled the notebook out of her hands. She turned her face away.

He shoved her notes back at her. 'I thought you'd learned shorthand? This is just scribble.'

She glared at him for a second and then stared at the polar bear poster. She imagined a real polar bear appearing in the office and tearing Mr Brown's head off. It still wouldn't help him to understand motivation.

'Does it matter? As long as I can write a decent letter?'

'I'm not happy with your attitude, young lady.'

'I can't learn shorthand instantly, can I?'

'Don't look at me like that.' He stared at her. His mouth twitched, as if he was trying to smile. 'I just want to help you to complete your placement successfully. Your mother persuaded me that you had potential, Miriam.' His voice had that sticky toffee sound again.

'Clare tells me that you were late back from your lunch again, Miriam. It's becoming a habit.' He put his hand on her knee. Her body tried to shrink away from his touch but she was trapped.

'Clare loves telling tales. She doesn't understand.'

Mr Brown touched Miriam's wrist. His fingers were sweaty. His lips were wet under his gingery moustache.

'You could be making so much more of yourself. Clare's just concerned about your productivity. Her prospects are excellent.'

Miriam backed away from him but now he was clutching her hand.

'God, what do you want me to do?' What did Clare have to put up with, just to keep in his good books?

'Respect the rules of this office. And make yourself more presentable. You'll never get ahead in business looking like that.'

He let go of her hand and reached forwards. Miriam tensed up. His fingers brushed against her breasts through her stained blouse. His hand hovered over the polyester material, as if it was stuck there by static. Mr Brown's legs were splayed apart.

She could let Mr Brown treat her like this and be guaranteed a job at the Mercia Building Society when she got her NVQs.

Miriam had tried complaining to Mum but she hadn't listened. She still thought that Mr Brown was a dynamic financial whiz-kid. She had worked with him ten years ago.

Now he was just a sad old man who touched up young girls. Miriam realised that she had a choice.

She stood up and shoved his hand away. Mr Brown looked surprised. Miriam pushed her shoulders back and looked him straight in the eye. He looked away.

Miriam took her ID card off and threw it at him. A warm glow rushed into her cheeks.

'Get stuffed!' she shouted.

'Miriam...' he said. He stood up and put his hand on her shoulder.

She pushed him away as hard as she could. He lost his balance and toppled back into his chair. It rolled backwards, crashing into his desk with some force. The polar bear picture fell off the wall and smashed on top of his monitor.

Mr Brown crumpled in the chair, his hands shielding his head.

Miriam ran out of his office. Her colleagues peered over their flimsy partitions like a family of startled meerkats.

'What the hell are you doing?' Clare asked, her hands on her hips.

'Leaving.' Miriam grabbed her bag.

Clare blocked her exit. Other people were moving towards her. Was she trapped?

Miriam barged Clare out of the way. She dodged under someone's arm, across the office and down the stairs. She needed her ID card to get out of the building but there was no going back. Miriam smashed the fire alarm button. The door automatically released and she escaped onto the street with the alarm ringing in her ears.

CHAPTER TWO
BELPER, DERBYSHIRE – FRIDAY 5TH MAY 2000

Paul watched the landmarks of the A6 through the windscreen of the lorry. There were some new houses where a factory had been but the way the road intertwined with the river and the hills was so familiar that it felt dreamlike.

He remembered sitting on the bus as a little kid, feeling safe as Mum pointed at the cows and sheep. As a seventeen-year-old, he'd driven too fast around the road's curves, thrilled by his new speed and independence. He wished he could stay in this lorry forever but it was already on the final stretch of road on the outskirts of the town, weaving around parked cars.

The lorry stopped at a pelican crossing. A young mum pushed a buggy across the road.

'This Belper?' the driver asked.

'Yeah.'

'You'd better get out here then, mate.'

'Cheers.'

Paul opened the door and jumped down from the cab. A jolt spread from the soles of his feet to his spine as he made contact with the ground.

He walked past the hospital, the old paint factory and the supermarket. He turned into the High Street and passed the off-licence where he'd tried to buy beer with his mates when they were fourteen. He'd snogged a girl down that alleyway. Her face was a blur but the touch of her lips was clear in his memory, the way he'd had to stoop because she was much shorter than him.

As he passed the Mason's Arms, he overtook an old lady struggling up the hill with a tartan shopping trolley. She half-smiled in recognition but he stared at the ground.

He kept walking until he reached the cul-de-sac of red brick council houses where he'd grown up. This was the corner where he'd crashed his BMX trying to do a wheelie. Paul noticed changes to the first few houses. He wondered who lived here now.

Paul broke into a clammy sweat when he saw his parents' house. The mundanity jolted him – the Creosoted fence and neatly mown lawn. The front border was crowded with bright bedding plants. An ageing but well-polished red Fiesta was parked beneath the car port.

He sniffed his armpits and hoped he still looked recognisable. He didn't even know if anyone was in, or even if this was still their house. Paul didn't know what he'd do if his dad answered the door.

Taking a deep breath, he stepped up to the front door. He could hear the faint murmur of the television. He pressed the doorbell. Its tinny noise made the nerves in his arms and legs tense up as he fought his compulsion to run.

A slim, well-preserved woman opened the door. She stared at him blankly.

'Mum – it's me…'

He remembered worry lines spreading around her eyes; split ends making her hair frizzy. Now her hair was elegantly cropped and her skin looked almost unlined under her make up.

'Paul?'

She reached out to touch him, as if she didn't believe he could be real. His mum took his hands and studied them in minute detail, as if she was reading his fortune in reverse, searching for clues of what had happened to him, staring at the dirt underneath his fingernails. She flipped his left hand round and saw the scars on his wrist. She quickly pushed back his shirt sleeve.

Mum let go of him. She sank heavily onto the low upholstered chair next to the phone. She stared at him, eyes wide. Paul didn't understand her expression. Her chest rose and fell quickly.

'Get me some water.'

Paul dropped his backpack onto the carpet. In the kitchen, he grabbed a pint glass from the cupboard. As he stood at the sink, he gazed at his father's work overalls flapping wildly on the washing line in the back garden, the trouser legs caught in a wigwam shaped trellis of sweet peas. Paul remembered being small, helping his dad to plant seeds and water them with his little plastic watering can.

The glass was overflowing into the sink. Paul realised that he was standing in his parents' house, as if the last seven years hadn't happened.

He carried the glass carefully into the hall. Mum grabbed it with both hands like a thirsty child and started gulping water. Paul noticed the new stair carpet. It had cream and beige swirls. The lounge door hung open. Soothing electronic music and a bossy sounding woman's voice drifted into the hall.

'Your bottom can start to sag as you get older, which is a very sad state of affairs. Yoga can hoist it up for you easily and simply. Try doing this movement as part of your routine every single day...' Mum's feet were bare, with pale pink varnish on her toenails.

'I thought you were dead.'

She put the glass on the telephone table and stood up. She wrapped her arms around him so tightly that his ribs felt crushed. He kissed the top of her head. Her hair smelled of fruity shampoo. She pulled away and examined him.

'I waited for so long. I knew you'd got mixed up in that -

15

thing your friends did.' Paul pressed his fists onto his legs, to stop himself from shaking.

'I had to protect them. I couldn't contact you.'

'The police found your car, with all your things in it. I told them you'd called - you'd got exam nerves and gone to live in Wales – you were always going on about that place with the windmills and solar panels.'

Paul felt a tiny surge of relief.

'Why did you cover up for me?'

She pulled a tissue from her tracksuit pocket and dabbed her eyes, smearing her mascara.

'Your dad doesn't know about the others.'

'Dad thinks I'm in Wales too?'

'He still thinks you ran off because of the argument.'

'I did – to begin with. I'm not scared of him, anyway.'

Tears squeezed out of Paul's eyes. He hung his head. He didn't want her to see him crying. She touched the faded scar on his cheek and wiped his tears gently with her thumb.

'Where have you been living?' She dabbed at her eyes with her tissue again. 'Why have you come back?'

'It's your birthday today, isn't it?'

She nodded.

'I can't believe I'm fifty.'

Paul rummaged in his backpack and pulled out a tired-looking Chocolate Orange. 'I'm sorry - it's not much.'

She shivered as he put it in her hands. Her eyes narrowed.

'I had seven years of inventing phone calls from you. I forged Christmas cards from you every year. But you're alive. That means more than…'

Paul swallowed.

'I'm sick of hiding. It's time to…'

'Please stay – even if it's just for tonight.'

'I don't want to see Dad.'

'I know he still feels bad about it.' She touched the scar on his cheek.

'He never apologised. Why do you put up with him?' His father's temper had always been volatile. Mum used to make Paul and Simon tip-toe around after Dad's night-shifts. One Saturday morning, they'd been watching a cartoon on TV. Dad had thundered downstairs in his pyjamas and ripped the plug out of the wall.

'Your dad's different now.'

'He still hates me.'

'You know that's not true.'

She led Paul into the lounge. Paul hoped there wasn't any mud on the soles of his boots. He didn't want her to see the holes in his socks.

She turned the television off, stabbing the buttons on the video recorder until the tape stopped whirring.

The room was painted a pale terracotta colour. Fussy ornaments had been replaced by candles and bowls of pot-pourri. There was a round tapestry rug over the spot where he'd bled on the carpet on Boxing Day, seven years ago.

☆

The fox streaked along the bare hedgerow. Paul nudged Gary and pointed, just as it reached the woods.

Gary pulled two garden spray containers out of his bag and thrust one into Paul's hands. He faced the other hunt saboteurs. Mark gave Paul a dirty look, disguised as a smile. Paul glowed with pride at being chosen. Gary was the main organiser of the Derby hunt-sabs group.

'Right, half of you surround the woods. Split up and don't

let them see you. Everyone else – distract the hunt and stop it coming up this way.'

Gary and Paul ran towards the woods, spraying a mixture of lemon oil and water at the edge of the field to disguise the fox's scent. The frozen wheat stubble closely matched Gary's bleached spiky hair.

Paul saw something gleam in front of Gary. It was half-hidden in the tangle of last summer's grass. He grabbed Gary's army coat, making him stumble. He glared at Paul.

'What the...?'

Paul pointed at the object lying in wait in the grass. It was an old iron trap, a dull rusty colour except for its jaws. Someone had taken a long time to shine them to a silver sheen, like a shark's grin. He held his breath, not daring to move.

Gary picked up a branch lying near the hedgerow and poked it into the trap. Its hinges snapped shut, breaking the branch in two.

'That would have been my leg if you hadn't stopped me.'

'I thought those things were illegal,' Paul said.

Gary kicked the sprung trap onto its side and into the ditch.

'That wasn't meant for the fox. It was for us.' Gary's face was pale.

The hounds were closer now, barking with excitement and confusion, as the other hunt-sabs blew horns and whistles. Gary and Paul carried on spraying, taking care to run on the stubble, rather than the long grass.

Near the woods, they turned a corner. Three policemen stepped out from behind a hedge and blocked their path.

Gary stopped. He looked relaxed, as if he was about to ask the police for directions. Paul wanted to run away.

'What do I do?' Paul whispered.

'Shh. Just copy me.'

Paul hadn't been arrested before. According to Gary, trying to resist arrest or run was stupid: coming quietly with a smile on your face really wound them up.

☆

'Your parents are here,' the grey-haired policeman said. 'You can go home.' Paul had been sitting in the bare cell for two hours, with nothing to do but listen to the tuneless singing of the drunk man in the next cell.

Getting arrested didn't seem to mean much. He hadn't been charged with anything. Paul felt relieved but also vaguely cheated. They had treated him like a novelty. He'd behaved exactly the way Gary had taught him – only giving his name, date of birth, address and a polite "no comment" to everything else. They hadn't found anything incriminating in his trouser pockets – just his wallet, house keys and a half-eaten bar of Fry's Chocolate Crème – Mum had given him loads of them for Christmas because they were vegan. Was it because he wasn't eighteen yet? They'd taken Gary more seriously, treating him like a criminal, even though he was only three years older than Paul. Maybe it was because he was the leader.

The Police Station car park was harshly floodlit. It seemed very quiet outside. Paul remembered that it was Boxing Day. Most people were at home, stuffing their faces with Christmas leftovers and chocolates.

He walked towards his parents' car. His mum looked worried. Her eyes were red and swollen. Dad glared at him from the passenger seat, his beefy arms crossed on top of his beer gut, looking uncomfortable in his new Marks and Spencer jumper.

Paul felt an arm across his back. Had the Police forgotten

something? But it was Gary.

'They decided to let me out too.'

'They called my parents.'

Mum beckoned Paul impatiently.

'I'll be home in ten minutes, if I walk fast.' Gary jerked his head to indicate the direction of his flat. 'A beer and a bath – lovely.' His angular features were set in deep shadow by the darkness and the bright lights.

'I wish I didn't live with my parents – my dad, anyway.'

Gary put his hand on Paul's arm.

'Thanks for what you did earlier. I'd be in hospital if you hadn't seen that trap.'

'It was just luck.'

'No. If you hadn't had your wits about you, someone would have got hurt.'

Gary squeezed Paul tightly. He pecked him on the cheek and grinned wickedly.

Paul glanced across at the car. Dad's eyes were blazing.

'I'd better go.'

'Are you coming out on New Year's Eve? You could stay at mine afterwards - save you the taxi fare.' Gary waved as he walked out of the car park.

Paul opened the rear door of the car, prepared for big trouble.

'Hi, Mum,' he said. She just turned the key in the ignition.

'Shut up and get in,' his father grunted. Paul could smell the whisky fumes from the passenger seat. The tension between them was like an unexploded bomb.

☆

Mum parked under the car port. Fairy lights twinkled in the

front window but Paul knew that the atmosphere at home wouldn't be very festive. Dad got out slowly but slammed the door so hard it made the car rock.

Mum sighed like a deflating Lilo. Paul half-expected her to collapse onto the steering wheel from lack of air.

'I'm sorry, Mum,' he said. 'I didn't mean to get arrested – I don't know why Dad's so bothered about it.'

'Please don't make it worse, Paul.'

Paul wished he could stay in the safety of the car all night. But he was tired of creeping around his dad, when all he'd done was stand up for what he believed in.

'I'll try. But everything I do makes him angry.'

'I know. It's stupid,' she said. 'I got you some Linda McCartney sausages. You could have them with the rest of that vegetarian stuffing you had yesterday.'

'Thanks, I'm starving.'

They came in through the back door, into the kitchen. Simon was sitting at the breakfast bar, still in his McDonalds polo shirt, the half-eaten turkey in front of him. Staring at Paul, he sliced off a strip of meat with a kitchen knife and dangled it into his mouth.

'That's disgusting. Haven't you had enough of meat at work?' Paul said.

Mum got the sausages out of the freezer and turned on the grill.

'Simon, you could use a plate at least,' she said.

'What happened? Got into trouble?' Simon asked, through a mouth of turkey.

'I've been out hunt-sabbing.'

'Did you get arrested or something? So that's why Dad's on the warpath!'

Paul shrugged. He filled the kettle. Bickering with Simon in

21

here was preferable to facing his dad but he wasn't going to let himself be intimidated any longer.

☆

He pushed open the lounge door, trying not to spill his cup of tea. He was ready to make peace with his dad, even though Mum had warned him to stay out of the way.

Dad stared at a quiz show which involved the audience members getting covered in green gunge. His favourite glass was in his hand, with a large measure of his Christmas whisky.

Paul sat down on the sofa.

'Alright, Dad?'

He only got a grunt in reply.

'I'm sorry you had to pick me up from the police station. I obviously spoiled your Boxing Day a bit.'

They looked at each other – Paul wondered if his father actually understood anything about him. He was sure his dad was thinking the same – doubting that he had anything in common with his son any more.

'It's all just a bit of fun to you, isn't it?' Dad muttered.

Paul leaned back on the sofa and pretended to watch TV – a man inside an inflatable pink costume was running around throwing custard pies at people. He needed to stay composed in the face of Dad's anger.

'Your poofy little mates can get arrested every day for all I care - but not you, okay?' His words were slightly slurred.

'It's alright, Dad. I told them I was a hunt-sab at that university open day in Manchester. They were quite impressed, actually.'

'You think you're clever, don't you?'

Mum said that Dad was proud of Paul's GCSE results and

the hard work he was putting into his A-Levels, so why was he incapable of showing it? He'd given Paul his old car so that he could drive to college but Dad seemed to resent him. Paul didn't seem to belong in this family any more. *Yes, I do think I'm clever,*' Paul wanted to shout back. *Why do you hate me for it?*' But he took a deep breath and made his voice stay quiet.

'You used to say fox hunters were just a load of toffs riding around, showing off. It's cruel. I want to stop it.'

'Foxes are vermin. They used to massacre your granddad's chickens.'

'That's just their nature. It doesn't mean that they deserve to get ripped apart by a pack of hounds.'

'I don't know where you get these funny ideas from.'

'I make my own mind up about things,' Paul sighed with frustration.

'These friends of yours put ideas in your head.'

'I can think for myself, Dad. Unlike you.' Paul sipped his tea and stared at the TV screen. He knew he'd made a mistake. Dad was rising slowly out of his chair. He stood in front of Paul, his shoulders stooped. He was starting to look like an old man.

'I brought up this family in difficult times. I didn't have time to faff about like you do. I had to work. I had to put food on the table.'

Paul had wanted to make up with Dad – have a proper conversation. But they couldn't stop winding each other up. Maybe he should just go to his room and stay there until the morning.

'It didn't mean you had to switch your brain off. I know you've got one in there, Dad.' He stood up and tried to walk out but Dad blocked the space, sticking his chest out like he was squaring up for a fight in the pub.

'How dare you talk to me like that, you stuck up little…?'
He pushed Paul and knocked the cup out of his hand, spilling the tea in an arc across the carpet.

Paul punched his dad hard in the stomach. His fist sank into the soft flesh. He retracted his arm, surprised at his own anger.

Dad stared back, frozen in shock. Then his eyes flashed with rage again.

'Hit me again, like a man.'

Paul threw another angry punch. Dad grabbed his arm, mid-swing. Paul tried to break free but Dad's other fist came flying towards his face.

The powerful impact knocked Paul backwards. The base of his skull banged against the edge of the sofa.

☆

Paul opened his eyes - or tried to. His right eye socket was full of something sticky. He sat up and some of it trickled into his mouth. It tasted salty and metallic – blood. Through his left eye, he saw Dad staring at him blankly, his arms swinging by his sides. The game show was still blaring away on the TV. The whole room seemed to be spinning.

Mum burst through the lounge door. Paul pulled himself back up. Blood ran down his cheek and onto the carpet. He tried to catch the blood with his shirt. He grabbed the back of the sofa to keep himself upright.

Mum tried to put her arms around him but he shrugged her off. He took a deep breath and ran upstairs to the bathroom. He slammed the bolt home and looked in the mirror.

Half of Paul's face was covered in blood, his blond hair on the right side stained dark pink. He gripped the washbasin, trying to stay calm.

He grabbed his towel from the rail, soaked it under the tap and dabbed at his face. There was a jagged cut on his right cheekbone, oozing blood. It looked dangerously close to his eye. He soaked a wad of toilet paper with warm water and tried to clean the wound. It kept bleeding.

His parents were shouting downstairs. The front door slammed. Someone ran up the stairs.

'Paul! Let me in! Let me help you!' Mum hammered on the bathroom door. 'He's gone now.' He could hear her sobbing.

Paul got the first aid kit down from the shelf. He found a long roll of fabric plasters. He hacked off a couple of wide strips with the nail scissors that were in the box and stretched them over the cut. Immediately, the pinkish material bloomed red.

He unlocked the door. Mum gasped when she saw his face.

'I'm going to stay at Gary's. I've had enough of this,' he said.

He walked into his bedroom and got a large holdall from the bottom of his wardrobe. He stuffed it with clothes, a few tapes and his course folders.

Mum walked into the room.

'Your dad says it was an accident. He didn't mean to hurt you like that. His ring cut your cheek. He's quite shaken up.'

'I can't believe you just take his bullshit.' He felt guilty for talking to her like that but why did she always forgive him? Why didn't she leave too?

'Paul – you can't drive in this state.'

She was right. His cheek throbbed and the back of his head felt numb.

'It looks worse than it is,' he lied. He would force himself to drive slowly and steadily. 'I'll call you in the week, when *he's* back at work.'

Paul's bedroom walls were plastered with anti-hunt leaflets

and posters of bands, dominated by a huge poster of Morrissey wearing an unbuttoned chiffon shirt. That must have given Dad some ideas but if he'd looked more closely, he would have found plenty of female pin-ups. They were just a bit more tasteful than the ones in Simon's room. Paul wondered if he would see his room again. Part of him wanted to shut the door and hide but that would only be a temporary solution.

As he dragged the holdall downstairs to his car, the smoke alarm started bleeping. The veggie sausages were burning under the grill.

CHAPTER THREE
UNCLE TED

'Your uncle Ted died in February - he had a heart attack.'

It was like earlier, realising that the old boiler factory had been demolished. Paul couldn't imagine Belper without his Uncle Ted. Surely he was a permanent fixture? He'd been well-liked behind the counter of his butcher's shop and in his favourite corner of the Mason's arms, holding court with friends he'd known since childhood.

'He left you something in his Will. I told your Aunty May that I'd written to you about it.'

'Can't we just stay here and talk?'

Mum pulled on a pair of bright white trainers. Her face was determined. She marched out to the hall and grabbed a set of car keys from a hook near the phone.

'May would love to see you. And she's not well.'

Paul swung his backpack over his shoulder again. He didn't want to argue.

When he sat in the passenger seat of the Fiesta, he felt like he was a teenager again. Mum still drove with one hand permanently gripping the gear stick.

'Your dad booked a table at that posh Chinese restaurant for my birthday – the one with red fans on the ceiling. Can you believe it? Mind you, he'll still order chips.' She chattered brightly, like this was a normal situation. 'I asked May to come but she's not feeling up to it. Simon's bringing Penny – that's his wife - and the kids.'

'He's got kids?'

'Did you think everything would stay the same?' She glanced at him sadly, before driving straight across a mini-roundabout. 'Simon's a catering manager at the hospital in Derby...'

Paul had still thought of Simon wiping tables and dressing up for kids' birthday parties at the MacDonalds near the supermarket.

'Shit. I mean – that's great. He passed his college course, then?'

'He's a trained chef. You said he was too thick to get anywhere.'

'Did I?' It was a shock to realise that Simon had achieved everything he'd wanted. The only thing Paul had achieved was to stay alive. And what good was that?

'They bought a house on that new estate where the factory used to be.' She parked, mounting the pavement of a street with a small row of old-fashioned shops. 'But you always wanted to be different.'

Mum opened the car door. 'God, this doesn't feel real,' she sighed.

The window of uncle Ted's butcher's shop was covered with faded sheets of the Derbyshire Times. A flimsy "For Sale" sign flapped in the breeze. Dandelions grew in the gap between the pavement and the doorstep. The door was graffiti-tagged.

Mum walked briskly down the passage, to the back of the house. She tapped at the kitchen door.

'May! It's Julie. You'll never guess who's here.'

A hunched shape appeared behind the patterned glass. They waited while May fumbled awkwardly with the lock.

'It's a pity you're not looking a bit smarter,' Mum said.

'This is smart, for me,' Paul mumbled. Yesterday in Somerset, he'd had a full strip wash in cold water, shaved off his straggly winter beard and put on hand-washed clothes. Earlier this morning, he'd brushed his teeth in a motorway service station.

May opened the door. She had lost a lot of weight. Her

elbows stuck out at sharp angles in her cardigan. She looked like a ghostly version of his mum. Her white hair hung around her ears.

She smiled slowly as she recognised Paul.

'You've come back to see us at last!'

☆

Auntie May's dusty Victorian sideboard was crowded with faded family photos. Paul stared at them as he sipped his black tea, perched on the high-backed sofa next to his mum. She looked as if she was waiting for something important to happen, her hands folded in her lap.

Paul spotted a school photo of himself aged eight: unruly sun-bleached hair, a gap-toothed grin, his tie wonky. At the front was a newly framed holiday snap of Simon and two smiling toddlers on a beach. The room smelled musty, with a faint hint of bleach and meat.

May came back into the living room and gave him a large brown envelope, before she collapsed into an armchair, exhausted with the effort of walking. Mum looked worried. Paul worked out that May was sixty five. She should have been starting a full retirement with her husband.

'I sorted everything out for you – We knew you'd come back. He didn't want to change his Will.' May's eyes closed, her eyelids creased and fragile like paper.

A solicitor's letter addressed to Paul at his parents' address was on top of a sheaf of paper inside the envelope. He read the letter dutifully, expecting to have inherited something useless. His mouth dropped open. Uncle Ted had left Paul his van. The smell of meat seemed to grow stronger. Paul took a deep breath. He leafed thorough the other documents – the MOT certificate and his uncle's insurance details. His mum smiled at him.

'But he can't have left it to me – I refused to be a butcher.'

May laughed, a spark of Paul's indulgent auntie creeping back. 'You couldn't help it. And before you went vegetarian…'

'Vegan.' Paul corrected her.

'- you were a great help in the shop.'

Paul couldn't believe he had weighed out bags of mince and sliced bacon without understanding the misery and pain those animals had experienced.

'At least you told him what you thought,' she said. 'Not like Simon. He was the same, you know? But he acted the hard man and never admitted it.'

'Simon's done very well for himself,' Mum protested.

May nodded. 'Ted was proud of him too. But Simon's got a decent car. What's he going to do with an old butcher's van? Ted knew that Paul might want it, living in that place in Wales.' She stared at the ripped knees of Paul's trousers. 'I could mend those for you.'

'I'm alright, thanks,' Paul laughed, surprising himself.

'How long are you staying here?'

'I can't stay - I've got to get back there tonight.' He glanced at his mum, to acknowledge her conspiracy but she looked disappointed.

'Is the van ready to drive?' he asked.

May stared at the blank TV screen as if it was hypnotising her.

'He died in the van. The doctor said he had high cholesterol - told him to stop smoking. He was going to sell up this year.' Her voice was flat.

Mum stared at him fiercely, as if he'd missed his cue.

'I had a lot of respect for Uncle Ted,' Paul told her. 'I knew he was testing me at that abattoir. Made sure I saw everything. Let me make my own mind up.'

It was still fresh: the cows kicking and struggling as they were hung up by their hind legs, eyes rolling, their tongues lolling. Throats slit by white-coated slaughter men, as they chatted casually to Uncle Ted about Derby County's poor performance in the First Division. Paul bolted outside and threw up his chocolate cereal on the concrete floor. The slaughter men laughed. His uncle had been kind but disappointed as he drove home. Ted had already explained to Paul that if he didn't want to become his apprentice, he would sell the shop when he retired. But on the bright side, Uncle Ted would be able to buy the apartment on the Costa del Sol that he and May had always dreamed of.

Paul had gulped fresh air from the van's open window, knowing that he would never eat meat again.

The key had to be turned in the ignition several times before the engine started. Paul wrestled the gear-stick into reverse with a grinding clunk. The engine roared unhappily as he tried to get the stiff pedals to biting point and he lurched backwards, relieved the van hadn't shot into the garage wall. Aunty May had given Mum the keys for the lock-up. She said she felt too poorly to leave the house.

Facing forwards, at the edge of the pavement, he put the hand-brake on and jumped down from the driver's seat. Mum pulled down the garage door and locked it.

He pointed to the windscreen.

'It's taxed until next January.'

She grinned. The wind tousled her hair, making her look

young and natural. He could hardly believe that she was fifty.

'That's good. Promise me you'll get the insurance sorted out too. I would have done it if I knew you were coming back.'

Paul shrugged.

'Your dad could get you a job at the factory,' she said.

The idea of making industrial hand cleaner for a living suddenly seemed like a state of blissful normality. Paul hesitated, imagining his dad walking into the living room tonight and seeing him sitting there; the gruff but heartfelt reunion, eating bean-curd in the Chinese restaurant while his dad tucked into chips and spare ribs.

'I can't. I've got to get back.'

'To what?'

'I've got friends, Mum. I'm not completely...'

'You're doing this to spite yourself, aren't you? I know the real reason why you ran away. I always hoped there was a chance that you weren't involved.'

Paul couldn't bear to look at her. The hills on the skyline seemed to glare at him.

'When you came round that time – and Gary made soup - the bomb was under the table.'

The colour drained from her face.

'They both seemed so nice – I thought you were safe.'

'We didn't mean to hurt anyone.'

'How did they drag you into it?' He saw tears in her eyes but she kept her voice steady.

'We promised to protect each other. I've told you too much already.'

'They called Gary evil in the news. I didn't want to believe it.'

The tears spilled down her cheeks. She ran towards her car, nearly tripping on a hole in the tarmac, and fumbled with the lock.

Paul stared blankly as she drove off, a cloud of exhaust fumes hanging in the air.

CHAPTER FOUR
ST PETER'S STREET

Miriam ran up the busy street, not daring to look over her shoulder. Everyone from the office would be waiting in the car park until the fire service came, even though they all knew there wasn't a fire. What if someone was chasing her? She slowed her pace as she walked into British Home Stores and took a winding route around the racks of clothing. She slipped out of the other side of the shop, into the indoor shopping centre and wandered without thinking where she was going. As long as she kept moving, they wouldn't be able to find her.

Her brain was overcrowded: the moment when she'd pushed Mr Brown looped in her head like a clip from a low-budget action movie. She tried to force her thoughts into some kind of logical order. What was she going to do now? She might be arrested. She couldn't go back home – it was Mum's day off. Mr Brown was probably on the phone to her already. The only option was to run away. She'd created the perfect excuse.

Relief hit her like a tidal wave. She stopped walking and laughed. Passers-by stared at her strangely. She didn't care. In that moment of anger in Mr Brown's office, she had taken control of her life and she couldn't stop now.

But what was she going to do? Where was she going to go? It didn't even matter. She had worked for almost two years, without being allowed to spend her wages. She had a ready-made escape fund. Maybe she would go to the railway station, stick a finger on the map and go there, wherever she fancied, for as long as she wanted.

Miriam found a cash machine and withdrew two hundred pounds. She wanted to fan the notes out in her hand, to know that it was hers and she could do what she liked with it but she stuffed it into her purse and clutched the shoulder strap of her handbag tightly.

She walked into Primark and grabbed a multi-coloured pack of pants, some stripy knee-high socks, a couple of plain t-shirts, a tight black top and a pair of combat trousers. She didn't want to queue for the changing room, so she bought the trousers in a size too big, just to be sure.

Miriam bought bright red hair dye. She imagined herself with shiny pillar-box coloured hair, people turning their heads to look. She wanted clothes that made people look at her. For now, she just needed a disguise.

Emerging from the shopping centre, the spring sunshine made her blink. She shivered in her polyester blouse. The breeze was cold. She remembered that her jacket was still on the back of her chair in the office. Her mum had chosen it anyway.

Miriam nipped into the Oxfam shop where she sometimes browsed, flicking through books and old records in hope of finding something – she didn't know what - a piece of Ruth? She couldn't resist a last look at their retro rail. She came out of the shop with a fluffy purple jumper and a long A-line skirt with big turquoise flowers. The handles of her carrier bags started to make a groove in her hands.

In the outdoor shop, she unhooked a green medium-sized backpack from the rack and took it straight to the counter.

'Camping trip?' asked the friendly grey-haired shopkeeper. She stared at him.

'Yeah, I suppose so,' she said. Maybe she would need more of this stuff. She picked up a sleeping bag and a pocket torch. A rail of German army-surplus parka coats distracted her. Ruth had saved her up her pocket money for one when she was fifteen. Mum had been totally bemused about her enthusiasm for a second-hand coat. Ruth had drawn her favourite band logos all over it in marker pen and her friends had copied her. But after a couple of years, her musical tastes had changed and she'd been embarrassed to wear it. Miriam picked one off the rail and tried it on, breathing in its familiar smell. It was too big, like Ruth's. The inner lining was soft and fleecy. The sleeves hung over her hands.

They had Docs too! They looked massive but she had to have them. Ruth had worn hers every day for years with everything from her school uniform to a vintage cocktail dress at her college Christmas party.

'Have you got any in size five?'

'Just wait a second.' The man shuffled into the back of the shop.

Miriam kicked off her flat court shoes and flicked through a tent catalogue until the man returned with a shoe box. The black Doc Martens nestled in white tissue paper. She sat on a stool and pulled on the new boots. The leather was like a stiff tube. She took a few steps across the shop. They held her up like scaffolding. She paid for everything without taking the boots off, emptied the contents of her handbag into her rucksack and asked the man to put the bag in the bin, along with her shoes. He looked surprised but she left them on the counter and thanked him nicely.

She walked up the road, to the block of toilets under the clock tower. The Ladies' seemed deserted when she got to the bottom of the steps. The floral curtains of the attendant's little room were drawn. Miriam checked her reflection in one of the highly polished sheets of metal they had instead of real mirrors. Her features were slightly distorted, stretching her mouth into a fishy shape. Apart from that, she was disappointed that she looked the same as usual, just a bit dishevelled and flushed. She was still wearing the hateful bank uniform. Miriam grabbed the blouse at the collar and pulled. The top button popped off into the sink.

Miriam opened the hair dye carton and arranged the tube of dye, the developing lotion and a sachet of conditioner on the edge of the sink. She put the plastic gloves on. She mixed the dye and started streaking her hair with it. It was dark red and dripped onto the shoulders of her blouse. The instructions said to use it all, so she squirted it onto her head, even after her hair was already slicked with it.

She checked her watch. It was nearly five. The hair dye took half an hour to develop. By the time she had chosen her destination and caught a train it might be too late to find somewhere to stay. Still, she had her sleeping bag.

A woman walked down the steps into the toilets while Miriam was wiping hair dye off the top of her ears with a hand towel. She stared at Miriam with horrified fascination, slammed the door of a cubicle and shot the bolt home. Miriam felt conspicuous now. She still had to wait for nearly twenty minutes. She took everything into a cubicle and changed into her new combat pants. They were loose at the waist – but they would have to do. She stuffed her skirt and camel-coloured tights behind the cistern.

Miriam heard the toilet flush. The taps gurgled. People would be leaving work – someone from the Mercia Building Society might see her if she wasn't careful. She needed to rinse her hair – it must be at least slightly red by now. Miriam pushed the door open. A large woman wearing an overall stood in front of the sinks, scrubbing at the red streaks that Miriam had left on the white porcelain. She turned round.

'What do you think you're doing? This is a public toilet, not a hairdressers.' She gawped at the red gunk on Miriam's head, streaking her blouse.

'Can't I just rinse it off?'

'You're not making any more mess in here. Clear off. These toilets are closed now, anyway.'

'Please?' Miriam stared at herself in the mirror behind the woman's head. She couldn't go out in public like this. Her plans were ruined. She was only two minutes' walk from the office. She felt her confidence drain away. The idea of running away seemed immature and stupid.

'If you don't leave now, I'm calling the Police.' The cleaner pulled a mobile phone out of her apron pocket, a stonily determined look on her face.

Miriam ran up the steps, her heart thumping. There were still lots of people around but they all seemed to be hurrying home. Most of the shops were shutting. It felt as if she'd been down there for hours, rather than forty minutes. She put her coat on and pulled the hood over her face. The hair dye would ruin the fluffy lining. What was she going to do? Stick her head in the river to rinse the dye off? She hoisted the rucksack onto her back and started running. Her trousers were falling down so she grabbed the waistband with both hands. She couldn't go home, not after what she'd done.

She ran the way she walked from work to the Flying Horse Café. Her feet automatically took her to the cobbled alleyway. Bella would help her. Miriam stopped outside the café window. The lights were switched off. She stood in front of the café, panting. There was a glow of light from the kitchen. They must still be clearing up. She came closer to the window and realised that Bella was sitting at one of the café tables, with a man. Lit from the back, Miriam saw them as silhouettes with a faint glow around the edges. Bella's rounded shape was unmistakeable but there was something different about her posture – leaning forwards slightly as if she was listening intently to what the man was saying. As the man spoke, he pushed dreadlocks back from his face, blond hair catching the light. He was hunched in his chair. Miriam felt guilty – she shouldn't be watching them but they seemed to be in the middle of something important.

Miriam felt a drip of hair dye on her forehead but she didn't want to interrupt them by banging on the door.

Bella stood up and disappeared into the kitchen, almost running. The man waited, with his head in his hands.

When Bella came back, she held a small white envelope. She gave it to him. Bella stood by the side of the table. The man slumped forwards, as if his spine had suddenly turned to jelly. Bella put her arm across his back, more tentatively than her suffocating, Mother-Earth hug.

Bella suddenly glanced towards the café window. Her mouth opened in horror. Miriam knocked on the window.

'It's me – Miriam! Please let me in.'

Bella unlocked the door. Miriam's hood slipped off. Bella's eyes widened with shock.

'What have you done?' she gasped.

The man stood up behind Bella. Miriam could see him properly now. The skin was stretched too tight on his face. He was tall - but too skinny. She could see the shape of his collar bone through his faded blue shirt. He stared at Miriam as if she was some kind of apparition.

'It's only hair dye,' she said, meekly.

'This is Paul,' Bella seemed keen to explain. 'He used to work in the café.'

Miriam remembered Ruth taking her to the café – the first time Miriam had visited the city centre without Mum; Ruth introducing her to the delights of record shops and alternative boutiques. Ruth was fifteen. It was the summer holiday before Miriam started secondary school. She had whispered to Miriam about the boy in the Smiths t-shirt behind the counter. Ruth was captivated by his deep blue eyes and shoulder-length blond hair. She had ordered extra drinks to make him smile at her again. Miriam had taken advantage of her sister's generosity and tried several flavours of soya milkshake. The boy behind the counter had laughed. Now Miriam stared at Paul. His eyes were blue.

☆

Bella enveloped the girl in a hug, not seeming to care that she ended up with a large smear of dye on her cheek. The girl sobbed something into Bella's shoulder. Hair dye – it wasn't blood after all – ran down her forehead. Underneath her coat, her pale blouse was covered in red stains.

'It's okay. We'll have all this cleared up in no time. Come upstairs with me.' Bella took the girl's hand and led her through the café. She paused and stared at Paul.

'Don't go anywhere.'

He nodded.

Bella took the girl into the kitchen, where Alan was washing up, not getting involved. Paul heard them going upstairs to the flat. The girl must be one of Bella's strays. Bella had an uncanny knack of picking out the customers who needed help. Paul had first come to the café a few days after his uncle had taken him to the abattoir. By the autumn, when he'd met Gary, Paul was already working here.

Paul stared at the photo of Gary in the newspaper cutting that Bella had given him. He was sure it had been doctored to create that look of menace in his eyes. It must have been taken by the police, on one of the many occasions that Gary had been arrested. He folded the clipping up, put it back in the envelope and shoved it to the bottom of his bag. His head felt numb, as if he'd stuck it in a freezer. Paul took a deep breath. Everything had changed. He totally understood why Gary had taken that decision. He wished he had the courage to do the same.

Before the girl had knocked on the window, Paul had been about to tell Bella everything, properly, the way he'd wanted to tell his mum. Maybe it was better this way. He'd come here because he'd been sure that Bella would know about Gary. She'd been close to him – he'd been one of Bella's favourite customers. Gary had discovered the café as a fresher.

It would be wrong to burden Bella – or his mum – with the knowledge of what had really happened. Let them jump to their own conclusions and get on with their lives. Why did Bella want him to wait? Maybe he should just go.

Footsteps thudded down the staircase.

'I don't want to go home and think things through,' the girl shouted. 'I can't go home – I'll get arrested.'

Paul stood up. Arrested? What had she done?

'You won't be safe.'

'I can look after myself.'

'You can't go off on your own.'

'You can't stop me.'

The girl marched back into the café, followed by Bella. Her hair had been washed and towel dried. Now it was a dark shade of red, sticking out around her face like an untidy halo. She seemed determined to storm straight out of the door, but she paused to stare at Paul again. He noticed that her rucksack still had the price label attached.

'Well, where are you going to go?' Bella asked.

'I don't know…' Miriam said. She hugged her coat in a bundle in front of her. The hood had been washed and water dripped onto the wooden floor. 'I was going to make my mind up when I got to the train station.'

'Have you ever been away from home on your own before?' Bella gave her a stern look.

'I can't go home, can I?'

Miriam gave Paul a sidelong glance.

'I think I remember you working here. My sister brought me here. Remember the milkshakes?'

Bella smiled.

'They were Paul's idea. He really helped us to get a younger crowd in here. Veggie burgers, potato wedges…'

Paul stared at Miriam. She looked too young to be arrested, the defiant look in her eyes dissolving into uncertainty. The police hadn't taken him seriously either.

'So what did you do?' he asked. 'Are you in trouble?'

'I smashed up my boss's office and set off the fire alarm,' she said. A blush spread across her cheeks.

'Criminal damage – they could charge you.'

Miriam nodded, gravely.

'Don't scare her,' Bella warned.

'I'm going, anyway.' Paul picked up his backpack. 'Thanks for earlier, Bella.'

'Where are you going?' Bella frowned. 'You shouldn't be alone.'

'There's a few of us in an old quarry near Bath.'

'You live in a quarry?' Miriam asked, her eyes wide.

'He's just inherited a van from his uncle,' Bella said.

'And you're going to live in it? Like Bella and Alan in the old days?'

Paul remembered Bella's stories about the Peace Convoy

and the photos of their beautifully painted bus. He took in Miriam's hopeful expression.

'No, not really. But it's safer than dossing in a shop doorway.'

'Can I come with you?' Miriam asked.

'I can't take you,' Paul said. His head was already a mess of confusing thoughts. He didn't even think he was capable of driving.

'I can help. I can read the map.'

'Can you drive?'

'No, but…'

'You don't even know me. I'm not…'

'Bella seems to trust you. Sounds like you were her star employee.' Miriam's arms were folded and she looked totally determined.

'I don't think it's a good idea, Miriam,' Bella said. 'Paul's just had a big shock.'

'Yeah, I didn't even know my uncle had died. I only came back for my mum's birthday.' Paul hastily covered up, in case Bella was about to tell Miriam his secret. Discretion had never been her strongest point. 'And now it'll be dark by the time I get home.'

'So he'll need someone to look after him then, won't he? Make sure he concentrates on driving properly.' Miriam had a point.

'And then what?' he said. 'You wouldn't want to live in the quarry.'

'Why?'

'Because there's nothing to do. It's cold and windy…'

'If I don't like it, I'll move on. At least I won't be stuck here with everyone breathing down my neck.'

Paul felt anxious. He'd stirred up the past by going back

home. The quarry was safe and quiet. He wished he'd stayed there, in his little bubble of oblivion. Miriam might stop him from doing something stupid tonight – he needed to get home. He needed time to think.

'Bella's right. You shouldn't go off on your own,' he said. 'And I suppose the worst that can happen to you up there is that you'll get a bit cold and wet. I've got friends there – you'll be okay.'

'So you'll take me?'

'I'm still not sure about this.' Bella looked worried.

'Stop fussing,' Miriam said.

'What about your parents?'

'I'll let them know.'

Paul almost laughed. She would be home soon enough anyway. She'd be tired enough of her little rebellion after a few days of roughing it at the top of that hill.

Alan came out of the kitchen. He handed a carrier bag to Paul. It contained a margarine tub and a square shape wrapped in tin-foil.

'It was your favourite – spinach and chick pea curry. There's a bit of left-over rice - and chocolate cake.'

Paul smiled, even though he felt like he'd never eat again. Alan had even packed a couple of napkins and plastic forks.

'Thanks,' Paul said.

Alan met his eyes. Paul realised that he must have heard everything from the kitchen – he knew all about Gary too.

Bella hugged him tightly, squeezing the air out of his lungs. 'I'm sorry we didn't have much time to talk. Forget about Gary,' she whispered. 'Look after yourself. And look after Miriam. I mean it. Or I'll…' Bella grabbed his arm. 'God, you're too thin.'

'I promise, Bella. She'll be fine.'

She hugged Miriam. Her slight frame almost disappeared in the folds of Bella's enormous bosom.

'Call me when you get there.' Bella pressed one of the business cards from the counter into Miriam's hand. 'And whenever you need to.'

CHAPTER FIVE
THE MOTORWAY

The van was parked on a side-street off Green Lane. The sign on its side read "T.B. Hackworth, Quality Meats, Belper." Paul unlocked the passenger door. Miriam felt unsure now she was alone with him. She climbed into the stale-smelling cab and dumped her bag on the seat next to the gear stick. The seats were upholstered in worn black vinyl.

'Your uncle was a butcher?'

'Yeah.'

Paul pulled a road atlas from underneath the driver's seat. He handed it to her. It was ten years out of date and scuffed at the corners, as if it had been kicked around the cab but never opened.

'I'm going to need your help. I can get on the ring-road but just make sure you're on the right page, okay?'

Miriam nodded. She buckled her seatbelt with a firm clunk. The engine rumbled loudly as they set off.

Paul was silent, staring straight ahead as he pulled onto the busy dual carriageway. Miriam shifted the position of her finger on the road atlas as Paul drove south. She kept glancing at Paul, at the look of strained concentration on his face. She tried to fight the knot of anxiety in her chest and distracted herself by looking down from the height of the van, staring at buildings and fields softening in the evening light. Her parents would be missing her by now.

Paul braked sharply at a roundabout junction, jerking Miriam forwards. The road atlas flew off her lap. Behind them, a car beeped its horn.

'Sorry. I haven't driven for years!'

'It's okay.'

Paul moved off again. His driving became smoother when he reached a straight stretch of road.

'I found some fags in the glove compartment. Can you light one for me? I daren't take my hands off the wheel.'

Miriam found a packet of cigarettes and a lighter amongst a stack of tapes and an ice-scraper.

'Do you want one? They must have been the last fags my uncle bought - before he keeled over at the wheel.' Paul was hardly selling the experience.

No one had ever offered her a cigarette. Miriam felt pleased that he'd treated her like an adult. Ruth had sometimes smoked out of her bedroom window, flicking the butts expertly into the gutter of next-door's conservatory.

'No, thanks.'

Miriam fiddled with the lighter until it produced a flame. She put the cigarette in her mouth and held the flame under it until the smoke got into her eyes and down her throat.

'Ugh,' she said. She handed Paul the cigarette. He snatched it from her but the van swerved towards the verge. Miriam gripped the door handle and shut her eyes but Paul managed to keep the van on the road. The cab filled with smoke, making her eyes water. Miriam wound the window down.

She looked through the tapes in the glove compartment. There was nothing that she would ever listen to.

'Pan Pipe Moods? Bagpipe Bonanza? Your uncle seriously liked this stuff?'

She heard Paul laugh for the first time.

'He used to hum along to that sort of stuff at top volume as he drove. Can you imagine the racket? The sound of massed bagpipes and my uncle – he wasn't even in tune.'

'I've got some of my own tapes – or I could just listen to my Walkman. I left a lot at home, though.'

Miriam took the small stack of tapes out of her bag, thinking regretfully of the ones she'd left behind – compilation tapes that Mike had made for Ruth. Paul probably wouldn't like her taste in music.

'What have you got?'

'Nirvana, Primal Scream…'

'I used to love Primal Scream. What album?'

'Screamadelica.'

'Perfect.'

Miriam smiled as she slid the cassette into the tape deck. Ruth had copied it from someone at school. She turned the volume up as the first song started. It was the first time she'd heard it so loud since Ruth died. She didn't care that the speakers were old and crackly. She smiled and leaned back on her seat. She'd listened to this tape over and over again on Ruth's Walkman, lying on her bed with her eyes shut, trying to imagine the life they were singing about - wild nights spent dancing.

'This came out the year I left school. You'd be too young though, surely?'

'These were my sister's tapes – and her Walkman.'

'That's generous of her. My brother wouldn't give me anything.'

Miriam fiddled with the hand-drawn tape inlay. Ruth had copied the CD cover in coloured pencils. It was faded but it was a small part of her sister that was still alive.

'How old's your sister?'

'She died six years ago. She was seventeen.'

Paul drove in silence for a few minutes.

'How did she die?'

'Ruth fancied you. Don't you remember?'

Paul shrugged.

☆

Paul noticed a stale blood smell coming from the heater vents, like the smell that used to come from his uncle's apron. They were on the M5, south of Birmingham. It was almost dark. They had listened to Miriam's Primal Scream tape at least three times without wanting to change it. He flicked the lights on and glanced at the dashboard. He realised that the van was almost out of petrol. The needle had dipped dangerously into the red and a warning light had come on. How had he not noticed? In frustration, he hit the steering wheel with both hands

'What's up?' Miriam sounded scared. He realised that she must have dozed off. He changed the heating control to cold, to keep them both awake.

'No petrol. I don't know how long we've got.'

She pointed to a blue sign. 'Look, services – five miles.'

'I haven't got any money.'

'I can pay. It's no problem.'

Paul was struggling to concentrate by the time he pulled off the motorway and parked at the services. His legs felt unsteady when he got out of the van. He took deep breaths of petrol-tainted air as he followed Miriam to the service station building.

'Meet you in the shop.' Miriam left him at the entrance to the toilets.

When he came out of the Gents, she was waiting for him by the self-service coffee machine, browsing through a music magazine.

'Do you want a coffee?' She grabbed a cardboard cup and pressed the "cappuccino" button. A torrent of coffee and foamy milk poured out. She moved the cup, pressed another button and chocolate dust covered the white froth.

'Just a black one for me, please.'

She gave him both cups to hold while they queued at the till. They were excruciatingly hot. She chose a large bag of cheese and onion crisps and a Lion bar.

'We can save Alan's curry until later.'

'Can I get some fresh air?' he asked. The bright lights hurt his eyes.

Miriam found a flood-lit picnic bench near the entrance. Paul sat down and blew on his coffee. He took a tentative sip, burning his lips. The cold breeze made him shiver.

'You must be freezing,' Miriam said.

She ripped the packet of crisps open and pushed it towards him.

'No thanks – they aren't vegan.'

Paul lit one of his uncle's cigarettes and inhaled the smoke deeply.

'I'll find a way to pay you for the petrol.'

'Forget it. We should ban money and just barter with each other.' Her hazel eyes widened with revolutionary fervour. Maybe she was quite good looking, in a gawky way. He tried to remember her sister.

'You've been reading those daft leaflets that Bella leaves lying around in the café. It wouldn't work – not on a large scale, anyway.'

'How do we know until we've tried it?' She picked up a large crisp and licked the flavouring off it. 'Is that what it's like – this travellers' site? Bella said…'

'Bella doesn't know what she's talking about. She gave up that life a long time ago. There's nothing much to see – just a few people trying to survive without the things that society takes for granted.'

'Like computers and designer labels and…'

'Water, electricity, heating.' Paul took a gulp of coffee. It tasted bitter but at least it was warm.

Miriam stared at him.

'Look, come if you want,' he said. 'But it's not an easy life.'

'So? You think I can't hack it?'

'Are you sure you want to run away? Surely if your boss deserved it, your parents won't be angry?'

'My mum thinks the sun shines out of Mr Brown's arse. She'd be on his side. There's no way I'm apologising or going back to the Mercia.'

'The Mercia Building Society?' Paul laughed. 'So you were trying to smash the capitalist system from within?'

'My boss was a sexist creep – and my mum forced me to work there. I wanted to do A-levels.'

'You should call someone – let them know you're safe. It'll be your last chance tonight unless you've got a mobile.'

'I'm in charge of my own life now. Bella knows I'm safe, doesn't she?'

Paul shrugged and drained his coffee. He ground out his cigarette on the gravel under the picnic table while Miriam stacked the empty cups and threw them into a nearby bin. They walked back to the van.

Paul drove into the petrol station. Just in time, he realised that the van's fuel was diesel, not petrol. He half-filled the tank. Miriam seemed happy to pay for it.

When they were on the motorway again, Miriam pulled out another tape. He glanced at the home-made cover and recognised the orange toy alien, drawn in faded felt-tip.

'Sonic Youth? Surely they're not your sort of thing?'

'They were one of Ruth's favourite bands.'

'But what music do you like?'

'Mum got this idea in her head that the music Ruth liked was a bad influence on her.'

'But that's stupid.'

'I listen to Ruth's tapes and the radio on Ruth's Walkman in my room. I like the Evening Session and the John Peel show.'

'You can't listen to it out loud?'

'Mum threw Ruth's stereo away. I rescued her tapes and the Walkman. Mum doesn't know. She wanted to get rid of everything that made Ruth who she was.'

Miriam changed the tape. The distorted guitars made Paul remember doing his A-Level homework, safely cocooned in his room, the stereo blocking everything out. He was starting to understand why Miriam wanted to escape her life.

He drove as fast as he could, spurred on by the music, willing the van to go above sixty miles per hour.

☆

Paul drove up the steep track that led to the site, the windscreen wipers batting away the rain that had started when they'd pulled off the motorway.

It was just past eleven according to the clock on the dashboard. Allie should still be up; maybe Miriam could sleep in her caravan for the night. Trev's bender might be too much of a culture shock for her first night away from home. Maybe she wouldn't mind – she was still fast asleep, despite the van bumping up the deep ruts in the unmade road. Paul imagined the surprised look on Trev's face when he turned up with the van. Trev hadn't believed that Paul was coming back.

Maybe he could get on with life here and try to forget about his family and the past. But that photo of Gary from the newspaper was stuck in his head now.

Paul braked sharply as the headlights illuminated two enormous boulders dumped in the middle of the track. His heart lurched. He put the handbrake on and jumped down from the cab.

CHAPTER SIX
THE OLD QUARRY

Miriam woke with a jolt. Her neck was stiff. The door on the driver's side of the van was wide open, the engine still running. Rain blew inside. She was on her own. Everything was totally dark apart from the headlight beam, illuminating two boulders in a narrow track with grass growing in the middle. The last thing she remembered was being on the motorway, passing a sign that said they were at the junction for Bristol.

'Paul. Paul!' Her voice sounded shrill and frightened.

Miriam turned the key in the ignition until the engine stopped. She was relieved that the headlights stayed on. The silence was unnerving. What should she do? What if Paul had got out of the van to try to move those rocks and been attacked by something? Miriam fished around in her bag until she found her new torch and the batteries she'd bought. She didn't want to stay in the van.

Miriam put the batteries in her torch and zipped up her coat. She could hear the rain drumming on the roof of the van and the wind in the trees. She pushed the door open quietly and stepped down from the cab, squelching into mud. Miriam walked around the van, shining the torch underneath it and into the woods on either side. There was no sign of Paul. She hoped he wasn't far away. The track seemed to slope downhill but the torch only illuminated a few metres.

'Paul!' she shouted. The rain blew into her face. Maybe she should try to see what was beyond those boulders.

She walked carefully. Bella had tried to put her off travelling with Paul but Miriam had convinced herself that she was on the verge of a big adventure. She should have followed her original plan and only trusted herself.

As she moved forwards, the trees seemed to thin out. The mud underfoot was churned up, as if a herd of cattle had been trampling through it. Her torch lit a wall of jagged rock. She remembered Paul saying something about a quarry. She flashed her torch around. There was a pale shape in the mud, moving. Miriam let out a small scream.

It was Paul. He looked up, holding his arm in front of his face to shield his eyes from the light.

'Where are we? What's going on?' she asked.

Miriam moved closer to him. He was soaking wet, patting the ground as if he was looking for something.

'This is it, Miriam. This was where I was living with my friends.' He sat on the muddy ground, hugging his knees. 'We've driven all this way for nothing.'

'Can't you find them again?'

'I don't know. Trev hasn't got a mobile. All his stuff's still here.' Paul pulled at a torn sheet of blue plastic. 'This was our home!'

Miriam stared at it, confused. It was just a broken home-made tent.

Paul was shaking. His soaked shirt clung to his skinny chest and arms. It was difficult to tell in the rain but he seemed to be crying.

'I just wanted to go home,' he said. 'Couldn't even do that.'

Miriam reached out and tentatively touched his shoulder. He didn't seem to notice. He crouched over the plastic sheet and scrabbled in the soil underneath it. He pulled out a mud-caked sock and stared at it.

'Paul – please come back to the van.' He didn't respond. She grabbed his hand. It was cold. She tried to pull him up but he didn't move.

Paul glared at Miriam and stood up suddenly. Her feet

started sliding but he grabbed her. She gasped, frightened. He supported her in his arms, keeping her upright.

'I'm sorry. I shouldn't have brought you here.'

They walked back to the van. Paul turned the engine on again, so he could get the heater running and they could sit with the light on. His breathing came in ragged gasps.

'You should change your clothes,' Miriam said.

'I'll be fine.'

☆

There was a dry shirt and a jumper in his rucksack. She was right. He'd feel much better if he wasn't soaked to the skin. What did it matter if he took his shirt off in front of her? She'd already seen him crying.

He changed as quickly as he could. But when he was bare-chested, she stared at his arm. She was the second person to see his scars that day. He quickly struggled into his dry clothes. He should never have left the quarry. What good had it done? Knowing about Gary just made things worse.

He turned off the engine and the cab light. The darkness was eerie.

'I'd better save the battery.'

Miriam turned her torch on and propped it on the seat next to her. It gave out a comforting, dim glow. He couldn't blame her if she was scared of being in the dark with him. Paul reached onto the dashboard for the cigarettes. His hand shook as he lit one. There was only one more cigarette left in the pack.

'What do we do now?'

'Sleep. There's nothing we can do until the morning.' He was too shaken up to attempt reversing the van down the hill in the dark. It was the only way they could get out.

Miriam took off her coat and picked at the knots of her wet bootlaces. She took her brand-new sleeping bag out of its compression sack and struggled into it. She curled up on the double seat with her head against the passenger door.

'Leave the torch on if you want,' she said.

She pulled out her Walkman, clamped the headphones to her ears and closed her eyes. He wondered what she was listening to but he couldn't hear anything apart from the noise of the rain on the roof of the van. The way she clung onto her sister's tapes was sweet but sad.

Paul smoked the cigarette down to the filter and threw the butt out of the window. He unrolled his blanket and pulled it over himself. He sat in the torchlight for a while, staring at the boulders, brought to stop anyone camping here again.

Every time he shut his eyes, he saw the picture of Gary. He took the newspaper cutting out of his bag and stared at the photograph. He read the story over and over. It didn't help. He put it away.

☆

The sun streamed through the windscreen of the van, waking Paul up. He ached all over and the blanket made him feel hot and feverish. He stared in disbelief at his soil-caked hands, ashamed that he'd made such a fool of himself in front of Miriam.

She was still huddled on the passenger seat, clutching her Walkman to her chest. If things had gone to plan, she wouldn't have been his sole responsibility any more. He tried to think of people who might know where the others were. Where had Trev gone, without any of his stuff?

Miriam stirred and opened her eyes. She looked surprised to

find herself here. She unzipped her sleeping bag, sat up and put her feet in her boots.

'Did you sleep well?' he asked.

She shrugged.

'I was tired out. I don't think I noticed. I need the loo.'

'You'll have to go behind a bush.' He pulled a wad of toilet paper from his bag, stolen from the service station. He handed it to her. She had a horrified look on her face. 'Don't worry. You'll get used to it.'

'Okay, whatever,' She left the van, her boots trailing laces.

Miriam stood in the centre of the old quarry. The things she'd glimpsed in torchlight last night now made sense. This would have been a good little camp; a bowl of grass sheltered by the rock walls and protected by the woods on the other side. There were several pale, light-starved rectangles, where shelters or vehicles must have stood for a long time, while the new spring grass grew around them. In the middle of the quarry was a blackened circle - a camp-fire, with logs around the edge for people to sit on. But it was all trampled, the ground scored with deep tyre tracks.

People's belongings were scattered on the ground. It looked like they'd been forced to leave in a hurry. It was like seeing the aftermath of a bombing raid on the news. A blue china plate had been crushed in the tyre tracks, making a pattern like an exploding flower.

Miriam trod on something spongy. She looked down. It was a toy monkey – handmade in brown velvet. Its trusting, muddy face stared up at her. She picked it up and squeezed rainwater out of it.

Paul was kneeling by the blue tarpaulin again. He folded it up, untangling it from snapped twigs and bits of string.

'Look what I found.' She showed him the toy monkey.

'Lil made that for Tom.'

'How are you going to find your friends?'

'Allie's got a mobile – and Lil. But I haven't got their numbers. We'll just have to keep looking for them – unless you just want me to drop you off at the train station?'

'No – I can help.' Miriam said.

Paul made a pile of meagre, mud-soaked items: a greasy frying pan, an old fleece jacket, a couple of blankets and a half-empty nylon holdall.

'Is that your friend's stuff?' she asked.

Paul nodded. His eyes were the same shade of blue as the morning sky. His face was still streaked with dirt from last night.

'I knew it was a mistake, trying to go back. I only wanted to…' Paul examined the ground closely, running his hand over the ruined grass. He lifted up a loose piece of turf and pulled out a small rusty tin, which he put in his trouser pocket.

'I'd better put this stuff in the back of the van. Then we can both sort out whatever's left.'

She followed Paul as he unlocked the van's back shutter and rolled it up with a loud rattle. The stale-blood smell that had been coming out of the heater vents was ten times stronger here. Blood-stained hooks hung from the van roof.

Paul turned away from the van. He crouched on the track, taking deep breaths.

'Are you okay?' she asked.

'This hasn't been opened since my uncle died. We're lucky there's not still a side of beef hanging up in here.' Paul's face was pale, sickened.

59

Near another patch of faded grass, Miriam found a washing line with clothes still attached: a pink leopard-print mini-skirt, black lacy underwear, a fuchsia t-shirt with zips sewn across the front and a pair of flared jeans with hand-painted flames coming from the hem. The clothes were too good to put in the back of the van with that smell, so she folded them and put them on the passenger seat.

'Everything's been smashed up. There's no point looking for anything else.' Paul sat on one of the boulders.

Miriam was sure there must be something else they had missed. She walked around the quarry, her eyes on the ground. She looked back towards Paul. There was something fluttering, tied to a branch of a young rowan tree near the track. Miriam ran back to the tree and held it still. It was a piece of coloured card, with "Paul" written on it in felt-tip, sealed inside a clear plastic bag.

'Look,' she said.

Paul sprang up from the rock. He cut the note down from the tree with a penknife that he got out of the rusty tin.

'Allie's left directions.' A relieved smile spread over Paul's face.

CHAPTER SEVEN
THE FIELD

The directions were written in clear, childish handwriting. Miriam hoped they were on the right road – this lane wasn't even on the road atlas.

'It says there should be something red hanging on the hedge where we have to turn off,' she said. 'It should be on the left soon.'

Paul slowed down while Miriam scanned the hedgerow. She spotted a child's t-shirt hanging limply on a sapling next to a gap in the hedge.

'Stop!' she said.

Paul's brakes squeaked as he brought the van to a halt. He turned off the road. Twigs scraped against the sides of the van. The track sloped steeply downhill between high earth banks. The tangled hedge almost met in the middle. Miriam felt completely cut off from the world. No one would find her now, unless she wanted them to.

The track flattened out, ending at a dilapidated wooden gate. On the other side was a gently sloping field, flanked by woodland. An ambulance and a shabby caravan with a battered estate car were parked by the hedge. A line of trees marked the bottom of the field.

'Is this it?'

'That's Allie's caravan.' Paul sounded excited. 'Open the gate for me.'

Miriam opened the door and climbed down from the passenger seat. She slipped the loop of frayed nylon rope over the wooden post and pushed the gate open. Paul drove through and parked it next to the caravan.

The caravan door swung open. A young woman holding a

baby on her hip stared at the van. She wore a blue mechanic's overall and red steel toe-cap boots. Her eyes locked on Miriam suspiciously.

'What do you want?'

Miriam's lips felt glued together. Paul jumped down from the van.

'It's okay, Allie, she's with me.'

Allie walked up to Paul and threw her free arm around Paul's shoulder. The top of her head only reached Paul's chest. She had long dark hair tied in a ponytail. She stepped back to examine the van, her mouth open with amazement. The baby clung to Allie's overall with its tiny hands and stared around solemnly. A dark-haired little girl ran out of the caravan and stood next to Allie.

'T.B. Hackworth Quality Meats?' Allie's daughter was wide-eyed. 'You stole a butcher's van?'

'My uncle left it to me.'

The little girl rolled underneath the van and seemed to be inspecting its workings.

'So where do you come in?' Allie asked Miriam.

She stepped forward to introduce herself. But Paul was staring at the man shambling towards them. He was wrapped in a muddy blanket, with an odd lump sticking out at the front of his chest. His face was weathered; tough-looking, topped by a grown-out Mohican haircut that flopped onto one side. His khaki trousers were torn and dirty.

'Trev!' Paul ran towards him. 'I was worried.'

Trev's blanket swung open. His left arm was in a plaster cast, bound tightly across his chest in a sling. He held a can of beer in his other hand.

'You got a van?'

'What happened to you?' Paul hugged Trev gently.

'He twisted my arms behind my back – this guy – built like a tank. I tried to struggle – then there was a crack – it bloody hurt. Allie took me to casualty. That was the worst bit. But she bought me the beer to cheer me up.' Trev laughed, his hardman's face transformed by warm brown eyes and a gap-toothed smile. 'Did you go back there?'

Paul nodded. 'It's a real mess,' he said.

'The owners of the quarry hired a security firm to evict us,' Allie explained. 'They didn't give us any warning.'

Trev staggered backwards to get a better look at the van. He stared at Miriam.

'Who are you?'

'Miriam,' she said.

Trev thrust his right fist in front of her eyes. She flinched, and then read the letters "TREV", crudely tattooed across his knuckles.

'Handy when I can't remember my name! Do you want some beer?' His voice had a Welsh lilt but it sounded mixed-up, as if he'd absorbed bits of other accents. Trev offered her his can of extra strong lager.

'Yeah, why not?' She didn't dare to refuse.

She took the can out of his hand and took a swig. It had a nasty metallic taste but she smiled and handed it back to him.

'I've got some more cans in my tent. You can have one.'

'Thanks.'

Paul took the rusty tin out of his trouser pocket. Trev grinned.

'The rest of your stuff's in the back of the van.'

Trev gave Paul a one-armed hug, spilling lager on his shirt. They looked as close as brothers.

'We need to start work on the bender.'

'We can live in the van now.'

Trev shook his head.

'Not on your life. You're not making me sleep indoors.'

'It's not indoors, it's a van.'

Paul unlocked the back of the van and pulled up the shutter.

'It stinks. I'm not sleeping in there,' Trev said. 'Those things would give me nightmares.' He stared up at the hooks hanging from the roof.

'I've got to clean it first.'

Miriam sulked. Paul had needed her help to get here. Now he was completely ignoring her. She could hang around feeling shy or prove to Allie that she was worth knowing. Miriam opened the van door and grabbed the clothes and the toy monkey from the passenger seat. She took a deep breath and walked up to Allie.

'I found this.'

The baby stretched his arms towards the monkey. His sad eyes suddenly shone. Allie grinned. She had a smudge of black oil on her nose.

'Tom's monkey!'

Miriam put the toy in the baby's hands. He immediately started sucking its ears.

'He loves it.' Allie gently tugged the mud-encrusted monkey away from Tom and tucked it in front of her overalls. 'But I should wash it, really.'

A tall girl barged in front of Allie. Her hair was an explosion of thick pink and white braids and her bottom lip was pierced in the centre with a silver ring.

'They're mine.' She snatched the clothes out of Miriam's hands.

'It's okay – she's with Paul,' Allie said.

'She can't be – how can she…?'

Lil stared at Miriam critically.

'How can he drag in that mousy thing?'

Lil clutched the bundle of clothes tightly as she walked to the ambulance. She slammed the door behind her. It didn't block out her scream of rage.

Miriam tried to keep her head up high. Maybe coming here was a mistake after all. Paul hadn't wanted her. She'd bullied him into taking her.

Allie stared at Miriam. 'Make yourself at home in my caravan for a minute.' She let herself into the ambulance.

Miriam noticed a rough shelter between the ambulance and the caravan – a groundsheet with one end tied to the hedge and the other edge pegged to the ground. An oak tree grew out of the hedge, its leaves still small and translucent.

Paul was with Trev, halfway towards the trees at the end of the field. Miriam thought about running after him but he'd forgotten all about her. She was mousy. People ignored her. She blinked back tears. Lil was shouting in the ambulance. Miriam couldn't make out what she was saying but she mentioned Paul several times. The baby started crying.

Miriam opened the caravan door. A small stove gave off glowing warmth and smelled like a bonfire. A tin pipe snaked out of it to the roof. There were two sofas covered in brown woolly material, with a table patterned in fake wood grain slotted between them under the window. At the far end of the caravan was a narrow bunk with a Scooby Doo duvet cover, half-hidden behind a curtain.

A small kitchen area had two gas stove rings, a sink and fitted overhead cupboards. Miriam opened one – it contained tinned food, a bottle of wine and a few cans of beer. In the cupboard under the sink there was a cool-box with milk, bread, margarine and a few vegetables. Miriam couldn't stop herself from being nosy. She pulled open a door next to a narrow wardrobe, revealing a tiny cubicle with a chemical toilet and a plastic baby bath hanging from a hook.

Miriam sat down on the sofa. Allie had left a paperback with a bright cover splayed out on the table. Miriam picked it up, keeping Allie's place with her finger. It was a travel book by a woman who had cycled through India. She started reading, allowing herself to get lost in someone else's world.

The door opened. Miriam guiltily put the book down in the same place she'd found it.

'I always thought I might do something adventurous like that.' Allie shrugged. She picked up the book and stared at the page where she'd left it open. 'But she gets very lonely.'

Allie pumped her foot furiously on a rubber stud in the floor until water came out of the tap. She filled an old fashioned iron kettle and put it on a hotplate on top of the stove. She brought two large enamel mugs out of a cupboard. Her baby was safely balanced on her hip while she did everything one-handed.

'So - how long have you known Paul?'

'I only met him yesterday. But I recognised him from...'

'Why did he bring you here?' Allie stared at her, hard.

'If I'm not welcome, I'll...' Miriam stood up. She would demand that Paul gave her a lift into the nearest town. She would catch a train somewhere.

'I didn't mean it like that – honest.'

'We both know a lady who runs a café in Derby.'

'Look – we're all a bit shaken up. And Paul doesn't know yet but this is just a temporary place. One of Lil's mates – some DJ in Bristol – he's holding a rave here next weekend. Lil's done a deal. We can stay here if we get the site ready.'

'Sounds great.'

'Yeah - but it was stupid of her to promise so much. We were desperate for somewhere to stay but they want us digging compost toilets and all sorts. How are we going to do that with Trev's arm in plaster? Lil was upset that Paul had gone but now he's back, with you, she's just going to sulk all week and not help and then Paul's going to get pissed and refuse to talk to anyone.'

'Did Lil and Paul go out with each other?'

'Nothing so simple.' Allie put tea bags into the mugs. 'Lil had a real thing about him last winter. God knows why. No one in their right mind would touch him with a barge pole. I mean, he could be good looking - but he's so messed up. I've learned to steer clear - after what happened with Flynn, my last bloke.' She laughed. 'Anyway, they slept with each other. You'd think that would cure her…'

Allie stood on a plastic footstool, fishing around at the back of an overhead cupboard. She found a half-empty bottle of brandy and poured a generous measure into each mug. Allie took a swig out of the bottle and offered it to Miriam.

'I try to keep things together normally but since the eviction…'

Miriam gulped a mouthful of brandy. It stung the inside of her mouth like TCP but a warm feeling spread down her throat and warmed her belly. Steam started coming out of the kettle.

'Hold Tom for a minute, will you?'

Allie put the baby on her lap. Miriam had never held a baby before. She tentatively put her arms around him so that he didn't fall off her knee. Tom was surprisingly solid.

'Bounce him up and down,' Allie smiled. 'He likes that.'

Miriam gently jogged her knees. The whole caravan vibrated slightly with the movement. Tom laughed and slapped the table with his hands, as if he was playing bongos.

Allie grabbed a tea-towel and gripped the kettle's handle. She added milk to the mugs and flicked the tea bags into the sink. Miriam stroked Tom's dark downy hair. Holding him made her feel sleepy.

'So what's the story with Paul getting the van?' asked Allie.

'His uncle died.'

'It sounds like it needs a good service. I know what I'm doing. But I can't get work when we're pushed around like this. I thought we were settled in that old quarry.'

'Can I help with the rave? I'd like to.'

'You don't look like you're used to hard work. We'll have to dig holes, chop wood…'

'Sometimes I surprise myself with my own strength.' Miriam thought of Mr Brown cowering in his chair.

'Alright, then!' Allie laughed.

☆

Trev leaned against the willow trunk, watching Paul saw through one of the thin branches.

'It's lucky you found the tools.'

'I can't believe you slept under that tarpaulin in the rain last night – one of the girls should have let you in.'

'The tree was sending out healing vibes through its roots.'

'Don't talk crap.'

'So you're going to live in that van now?'

'I thought – once it was cleaned up – there's plenty of space for both of us.'

Trev shook his head. He took a swig of lager.

'Why don't you ask Miriam?'

Paul stared into the river, flowing swiftly after last night's rain, sucking at the half-submerged willow roots. He stripped the new leaves and side-shoots from the branch with Trev's penknife. Its steel handle warmed to his touch.

'I hardly know her. But there's nowhere else for her to stay.'

'What about Lil, though?'

Paul cut two more branches and piled them up with the others. They were nearly ready to make the bender. He had a feeling the weather was going to turn bad again. There was a sharp wind that might blow a storm into the valley.

'I don't know what she expected. I wish we could all just forget about it.'

'You hurt her.'

'I didn't mean to – we were both off our faces. She's the one who…'

'That's not the point.'

Paul wrapped a strip of cloth around the saw blade and slipped the knife into his pocket. He gathered the long willow poles into a bundle and hoisted them onto his shoulder. It felt strange to be doing this without any help. Trev watched him so critically, it felt like an exam in bender construction.

'Miriam just needs somewhere safe to sleep.'

'And you reckon she'll be safe with you?' Trev frowned.

☆

Miriam stared through the window at Paul and Trev. They were sticking long poles into the ground between the caravan and the ambulance, as if they were going to plant runner beans. Paul was doing most of the work, while Trev talked and pointed. Paul hadn't said a word to her since she'd opened the gate. The warmth from the stove made her too lethargic to go and talk to him.

Allie wrung water and soaps suds out of the toy monkey. Tom squirmed on Miriam's lap as she twisted its velvet body. She tied string to its legs and attached it to a hook in the ceiling above the stove.

'Look, Tom – the monkey's bungee jumping.' Allie's daughter Heather looked up from the battered Jacqueline Wilson book she was reading. Heather was delicately built, like Allie. Miriam guessed she was about eight years old but she had a wary look that belonged to someone much older.

Water dripped out of the monkey, making the hotplate sizzle. Tom gurgled.

'You may as well stay in here tonight; there's lots of room,' Allie said.

'Where?'

'The sofas fold down to make another bed.'

'Haven't you stayed in a caravan before?' Heather asked.

'No – but I've been camping a few times.'

'We bought this caravan from an old man. Guess how much it was – and the car too?' Heather looked at Miriam expectantly.

'I don't know.'

'Two hundred pounds. I'm not kidding.'

'But we had to put new tyres on and get rid of the damp in the caravan. And it was bloody freezing in here before we got the stove fitted,' Allie explained. She leaned across the table to get a better view of Paul and Trev.

'Paul's not going to get that bender finished before it starts raining,' she said.

'What's a bender?' Miriam asked.

'I lived in one for a while. Ours had windows and a front door we'd got out of a skip.'

Paul looked like he'd forgotten what to do with the stick he was holding. Trev waved his unbroken arm angrily. Suddenly, he marched off towards the woods. Paul sat down behind the willow poles, hugging his knees. It looked like he was in a cage.

'They haven't been able to stop arguing since Paul slept with Lil. No wonder he wanted to go back home,' Allie smirked.

'I'm going to help him,' Miriam said. She passed the baby back to Allie.

Miriam stopped, mid-stride, as she walked towards Paul. He was staring at a fresh cut on his left arm. She wasn't going to pretend she hadn't seen his arm last night: the mess of criss-crossing scar tissue and red, raw cuts. She walked right up to him, determined to say something but he pulled his shirt-sleeve down and put the knife in his pocket.

'Do you want a hand?'

Paul shrugged.

'Just take some of these sticks and push them into the ground – like this.'

She followed the circular shape of the sticks he'd pushed in already. The ground was quite soft and the sticks had sharp points, so it was fairly easy. They worked at opposite ends of the circle, until Paul almost bumped into her at the opposite end.

He picked up a ball of string and cut several lengths with the knife.

'You've got blood on your sleeve,' Miriam said.

'I caught myself while I was whittling the end of the poles.'

If he wanted to lie, that was his problem. He didn't look at her. He started to tie the ends of the branches together at the top, making a dome shape. He cut her a few pieces of string.

'Have a go. It's easy.'

She tied a few branches, trying to make tight, neat knots. Paul smiled in approval. She felt a glow of pride that was almost as warm as the brandy.

'I've not made anything like this since Guides.'

'You made benders in Guides?'

'Just stupid girly things like washing up stands.'

'I'm going to clean the back of the van tomorrow,' he said.

'Allie told me about the rave. I'm going to stick around and help.'

'Borrow Allie's phone and tell Bella where you are. She was expecting it.'

Miriam shrugged. She wasn't ready to tell anyone where she was yet. It was still a shock to realise that she wasn't trapped at home.

'Do you want to live with me in the van?' he asked.

She stared at Paul. He smiled, a hopeful look on his face. He seemed totally casual about it. She tied a few more branches together, trying to ignore the rush of blood to her cheeks. She turned away from him, not knowing what to say or think.

The space became more constricted as more branches were tied together. She brushed one of Paul's hands accidentally. He pulled away from her.

'I'm sorry. It was a stupid idea.'

'It's a bit sudden. You only met me yesterday.'

'You've been listening to Allie, haven't you? Just as mates – friends – that's all. We can sleep at opposite ends of the van.'

She looked at him and laughed with relief.

'Yeah, why not?' she said. He started laughing too but his blood-stained sleeve bothered her. There seemed to be a lot she didn't know about him.

☆

Rain drummed steadily on the roof of the caravan. Allie was heating up the leftover curry from the Flying Horse Café on the hotplate. The glow from the stove and the electric wall-light made the caravan seem like a bubble of civilisation. It had only just got dark but Miriam had been awake since dawn and she was fighting to stay awake, despite her hunger.

Allie scooped up a spoonful of mashed carrot and made car noises as she moved it towards Tom's open mouth. When she had finished, she checked his nappy, changed him into a Babygro and laid him in a Moses basket on the floor near Heather's bed. She leaned back on the sofa cushions and sighed.

Miriam checked the curry. It was in danger of getting stuck to the bottom of the pan. It looked okay mixed in with the rice. She took it off the heat and spooned it onto the enamel plates that Allie had put on the table. The smell of the curry made Miriam feel guilty. She hadn't called Bella. She wasn't sure she wanted to yet. Allie had said that the only mobile reception was right at the top of the lane and it was too wet to leave the caravan.

'I'm warning you. This wine was the cheapest they had in NETTO – and that's saying something.' Allie opened the bottle of white wine from her cupboard and filled two plastic glasses.

'That's okay.'

'You haven't tried it yet.'

Miriam took a sip of wine. It tasted sour, like pear-drops. She looked enviously at Heather's orange squash.

'This is lovely.' Allie made appreciative noises as she ate her curry. Paul had told Miriam that he didn't want any. The bender had been like a small cave when they'd finished making it. He must be sleeping already.

Someone knocked urgently on the door. Heather dropped her fork with a clatter. Allie approached the door warily and opened the top half. The sound of rain became louder.

'God, sorry, come in. My nerves are still shot. I should have invited you round. But I thought you were still…'

73

'Pissed off? Yeah, well.'

Lil pulled her hood down and stood dripping on Allie's welcome mat in a long black PVC raincoat. She stared at Miriam.

'I see you're still here.'

'I've got nothing to do with Paul.'

'Apart from the fact that you're going to be sharing that butcher's van.'

'It's not like you think. He promised Bella he'd look after me.'

'Who's Bella? Another woman he's got on the go?'

Miriam laughed. The idea of Bella and Paul as lovers was ridiculous.

'No – she's got a café in Derby. That's where I met Paul. They gave us this curry last night.'

'And it's getting cold,' Allie said. 'Sit down – I bet you haven't eaten yet.' She gave Lil the saucepan with the rest of the curry and a fork. 'Sorry – I've run out of plates.'

Miriam shuffled towards the window to make room for Lil.

Lil took off her raincoat, kicked off her bright pink wellies and sat on the sofa. She wore heavy foundation and eye-liner – even though she was in a field in the middle of nowhere. Allie poured wine into a plastic glass with a picture of Winnie the Pooh. Lil drank half of it in one gulp. Allie gave her a sharp glance.

'It doesn't taste as bad if you down it in one,' Lil said. 'I've got some proper wine we can drink later.'

'Sounds like a deal,' Allie said.

Miriam focused on her food. Lil's fork made a horrible scraping sound on the saucepan. When she finished eating, she played noughts and crosses with Heather on the window condensation.

'So Paul's babysitting you, then?' Lil asked. Miriam stared back at her.

'Actually, I'm on the run from the police,' Miriam said. Lil raised one of her over-plucked eyebrows. 'My boss was feeling up all the girls at work. He tried to do it to me. So I smashed a picture frame over his computer monitor – and then I kicked him in the balls.'

Heather gasped.

'Really?' Lil asked.

'Ask Paul if you don't believe me. I've got to lie low for a while.'

Lil poured wine into Miriam's glass.

'Nice one.'

'That's what I call girl power!' Allie laughed.

Miriam felt her cheeks growing hot. She was unsure if it was the effect of the wine and curry – or was it because she had exaggerated so much? She decided that she didn't care. She'd got their attention at last.

CHAPTER EIGHT
MINEHEAD

Miriam's mouth was dry, her temples throbbed and there was bright sunlight behind her closed eyelids. She was lying on a bed but she definitely wasn't at home. She pulled her sleeping bag over her face and tried to sleep.

A baby started crying. A woman swore softly and started moving about. The mattress wobbled. Miriam blinked her eyes open. Allie was changing Tom's nappy on the bed. Miriam sat up and opened the window wide to get rid of the smell.

'We've made a load of promises we can't keep. We can't help with this rave. We'll have to find somewhere else,' Allie said. She threw the dirty nappy into a bucket and dumped it outside the caravan door. She expertly pinned the clean towelling nappy into place and dressed Tom in a clean Babygro.

'I said I'd help,' Miriam croaked.

'I've been trying to save money for the start of the festival season but it's not enough to run a bar – look.'

Allie handed Miriam a cash-and-carry catalogue. She had ringed the prices of crates of beer in Biro and scribbled sums next to them. It worked out at about fifty pence per can.

'I've got just over two hundred quid – Lil's putting in a hundred. Paul said I could use any money I'll get for selling the refrigeration unit from his van. That's only going to be about six hundred cans of beer.'

'How many people are meant to be coming?'

'Lil's mate said they were expecting about three thousand. We're just going to look stupid.'

'How much were you going to sell them at?'

'Two quid. They'll pay that. But what's the point? We can't do it.'

'I'll put some money in,' Miriam said.

'Yeah, thanks. But it won't make much difference.'

Miriam studied Allie's sums. She wanted to show that she wasn't just some silly little kid.

'What about two thousand pounds?'

Allie's mouth gaped. Miriam hoped she hadn't gone too far. It hadn't seemed like much money when she was earning it, watching it stack up in her account without being able to spend it on things that other teenagers wasted money on. It felt deliciously ironic that she was about to give a good percentage of her earnings to buy beer.

Heather sat up in her bunk and stared at Miriam.

'Are you a millionaire?'

'What did you do, rob a bank?' Allie sounded choked.

Miriam laughed.

'Remember? I worked at the Mercia Building Society.' Allie stared. Miriam grabbed Tom before he crawled off the edge of the bed. She sat him on her knee.

'Why don't you buy a plane ticket and see the world instead of being stuck here?'

'I might do.'

'You could take me to Disneyland,' Heather said. She bounced up and down on the big bed.

'God, the things I would have done with thousands of pounds in the bank at your age.'

'I haven't made any plans yet. But if I can invest it...' Miriam stopped. She sounded like Mr Brown giving advice to one of his business customers.

'You hardly know us. Are you sure?' Allie filled the kettle.

Miriam watched Paul emerge from the bender. He walked towards the field gate, swinging a wood saw in his hand. He glanced at the caravan. They made eye contact. A smile flickered on Paul's face. He was still wearing the blood-stained shirt. The bender looked very small. She hoped it hadn't leaked on Paul and Trev overnight.

☆

The smell of pine-scented bleach clung to Miriam's clothes. At least the van was clean now. The refrigeration unit and the old meat hooks were in the boot of Allie's car, ready to be sold as scrap.

'The back of this van gives me the creeps.' Trev shuffled along with an old tea-towel under his bare feet to dry the floor. Miriam tried not to look at his overgrown toenails. 'And I'm not even a vegan.'

'It'll be better than the bender,' Paul said. He rinsed his cloth in the bucket of soapy water. He'd scrubbed until the aluminium surfaces were shiny.

'It just needs some furniture,' Miriam said.

'We should cover the walls with something.' Paul's voice echoed with a metallic ring.

'Let's see what we can pick up in Minehead,' Trev said.

'Take me with you. I've got stuff to do there,' Miriam said. She couldn't live in the van without anything to make it more comfortable.

☆

Paul dropped Miriam off near the High Street. He followed the signs for the industrial estate and drove slowly along the deserted road.

'Stop!' Trev shouted. Paul braked sharply.

'You saw a skip?' he asked.

'It was down the side of that building. It looked full.'

Paul turned the van around and drove into the forecourt of the warehouse building that Trev had pointed out. The skip was full of pallets and planks. Paul parked in front it.

'I suppose this is the advantage of having a van,' Paul said.

'I'm still not sleeping in it, though.'

Paul jumped down from the driver's seat. He pulled up the shutter and started loading the pallets into the back of the van. Paul felt tired and slow. The last thing he'd eaten had been a piece of Alan's cake yesterday morning. Allie had offered him breakfast but Paul had made himself busy, chopping wood and digging out turf for the fire pit. Then he'd cleaned the back of the van. If he stopped, he might think about Gary again.

Trev quickly developed a one-handed technique for picking up pallets, using his head to take the weight as he lifted them up. He got into the back of the van and stacked the pallets neatly.

Paul drove back into town. They scanned the Victorian streets until they found a skip on the pavement, piled high with an intriguing jumble of items. Paul pulled into the space in front of the skip. His tyres scraped against the kerb as he tried to straighten up.

'Don't take any old crap just because we've got room for it,' he said. Trev grinned.

Paul got out of the van and looked around. The skip was outside a house with a faded B&B sign on the gate. It was covered in scaffolding.

'You've got to have this!' Trev patted a floral sofa bed balanced on top of the skip, releasing a cloud of dust. 'It looks really comfy.'

'Okay,' Paul agreed. He didn't have the energy to argue with Trev. He helped him to move it into the back of the van.

'I think I'm getting pretty good at only using one arm. Do you reckon people would feel sorry for me if I tried busking?'

'No, probably not.'

Trev rummaged through the skip, finding a Formica bedside cabinet, some dusty orange curtains and a shaggy brown rug. Paul loaded everything into the van.

'Miriam's going to love this.' Trev said.

'She'll probably have an asthma attack.'

Trev stuck a red fringed lampshade on his head, like a fez.

'What do you think? For the rave?'

Paul shrugged.

'You're a barrel of laughs,' Trev said.

There was nothing left worth taking from the skip. It was mostly rubbish now; lumps of plaster and broken bathroom fittings.

Trev sighed heavily.

Paul stared at him. He wiped the plaster dust off his hands, onto his trousers. He wished he'd never asked Miriam to share his van. It was a responsibility he didn't want – and the van complicated things too much. He couldn't sleep in it alone, imagining the ghostly headless carcasses of pigs and sheep swinging around in the dark.

'I'm fine,' Paul snapped.

'Lil said that Miriam's on the run from the police.'

'She's entitled to her story,' Paul said.

☆

Miriam put down her shopping bags and sat on a bench on the sea front. She took the postcards out of her rucksack. She addressed the card with the photo of an Exmoor pony to the Flying Horse café and wrote: *To Bella and Alan! Hi! I made it. No phone reception – sorry! There's going to be a rave next week! I'll call soon. Luv Miriam xxx.*

The other postcard had a more anonymous photograph of a sandcastle, with a strip of sand and sea in the background. Miriam stared at the wooded headland that looked like a green dragon rising out of the bay. She took a deep breath and scribbled the address and her message without trying to think too much. *Dear Mum and Dad. I'm fine. Please don't look for me. Don't worry about me. Love Miriam xxx*

Miriam stuck a first class stamp onto both cards and slipped them into the nearby post box. At least they would know she was alive. She panicked as she realised the postmark would give her away. Maybe she should come back tomorrow morning and intercept the first collection? Or Allie might have something she could prise the door open with. She told herself not to be stupid. Even if the postcard arrived with Minehead stamped on it, they wouldn't be able to find her in that secret valley.

The van pulled up. Miriam checked her watch. They were early. Miriam gathered up her shopping.

'What's all this?' Trev asked. He took a bag. 'Argos?'

'I got a camping stove – and a couple of air-beds, so we can sleep in the van.'

'You shouldn't have done that,' Paul muttered.

'We've already got it sorted,' Trev said. 'Look.'

Trev pulled up the shutter. The back of the van was piled high with wooden pallets and old furniture. He helped her to put her bags inside the van.

'You've been busy,' she said.

Trev pointed at a faded sofa bed proudly with his good arm, like he was showing off a game-show prize.

'It's a double – plenty of room for you and Paul on that.' He winked. Miriam ignored him.

'I got some food and beer too,' she said.

'You didn't need to get that.' Paul looked angry. 'You shouldn't have bought me anything.'

'I bought you a sleeping bag as well. I thought you needed one.' She held it out to him. The compression sack made it look like an out-sized Easter egg.

'Take it back. Don't waste your money on me.' He leaned against the van, his arms folded, not even looking at it.

'It was a surprise.' She threw the sleeping bag angrily into the van. It bounced off the back wall and wedged itself between two pallets.

'You're an ungrateful sod,' Trev told Paul. 'You can buy me beer any day, love. I'm sorry about that miserable git.'

Miriam pulled one of the air beds out of the Argos bag. She offered it to Trev.

'Thanks for finding the sofa bed. It looks great. I'd like you to have this. Please don't be offended.'

He gave her a clumsy, one-armed hug. Her chest bumped against his plaster cast. He smelled of sweat and dust.

'Thanks a million. But we just get everything out of skips.'

'We survive by living off all the crap that people throw out,' Paul said.

'It's better than that. It's a whole way of life. We don't need money.'

'We've got the van now. It needs diesel. And a whole lot of other stuff.' Paul glared at Trev.

'Ignore him, Miriam. If we do need to buy things, I've got a penny whistle, so I do a bit of busking.'

'People give him money to stop him playing.' Paul looked at her hopefully, as if he was attempting to apologise.

'Paul's role is to look as miserable as possible and do the whole "homeless and hungry" routine,' Trev said.

'Begging?' she asked.

Trev shrugged. Paul stared at his boots. Miriam tried to hide her shock. The beggars she'd encountered in Derby city centre were pleading, unsavoury characters. Her ex-colleagues at the Mercia Building Society said they were spongers who spent all the money on booze and drugs. She stared at Paul and Trev, realising that was exactly how Mum or Mr Brown would see them.

'Only when we're desperate. Normally there's no need.' Trev grinned. 'Do you want to see how we get free food?'

☆

'Is this illegal?' Miriam asked. 'Will they catch us on CCTV?'

Paul parked near the delivery entrance of the supermarket.

'Technically, it's stealing,' Paul said. 'But they're just throwing it away.'

Trev and Paul jumped down from the van and walked towards a large metal wheelie bin. Miriam was glad she'd bought packets of super noodles and tins of beans, soup and tomatoes. It would save her from eating mouldy, rotten food.

'Some shops padlock their bins. Sometimes they deliberately pour bleach over the food,' Paul said.

'Why?'

Paul pushed the bin lid back with a heavy crash. It was full of black bags. It smelled stale but not totally unpleasant, like a mixture of vacuum cleaner bags, banana skins and strong cheese.

A baguette lay on top of the bin bags. It was still in its paper wrapper, with a "price reduced" sticker on its side.

'Try it.'

Miriam sniffed the bread. It was freshly baked. The loaf was just a bit bent in the middle. She tore off a bit of crust from the end and put it in her mouth. She chewed it, realising that she was quite hungry.

'Want some?' she asked. She broke off a piece of bread for Trev.

'If you don't buy it, they just throw it away – then you can have it for free.' He pulled some carrier bags from his trouser pocket and gave one to Miriam. 'See what else you can find.'

Paul was already sorting through a bin bag. He pulled out pre-packed salads and florets of broccoli.

'If it's past its sell-by date, or there's something a bit wrong with it, they just throw it out.' He showed her a box of fresh mushrooms. Its cellophane top was ripped.

Trev struggled to open a bin-liner. Paul helped, deftly tearing a hole in the plastic.

'Ugh.' he grimaced.

'Excellent!' Trev pulled out a semi-transparent plastic bag containing thick, speckled sausages. He held them above his head, like someone showing off a winning lottery ticket.

Miriam's mouth watered, despite the leaflets she'd read in Bella's café about the evils of the meat industry. Trev pulled out a bag of sliced ham. He sniffed it, shrugged and stuffed a few slices into his mouth. Miriam delved into the bin-bag. She found a plastic container of stuffed olives in oil. It had leaked onto a large block of unwrapped cheddar. The cheese felt slimy.

'It'll be fine on the inside.' Trev handed her another carrier bag to wrap it in.

Paul found a large red cabbage and bags of potatoes and carrots. Trev found a paper carton of doughnuts and some burger buns.

'We hit the jackpot with this bin. Sometimes we have to pick out loads of crap first,' Paul said. 'We make sure there's plenty of food for everyone.'

'When I was a kid, I wanted to be a Womble,' Trev said. Miriam laughed.

'I think we've got enough.' Paul glanced around nervously but the car park was still deserted.

'You've done well, Miriam,' Trev said. 'The girls will be really chuffed.'

Miriam smiled, glad that they were including her in their world.

CHAPTER NINE
THE FEAST

Paul arranged Miriam's plate artistically with mixed-leaf salad, olives and a jacket potato. He had wrapped potatoes in foil and cooked them in the fire for everyone.

'It looks lovely,' she said.

'I'm sorry about earlier. But don't buy anything for me again.'

'Why?'

Paul shrugged.

Miriam sawed through the jacket potato skin with the plastic knife from the picnic set she'd bought from Argos. She reached for a handful of grated cheese from the bowl on the ground. It was quiet round the fire, a circle of contented munching. But Paul had just given himself a plain potato. He cut it into small segments and ate them slowly, one by one.

One of the sausages in the frying pan popped loudly. Allie jumped off the plastic bucket she was sitting on. Salad leaves flew off her plate, onto the grass.

'Shit!' she gasped, her hand against her heart.

'God, Allie, you're paranoid,' Lil said. She helped herself to a slice of ham. Allie sat down again, laughing nervously.

Trev prodded the sausages with a sharpened stick.

'I think they're done,' Trev said. 'Anyone want one?'

Miriam nodded, her mouth still full of potato. She held her plate out. Paul shot her a disapproving look. She looked at the unappetizing plain potato on his plate.

'Why don't you have some salad?'

'I don't want any.'

'You must be hungry.'

Paul stared at his potato and started chewing another

mouthful.

Miriam took a bite out of the sausage. It was good. But she felt bad about Paul. He'd put so much effort into making sure there was enough food for everyone, cooking the potatoes and picking the wilted bits out of the salad.

'Paul's disappointed in our lack of morals,' Lil said. 'The rest of us eat anything we can get our hands on.'

Paul dropped his plate and walked towards the river. Miriam watched him disappear into the dusk. She stood up, wanting to chase after him.

'Just ignore him,' Lil said. 'Or he'll drive you mad.'

'Why did he just have a potato? There was loads of food he could have eaten.'

Trev shook his head. 'Sometimes he doesn't eat for days. I have to make him.'

'What's for pudding?' Heather asked, through a mouthful of ham.

Trev held up the doughnuts.

'Freshly baked today.' He seemed relieved to change the subject. 'Paul found some strawberries, if anyone wants the healthy option.'

'And I bought some beer,' Miriam said.

'Another cunning aspect of Trev and Paul's philosophy. They get everything for free but expect other people to buy the booze,' Lil said.

Trev just smiled, like he was enjoying the attention.

'No, I bought it myself. To share.' Miriam stared at Lil.

'I'm surprised you got served. But thanks.'

The darkness of the valley and the cold night air made Miriam want to stay close to the fire. Without the glare of street lights, the stars were bright. She pulled her purple jumper over her knees and warmed her hands on the fire. Paul was on his third can of lager, staring into the fire. Miriam couldn't work him out at all.

'Come to my van. I've got something to show you,' Lil said.

'What, now?'

'Yeah, why not?'

Miriam wasn't convinced by Lil's friendliness. Her anger might erupt again. She followed Lil warily into the ambulance.

Lil switched on a table lamp and a string of battery-operated fairy lights. Miriam blinked.

'Wow. It's very - pink.'

Pink Barbie doll patterned curtains hung at the windows. The bed was covered with a pink mirrored throw made out of sari material.

'I'm glad you like it.' Lil slipped off her wellies. She sat on the bed, leaning on a large satin cushion in the shape of a pair of lips. 'I really wanted to make a statement – be a bit different. Sit down – take your boots off, though.'

Miriam unlaced her boots and stepped onto the pink fluffy carpet. She perched awkwardly on the edge of the bed. She noticed how the ambulance had been cleverly converted into a camper van. The wardrobe had a full-length mirror on its door. Miriam hadn't seen her reflection since Friday night, in Bella's flat. She just looked like a scruffier version of herself, her unbrushed hair sticking out like a bush.

An antique hand-driven sewing machine stood on a fold-out table, surrounded by lengths of brightly coloured material and tangles of net and lace. Lil smiled.

'I'm making some tutus to sell at the rave. I thought maybe I'd charge a tenner each – it's not too much, is it?'

She held one up. It was made of blue and green net, with scraps of iridescent material and silver spangles that caught the light.

'It's pretty.'

'I made loads of earrings last winter – recycling them from old bits and bobs I found at jumble sales. And I do UV face-painting and hair-braiding.'

'Cool.'

'I thought I'd be all set up by now but I'm just scraping by. Last winter was harder than I thought.'

Lil opened a cupboard and brought out a large, hard-backed sketchbook. The pages fanned out stiffly, samples of material sticking out of the sides. She opened the book on a page with a watercolour painting of a woman wearing a long red dress. She was dancing, wild auburn hair whirling around her head as her embroidered skirt swirled.

'You drew this?' Miriam gasped.

'I want to have my own boutique – tour it round the festivals. I'm building it up slowly, small stalls at places like this. It's going to take years at this rate. Have you got any idea how much a stall at Glastonbury costs?'

Miriam shook her head. She flicked through the pages of the sketchbook. The designs were fresh and unusual. The women in Lil's paintings were dancing, flirting and chatting, looking like they were having a fabulous time.

'These are brilliant,' Miriam said.

'Allie said that you're helping out with the bar.'

Miriam nodded. Lil stared keenly at Miriam. Suddenly it was obvious that Lil wanted to ask her for money. Lil was so talented, she deserved to get her ideas off the ground. But if Miriam was going to give her anything, Lil would have to earn her trust; offer her something in return.

Lil seemed to be waiting for Miriam to say something. She turned the tutu round in her hands like she was inspecting it for faults. Miriam stared at a design of a woman in a short black dress.

'I'm sorry about what I said yesterday. The eviction stressed us all out. Allie's the only who tries to hold it together.'

'She's tough.'

'Allie's had a hard time. I first met her on a site near Bristol. She was with this bloke who knocked her about. She was pregnant but he wanted to go off to Finland with his mates – for cheap old army trucks and drugs, probably. Allie stayed behind at the last minute. We decided to go it alone.'

'What about Paul and Trev?'

'Allie's ex and his mates were always competing about who had the biggest and best truck, going on about engines. Paul and Trev are different. We felt safe with them.'

'They're skint though, aren't they? They've got nothing to show off about.'

'Trev looks like someone you wouldn't mess with but get him pissed and he just talks about trees,' Lil laughed.

She opened her wardrobe and pulled out the pink leopard print mini-skirt that Miriam had found yesterday. Miriam had seen Lil hanging it up to dry in the sunshine earlier.

'I want you to have this. It's one of my old favourites. Go on – try it on.'

Miriam pulled on the skirt. The waistband of her combat pants bunched up underneath it.

'That's not working. Take the trousers off.'

Miriam turned away from her and unzipped her trousers. Her purple jumper was too long. She pulled it over her head, even though it was cold in the ambulance.

'Great legs.' Lil smiled. 'You've got a really good figure.'

'Don't you think I'm flat-chested?' She stared at Lil's generous cleavage.

'How many supermodels have you seen with enormous boobs?' she laughed. 'I'd like you to model some of my designs.'

Miriam couldn't remember the last time anyone had complimented her, even though she wasn't sure that Lil meant it. The skirt hung low on her hips. It went well with her tight black top, though. She smiled at her reflection, impressed.

'That baggy jumper made you look...'

'Mousy?' Miriam glared at Lil in the mirror.

'I was bang out of order yesterday. Why should I care what Paul does?'

'He's not interested in me anyway,' Miriam said.

'Don't you want him to be?'

'At first I thought I got on really well with him. Now he can't even be bothered to talk to me. But sometimes you get flashes of what he could be like and...'

'Allie says he's not worth it.' Lil sighed. She stood behind Miriam and smoothed her hair; held the ends between her fingers as if they were scissors.

'I know what you mean,' Miriam said.

'I made the mistake of thinking he was deep and mysterious, when he's just...'

'A mess?'

Lil nodded, her eyes on the floor. Miriam watched her in the mirror. She looked like she was going to cry. Miriam turned round. Lil pasted a too-bright grin on her face.

'Let's do something with your hair,' she said. 'The colour's not too bad.'

'It was an accident – it was meant to come out brighter.'

'It needs punking up a bit. I promise I won't make it too

short.'

'You're going to cut my hair?'

'I know what I'm doing – I started cutting hair when I was fifteen.'

'Now?'

'We can surprise everyone.'

Miriam sat on the bed again, letting herself get caught up in Lil's enthusiasm. Lil draped an old towel over Miriam's shoulders. She sprayed her hair with water and brushed it, surprisingly gentle when she pulled out the tangles. Miriam wondered if Lil would deliberately give her a ridiculous haircut but she didn't really care. She just wanted to look different.

☆

Miriam balanced her torch on the bedside cabinet. Paul tried not to look at her as she changed for bed. The light cast a huge shadow on the wall of the van as she pulled off her jumper and put on a baggy t-shirt. She wriggled into her sleeping bag and lay down on one side of the sofa bed. Paul unlaced his boots.

'It's much nicer in here now,' she said. 'I like what you've done with the curtains.' All he'd done was tape them to the walls to hide the aluminium but the orange colour made the van seem warmer.

He didn't like the way that Lil had taken control of her, cutting her hair, giving her clothes, like she was a doll. But the angular bob gave her an elfin look that suited her. Her eyes looked enormous in the torchlight.

It felt strange to be sleeping in the same bed as her. He could sleep on the floor but that would seem stupid. Neither of them needed that air bed now. She had wasted her money.

'You'd better not sleep under that ratty old blanket. It's a nice sleeping bag.'

Paul reluctantly undid the straps on the compression sack. He felt the soft, shiny material of the sleeping bag. He was used to sleeping fully-clothed, pulling the blanket over himself, but that would make it too warm in the sleeping bag. He wished he'd drunk more - enough to go to sleep - but not so much that he'd do something stupid. Three cans of lager really weren't enough. He took off his jumper and shirt. Miriam gave him a sidelong glance.

'Don't look at me,' he said.

'I wasn't.'

Paul took off his trousers, conscious that she was still staring at him. He got into his sleeping bag as quickly as he could, feeling vulnerable in just a t-shirt and boxer shorts. The sofa bed was comfortable but he felt as if he was sinking into the foam. It smelled musty. Miriam put her headphones in her ears.

'I'll switch the torch off, then,' she said.

'Okay.'

Paul lay awake with his eyes open. But with the door shut tight, the van was absolutely dark. His eyes grew accustomed to the darkness but he couldn't make out anything. He held his hand in front of his face – he couldn't even see that. He concentrated on the muffled sound of Miriam's tape, trying to work out what she was listening to. When the tape stopped, he heard an owl hooting in the woods. He tried to tune into its irregular rhythm, tried to match it to the sound of Miriam's breathing.

Paul was starting to drift into a light sleep when he heard a fox scream. He sat up, not knowing where he was. He felt trapped. Then he realised that he was in the back of the van. He lay down again but the sound of the fox made him think of Gary – and Mark. If only Paul hadn't got drunk and let his mouth run away with him...

☆

'We need to do something,' Gary grabbed a handful of Paul's chips. They walked home unsteadily from the Rock House, weaving through streets crowded with New Year's Eve revellers. It was still a thrill for Paul to call the flat his home.

Paul had seen his college friends for the first time since Christmas. He'd found himself telling them that he'd left home after a fight with his dad, almost showing off. The livid scar on his cheek didn't seem to put the girls off either. He'd snogged Emma, the girl he'd fancied for ages from his history class. He had her number in his pocket.

'What about?'

'I mean, it's just got worse and worse. There was that guy with the baseball bat, then the slashed tyres on the mini-bus – and now the man-trap.' Gary was really wound up. 'It's the hunt master – Lord Roderick Engelby.' Gary said the name in a mock-posh voice. 'He hires scum to do his dirty work.'

'What can we do? The police are on their side.'

'Exactly.'

Gary staggered slightly along the pavement as he walked. It was quiet now they'd got away from the taxi queues, into dark streets of run-down houses.

Mark marched down the street fifty metres ahead of them, too impatient to walk at Gary and Paul's drunken pace. His polished boots reflected the glow of the street lights. The slogan "Meat is Murder" shone starkly in white paint on the back of his second-hand leather jacket.

'It's my New Year's Resolution - to do something about it.'

'Yeah – why not?' Paul clapped Gary on the back.

☆

Mark was already sitting on the sofa, unlacing his 10-hole Doc Martens. He'd put one of his hardcore punk CDs on the stereo. Mark said the lyrics were really political and profound but all Paul could make out was shouting over dissonant guitar chords.

Paul sat down on the carpet and warmed himself by the gas fire. Gary went straight to the kitchen.

'Enjoy yourself?' Mark asked.

Paul nodded. He'd hardly seen Mark inside the Rock House. Gary had danced and chatted to Paul's mates but Mark had hung around near the pool table, as if he was ashamed of being seen with kids who were still doing A-levels.

Gary came into the lounge with three small glasses of purple liquid. It looked like Ribena. He handed one to Paul. He took a gulp. His throat felt like it was on fire. Gary laughed as Paul spluttered.

'I should have warned you - it's that elderberry vodka I made in September. I forgot about it until now.'

Paul took a cautious sip. It was sweet but very strong.

'I wanted to make a toast,' Gary said.

'What to?' Mark asked.

'To Ninety Three – the year we finally get the Derbyshire Hunt on the run.'

They stood in the middle of the lounge and clanked their glasses together.

'Cheers,' Paul said.

'Smash the hunt!' Mark raised the glass to his lips.

'I want to do something big,' Gary announced.

'Yeah - but what?' Paul asked.

'We could get the hunt-sabs from Nottingham and Sheffield

to come – we'd outnumber the hunt,' Gary said.

Mark smiled, like he'd thought of a joke.

'We've been doing that for years – getting nowhere. We've got to surprise them. Use different tactics. Who's got all the wealth and power in the hunt?'

'Engelby.' Gary said.

'We've got to target him directly. Hit him where it hurts.'

'Literally?' Paul asked.

Mark nodded.

'What about non-violence?'

'What about the animals he's murdering?'

Gary sat on the edge of the armchair, his eyes burning with passion.

'Damaging possessions, property – as long as we don't physically hurt anyone – even Engelby.' He was absorbed in his own thoughts.

'What does he love more than anything?' Mark asked.

'His car. That Rolls Royce,' Paul said. On several occasions, he'd watched Engelby arrive at the hunt in his shining chauffeur-driven Rolls-Royce, immediately mounting his hunter, held still by a groom, its coat polished like a conker.

'Maybe we could throw paint at it.' Gary suggested.

'We could blow it up,' Paul said.

Mark hugged Paul tightly.

'That's it. You've got it! That's brilliant.'

'You think we can pull it off?' Gary's eyes were wide with surprise.

'But I didn't mean it – it was a...' Paul put his drink down on the coffee table. His head was spinning.

'Paul, you're a genius.' Mark grinned. 'It's a step up from supergluing the locks at McDonalds but we can do it.' He patted Paul heavily on the shoulder.

It was the vodka – and six pints talking. He hadn't expected them to take him seriously. He hoped that they would forget about it by the morning but Mark was already scribbling in his notebook.

CHAPTER TEN
THE RAVE

The farmer was waiting by the gate, collecting five pounds from each car in parking fees. People didn't seem to mind much. They spilled excitedly from the cars parked by the back hedge, carrying camping equipment.

'Greedy bastard. He's making a fortune out of this,' Allie said.

'We're using his field. And we're making money too,' Miriam pointed out.

'We've been working hard all week. He should be paying us, not moaning about us being on his land. I don't trust him.'

The deep thump of dub reggae came from an old army marquee. The people Lil knew from Bristol had arrived yesterday with hired Transit vans and equipment crammed into cars. They'd set up a main stage with speaker stacks covered by garden gazebos. A band was soundchecking. Bursts of distorted guitars interrupted the dub. There was already a smattering of people in front of the stage, waiting for something to happen. There was an ice cream van and a stall selling veggie burgers.

'Never mind him. This is great,' Miriam said. The flower garlands on Allie's awning fluttered. The sky was blue.

'Yeah. I can't believe it's the same soggy field.'

'It's like magic.'

'You're looking pretty different yourself.'

Miriam had agreed to wear one of Lil's tutus – fluorescent pink, with silver tights. Lil had sprayed Miriam's hair silver and pinned it into punky little twists. Her eyelids and lips were painted silver to match. She'd felt outrageous and confident earlier but now she felt silly.

'Are you sure it's not too much?'

'You look pretty,' Heather said. Lil had made her a pair of glittery wings and she wore them with a purple t-shirt embroidered with a butterfly. She had nearly finished painting the word "Bar" in two-foot high letters on a big sheet of hardboard that Paul and Trev had found.

A young man with dark shoulder-length hair walked up to the bar. He looked at the price list that Miriam had chalked on Heather's blackboard.

'Four cans of Fosters, please,' he said. Miriam reached into the old bath. It was full of cans bobbing around in cold water. She pulled out four cans of lager. He gave her a ten pound note and she gave him his change. He barely gave her a second glance. Miriam stifled a giggle.

'Thanks,' she said. She watched him carry the cans back to his friends lounging on the grass.

'Hey, Lil,' Allie shouted. 'That was our first customer.'

Lil had set up her stall next door, under a gazebo. Rows of tutus sparkled in the sunshine. She had spent most of the morning arranging her display of earrings.

'How about a photo?' Lil's pink PVC top was so tight and low cut, it looked like it had been sprayed on. 'You take it, Allie. You couldn't be bothered to dress up.' She handed her camera over.

Miriam picked up Tom from his buggy and held him on her hip. Lil had made him a romper suit in black and yellow bumble bee stripes. They posed in front of the "Bar" sign. Heather held her paintbrush and showed off her wings. Lil put her arm around Miriam's shoulder.

'Now everyone – say "sex"!' Lil said.

'Sex?'

'Anything's better than "cheese!" Are you ready? One...two...three...SEX!' Lil shouted. Miriam joined in. Heather erupted into helpless giggles.

☆

The organisers had asked them to direct traffic from the road so that people didn't get lost and miss the turning, but so many cars were now queuing on the lane there was a traffic jam. Paul sat on the grass verge. Exhaust fumes and the thump of dozens of car stereos drained him. He knew he wouldn't be able to cope with the rave.

Trev chatted to a car-load of people, keeping them entertained as they waited. Lil had given him a skull and cross-bones flag this morning to replace the filthy sling he'd been wearing since he broke his arm. He seemed ridiculously pleased about it.

When the traffic started to trickle down the lane again, a girl in the passenger seat of the car handed Trev something through the window.

'Ta. See you later. Have a good one,' he said.

He sat next to Paul.

'Custard cream?' He held out an opened packet of biscuits.

'They're not vegan.' Paul shook his head.

'I can't see the vegan police anywhere. What difference does it make, Paul?'

Trev ate a biscuit, pulling the two sides apart carefully and scraping the yellow filling off with his teeth. Paul looked away in disgust.

'We've done quite well for free stuff,' Trev said, spraying crumbs. 'Two cans of cider, a kiwi fruit, a glow stick – and these glasses.' He pulled something out of his sling – cardboard glasses with cellophane lenses. Trev put them on. He looked ludicrous. 'Now everything's swirling around – it's brilliant! Try them.'

He placed them on Paul's head. Paul suddenly saw a thousand hexagonal shapes full of Trev's face. He snatched them off, feeling disoriented.

'I wish you'd tell me what's wrong.' Trev put his hand on Paul's shoulder.

'I'm fine,' Paul snapped. He felt shivery, even though the sun was blazing. Trev was bare-chested beneath the grubby hi-vis vest they'd given him.

'Something happened, didn't it? When you went back?'

Paul shrugged.

'Was it your dad?'

'I didn't have the guts to face him. I just ran away again.' He'd stretched the truth so much it was grotesque. Trev didn't know his secret. It was like a barrier between them.

Paul knew about Trev's past. He'd been in a young offender's institute for three years, after stealing and crashing a car. Trev was afraid of being indoors now. He'd told Paul all about it when they'd first met. Paul envied his honesty.

Trev's expression softened.

'But you tried.' He gave Paul a one-armed hug.

☆

Trev waited his turn in the queue for the bar.

'If you want a freebie, forget it.' Allie folded her arms. 'We haven't got any to spare.'

The cash box was almost full. Miriam had been worried about storing the money safely. Allie said there was a secret hiding place in the caravan. The bar was so busy, they might run out of beer after all and it was only early evening.

'Miriam, I need to talk to you.' Trev looked serious.

'Can't you come back later?' Allie said. Trev turned away. Miriam felt annoyed – what gave Allie the right to talk on her behalf? She dashed out from behind the bar and stopped Trev before he reached the field gate.

'What is it?'

She followed Trev into the copse where they had been collecting wood for the fire-pit. The noise of the rave faded into the background. The loudest noise was a woodpigeon calling from the top of a beech tree.

'Paul's getting depressed again,' he said. 'I saw blood on his sleeve last week.'

'It was when he was building the bender.' Miriam sat down on the trunk of a fallen tree. 'And I think he's done it again since then. He's hardly spoken to me all week. He must regret asking me to share the van.'

Trev took a packet of custard creams out of his trouser pocket and offered it to her. She took one and ate it greedily.

'He was so brave, deciding to go back home. His dad beat him up when he was a kid. But since he came back, I can see the signs.'

'So it's not me?'

Trev put his arm around Miriam. She leaned her head on his shoulder.

'Of course it isn't you. It's Paul. Promise you'll tell me if he does anything to himself?'

'I've been watching him. He keeps walking off towards the river,' Miriam said.

'I'm sorry – you should be enjoying yourself. He's not your responsibility.'

'I'm glad you're looking out for him too.'

☆

It was dark. A ska band with a row of dancing trumpeters was playing on the main stage. Miriam bounced along to the music as she served customers. The bar was still steadily busy.

'I'm going to pack up soon,' Lil called over. 'I think I've had enough.'

Miriam had noticed a few girls wearing Lil's tutus and the earrings had sold well but now her stall was quiet. Lil wandered over to the bar.

'Are you both going to work all night?' she asked. She seemed lonely, even though lots of people she knew from Bristol had come up to her stall, including the good looking DJ who'd organised the rave.

'Go and enjoy yourself, Miriam,' Allie said.

'Are you sure?'

'I'll send Heather to find you if I need help. Take a few cans if you want.'

'Okay. Thanks.'

Miriam put some cans of cider in her bag. She helped Lil to pack her stall away.

'It's important to keep the price just right and have things displayed nicely,' Lil said. 'I think it went quite well.'

When everything was inside the ambulance, Lil lay back on the bed and closed her eyes.

'It's knackering, though, keeping a smile on your face all day.'

Miriam perched on the end of the bed. She fought the urge to yawn. They'd opened the bar at midday. Now it was nearly nine o'clock. What she really wanted was a long hot bath. The closest she could get to that was to stand in Allie's plastic baby bath, pouring warm water over herself.

'I've got something to perk us up – I've been saving them

since last summer.' Lil rummaged in the bottom of her wardrobe and produced a pair of salmon pink stilettos.

'I'm not wearing those.'

Lil stuck her fingers into the pointed toe of one of the shoes and pulled out a twist of tissue paper. She undid it and showed Miriam two small white pills.

'Go on, take one. You'll need it.'

Lil swallowed her pill quickly, with a swig from her water bottle. She held the other one out to Miriam, in the palm of her hand. Miriam hesitated.

'Suit yourself,' Lil said. 'But you'll probably be asleep before midnight without it.'

Miriam stared at Lil – she wasn't sure if Lil genuinely liked her but she wanted to have a good time tonight. It felt like she was finally in the world that she'd dreamed about. She opened one of her cans of cider, put the pill onto her tongue and swallowed with a gulp. There. She'd done it. She hadn't even asked what the pill was. Miriam felt a moment of panic but was determined not to show any weakness in front of Lil. She took another swig of cider to get rid of the aspirin-like taste. Maybe that was all it was. But she doubted it somehow. Lil had a wide grin on her face.

'Are you coming up yet?' Lil shouted in her ear. It was hot in the reggae tent, heavy with smoke. Miriam felt waves of tingly warmth spreading through her body, like bursts of excitement.

'I don't know. Maybe.' Miriam didn't know what Lil meant. It must be something to do with the pill.

'Want to see what's happening on the main stage?'

'Yeah, okay.'

They left the tent. The cool night air felt exhilarating on Miriam's bare arms. She heard a liquid bassline pumping out of the main stage speakers. She grabbed Lil's arm and pulled her towards the music. Miriam just wanted to dance.

They weaved between dancing people until they were at the front. The DJ was Lil's friend from Bristol. Lil caught his eye and waved at him. He grinned at her, running his hand through his tousled hair.

'He's on early. I would have been gutted if we'd missed him,' Lil shouted into her ear.

The DJ took a record out of the box. He danced with it in his arms before he put it on the turntable. Miriam felt herself become totally absorbed in the hypnotic bassline and the sounds that were layered on top of it. She felt waves of affection towards the DJ, Lil and all the strangers dancing in the field.

Miriam saw an odd figure wearing cardboard sunglasses, with a lampshade on his head, dancing in the middle of the crowd. She realised that it was Trev. He waved his right arm around manically, swaying so that other dancers had to move out of his way. He had a childlike smile, completely absorbed in his own world.

'God, he's so embarrassing,' Lil laughed.

For a moment, Miriam wondered where Paul was but the music enveloped her and she was totally sucked back into it again.

☆

The music was a dull thud in the background. The sounds of the river were soothing: the soft gurgle of the flowing water, the wind rustling the leaves of the willow tree. Away from the flashing lights, the sky was bright with stars. The moon shone on the rippling water.

No one would miss him tonight – they were all off their faces. He'd walked past the stage and seen Trev wearing that idiotic lampshade on his head and Miriam and Lil pushing into the middle of the dancers, wild looks on their faces. In the dawn, Miriam would find the newspaper cutting he'd left on their bed. By then it would all be over.

He took a gulp of White Lightning, holding the two litre bottle with both hands. He shuddered at the taste – he'd never got used to it but he needed it tonight. By the time he got to the bottom of the bottle that would be it. Coming back to Trev and the others had shown him that his life wasn't worth living. It was just a tiresome series of disasters. It was his duty to do this. He owed it to the little girl – to Gary – to do what he'd been too much of a coward to do years before.

Paul gave into self-pity and let the tears flow down his face.

CHAPTER ELEVEN
THE WILLOW TREE

Lil climbed onto the stage and gave the DJ a massive kiss as soon as he finished his set. She chattered to him as he packed away his records. Miriam waited. Lil hadn't even glanced back in her direction.

Miriam tried to dance but the music didn't move her now, even though the DJ who'd taken over from Lil's friend was quite good. She shivered, wishing she'd brought her jumper with her. It would only take a few minutes to walk to Paul's van and come back again.

Someone put their arms around her. At first, she thought it was Paul but these arms were unscarred, lightly tanned, with dark hairs. His t-shirt smelled of washing powder.

'Love the tutu,' he said. 'I was watching you behind that bar all afternoon.' She felt his lips brush the back of her neck. She turned around, startled.

It was her first customer – the guy with the dark shoulder-length hair. He grinned at her.

'Fancy a stroll down to the river – a bit of fresh air?'

'It's freezing.'

He untied a black hooded top from around his waist and gave it to her.

Paul heard people walking through the long grass, towards the river. He crouched in the deep shadow of the willow tree, cradling his cider bottle.

'Wow – it's beautiful. We've been here for a week but I've never noticed the river in the moonlight.' Paul realised that it

107

was Miriam. Why wouldn't she leave him in peace?

'I couldn't stop looking at you. You're gorgeous.'

Paul didn't recognise the man's voice. He heard the wet sound of kissing. He wished they would go away.

Miriam gasped.

'Let me come up for air for a second,' she giggled. That meant she must be nervous. 'I don't even know your name.'

'It's Gavin.'

'I'm Miriam.'

'So you're one of the travellers, then? Got your own van?' Paul knew what he was really asking. She would take this man back to the van and find the newspaper cutting too early, before he had time. Or maybe they would just shag on top of it and never even notice. Why should it matter now anyway?

'I'm sharing a caravan with a friend at the moment. She's got kids, though. They'll already be in bed.' Paul didn't know why she'd lied but he was grateful.

The cider bottle slipped out of his hands with a dull thud. Paul stopped it from rolling down the river bank with his foot. It was still a quarter full.

'Did you hear something? It came from over there.' The man sounded jumpy. Paul held his breath and crouched in the shadow of the willow.

'It was just an otter or something.'

'Come back to my tent. There won't be any scary noises.'

'Are you sure about that?' she giggled.

'We could start making some of our own.'

Paul couldn't believe that Miriam had fallen for a guy who seemed so pathetic. Paul took a deep breath. He had no right to judge anyone. He waited under the tree until their footsteps were just a faint swishing in the distance.

☆

Gavin unzipped the tent and fumbled for his torch.

'Is there room?' Miriam's heart was thumping. She was still shivery, despite Gavin's hoodie. He crawled inside his dome tent.

'Come on,' he said.

She unlaced her boots and followed him inside. She hadn't wanted to take him back to the van. Paul might be there. She didn't want to explain why she was sleeping on a sofa bed with a man who wasn't even her boyfriend.

Gavin tied his torch to a loop at the top of the tent. She banged her head on it as she sat down, making the light swing around wildly. Gavin laughed.

'Yeah, it's quite small in here. It'll be okay if we lie down, though.' He leaned forward to give her a long, lingering kiss, pulling her towards him. His mouth tasted of beer. He unzipped his sleeping bag and laid it out on the groundsheet. Miriam lay back, uncertain about what was going to happen next.

Gavin suddenly wriggled out of his jeans. The torch lit up the bulge in the front of his tight black boxer shorts. She took off the hoodie and started to pull off her tutu. Gavin put his hand out.

'No – leave it on. Take everything else off,' he grinned.

A stupid, childish-sounding giggle escaped from her lips. Part of her felt scared. But she'd chosen to come to Gavin's tent. If she changed her mind now, she could just put her boots back on and go back to the rave as if nothing had happened. This was the point of no return. She took a deep breath and peeled off her t-shirt.

Gavin put his hands on her breasts. She gasped at the cold

touch of his fingers but tried to breathe more slowly, telling herself to enjoy this; that it was normal.

☆

Paul felt strangely calm as he took off his boots. He undressed quickly, hanging his clothes on the low branch of the willow tree. The cold air pinched his skin but he was numb from drinking the bottle of White Lightning. He wasn't even sure why he'd taken his clothes off. It just seemed like the right thing to do.

He scrambled down the bank to a point where the water looked deep and waded in. He was thrown off balance by the strong current. The water was so cold, it seemed to knock the air out of his lungs, but it only reached his chest. He lay face-down in the water and was swept downstream. An impulse to swim took over. He became entangled in the hanging branches of the willow tree.

If he lay here, the branches would stop him from being carried along by the current. He hoped that his body would sink before dawn and be pushed down to the mouth of the river and into the sea. Paul floated on his front and opened his mouth so the water gushed in. He reacted instinctively, choking and gasping.

Paul lifted his head out of the water and thought about Gary. He'd gone through with it. He hadn't been a coward. Determined, Paul put his face beneath the surface again.

☆

'It's your first time? Why didn't you say?'

Miriam gripped the condom uncertainly between her finger

and thumb.

'I didn't want to put you off. I've only ever put one of these on a banana. You know, at school.'

Gavin propped himself up on one elbow.

'Seriously?' he laughed.

'I'm sorry.'

'But – I thought you were really up for it.'

'I was – I am. I'm just a bit nervous.'

'But you looked so…'

'Like what?' She sat up and pulled a corner of the sleeping bag over her chest.

'I didn't think you were a virgin.'

'Why?'

'The moment's gone now. It was nice while it lasted.'

'We could still do it.' She had ruined it by fumbling with the condom. Her nerves had been too obvious.

Gavin shook his head.

'It wouldn't be right. I didn't tell you but I've got a girlfriend in Bristol. I mean, I really fancy you but I just wanted a bit of fun.'

Miriam dropped the condom onto the groundsheet and put her knickers and t-shirt back on. She struggled into the silver tights. It was a massive anti-climax but she also felt relieved.

'That's honest of you.'

'I'm too pissed, anyway. Your fault for selling me all that beer. I just wanted to talk to you.'

'We're meant to be clearing up the site. Maybe I'll see you tomorrow?'

'Maybe.'

Miriam put her unlaced boots on and half ran, half stumbled towards Paul's van, tripping over guy ropes. She pulled the shutter up. Paul wasn't here.

She threw herself onto the sofa bed, sobbing. She didn't know what she'd been thinking. She'd been caught up in the moment with Gavin and the excitement the pill had given her. It was all Lil's fault, encouraging her to dress up like an idiot and then abandoning her while she chatted up that DJ. She should have stayed safely behind the bar with Allie.

She felt a piece of paper crumple under her hand. Miriam sat up and switched on her torch. It was a grubby white envelope. There was a note on it, scrawled in Biro.

Trev needs to know what I did. I should have told him years ago. You can do what you like with the van. I've got to do what Gary did. I'm sorry.

Who was Gary? She opened the envelope. Inside was an old newspaper cutting, yellow and brittle. The young man in the photo stared back at her with deep-set eyes.

SIGNED SUICIDE CONFESSION OF ENGELBY BOMBER

Early this morning, the hunt for the killer of tragic bomb tot Kelly Andrews, 4, came to a dramatic conclusion. The car bomb mastermind's body was found hanging from a tree in a park near his student flat in the Normanton area of Derby.

Engineering student Gary Hirst, 21, an animal rights extremist, left a suicide note containing a full confession to Saturday's bomb attack on a vintage Rolls Royce belonging to the Master of the South Derbyshire Hunt, Lord Roderick Engelby.

Instructions for home-made explosives, bolt clippers and paramilitary style clothing were also found at the flat.

The grieving father of murdered toddler Kelly, chauffeur Ken Andrews, made the following statement: "My daughter was an innocent little girl. The man who planned this attack was pure evil."

Inspector Steve Tanner, from Derbyshire Constabulary

commented: "This is one of the most severe acts of terrorism ever committed in the region. We are probing all known animal rights groups in the area for any links with Hirst and this attack."

Miriam stared at the newspaper cutting. She jumped down from the van and ran, still clutching her torch.

It didn't take her long to find Trev. He was swaying slowly at the edge of the crowd. He still had the lampshade on his head. Miriam stood in front of him. Trev looked at her blankly. She grabbed his good arm and pulled him away.

She held out the newspaper cutting and the envelope. The paper flickered under the strobe lights. Her hand shook.

'Paul's going to kill himself.'

Trev threw the lampshade onto the ground.

'He left this for you,' she said.

Trev took the envelope and the cutting. He seemed to stare at them for a long time. He folded them into his trouser pocket.

'Where is he?'

'I haven't seen him for hours. But I was near the river a while ago and I heard a noise.'

'Do you think he's gone down to the willow tree?'

'Maybe.'

Trev sprinted towards the river. Miriam ran after him. The beat of the music grew fainter, replaced by the thump of her heart.

Miriam switched her torch on. The light caught something white flapping in the branches of the willow tree. The flow of the water rushed in her ears. The rave felt a million miles away.

'Trev!'

There was a t-shirt and Paul's ripped combat pants hanging

over a branch. Trev snatched the torch out of her hands and shone the torch up into the branches of the tree.

'God – please,' he muttered.

Miriam ducked under the overhanging canopy of the tree. She saw a shape floating at the point where the branches dipped into the water. The silvery leaves reflected the moonlight.

'It's too late,' Trev sobbed. He dropped the torch and sank onto the ground next to her.

'Don't give up,' she said. Her body seemed to act automatically. She kicked off her boots and struggled down the river bank. She slipped and fought to keep her balance as she made her way towards Paul, crawling over the roots of the willow tree, entwined just under the water. She hooked her legs over one of the roots, reached out and grasped a handful of Paul's dreadlocks. She pulled him towards her, grabbed him under his armpits and flipped him onto his back. It took all of her strength to pull Paul onto the platform. The water was only a few centimetres deep. She gasped for air.

Paul's legs were still underwater. The dappled moonlight shone on his pale skin, making it look like marble. Miriam touched his face. He was cold, like the rubber mannequins that she had used on her first aid course at work.

Suddenly, Miriam remembered everything.

'Paul. Paul!' she called. There was no response. She put her hand on his chest. He wasn't breathing. Miriam tipped his jaw back and pinched his nostrils with one hand. She put her lips to Paul's and breathed into his mouth twice. She couldn't stop shivering but somehow she had to keep going.

She felt his chest. There was no movement. The moonlight disappeared. She had to do everything by touch. She breathed into his mouth and put her hand on his chest again. She had to keep hoping - but Trev was right. They hadn't reached him in time. He might have been in the water for hours. Paul was dead.

Miriam felt Paul's chest rise slightly. It must be a reflex movement from her mouth-to-mouth breathing. Then it convulsed with a sudden spasm. She tried to roll Paul onto his side, her fingers slipping on his skin. The moon came out again, as he spewed foul-smelling river water.

'Trev – help!'

Paul realised he was throwing up vast amounts of liquid. He lay awkwardly on his side, on what felt like a pile of bones under a layer of shallow water. There was nothing left inside him and his chest burned with every breath he tried to take.

'He needs an ambulance.' A girl's voice.

'No,' he croaked.

'I thought you were dead.' That was Trev.

Paul opened his eyes but everything was dark. He forced himself into a sitting position. Pale light filtered through the branches of a tree. His bare legs looked strangely white in the moonlight.

'Come on, mate.' Trev said. He grabbed Paul's arm and put it over his shoulder. 'You'll be alright.' Someone else – the girl? Was it Miriam? - took his other arm. He made no attempt to struggle. He felt himself being pulled upwards until he was lying on the grass, his back throbbing from being dragged over the roots sticking out of the riverbank. For a few blissful seconds, he was unaware of everything except the pain.

CHAPTER TWELVE
ENGELBY HALL, APRIL 1993

Paul stared at his reflection. The cut on his cheek had healed into a jagged red scar. It made him seem harder than he really was, like he'd been in a knife fight. Gary and Mark seemed so sure, but Paul had shadows like bruises under his eyes. He'd been unable to sleep for weeks, worrying if this was an heroic thing to do; or just stupid and dangerous.

He didn't even look like himself. Mark had lent him a pair of combat trousers; Gary had given him a plain black hooded sweatshirt. He wore two layers of long sleeved t-shirts underneath, to keep out the cold night air. Paul held the balaclava. He stuck his fingers through the small holes that he was supposed to see and breathe through.

He pulled it over his head. The acrylic wool was harsh and itchy against his skin. In the warmth of the flat, he could already feel a prickle of sweat on his scalp. His eyes were the only thing he recognised in the mirror. He didn't belong in this tiny box room. He was a bank robber or a terrorist.

They would go to prison if they were caught blowing up Engelby's car. Paul's A-Level exams were only a few weeks away. He'd already been provisionally accepted by Manchester University. He'd worked hard at his revision and coursework since leaving home. He was an adult now, in charge of his own destiny. The bomb could totally screw everything up.

He'd meant it as a joke. Why did Mark have to take everything so seriously? Gary had got sucked up in his enthusiasm, until Paul had kidded himself that it was a good idea. A few weeks ago, bomb-making instructions had arrived in a brown envelope. Paul had found himself stripping wires and cutting up pieces of duct tape at the kitchen table, while

Gary pored over the complex diagrams. He had lent his car to Mark for reconnaissance missions.

Paul pulled the balaclava off and stuffed it into his trouser pocket. He felt safe in here. He lay on his sofa bed, staring at the patterns in the textured wallpaper. If he didn't move, maybe it would never happen.

He was woken by a knock on his door.

'Paul! Are you ready? We should get going.'

'He's fallen asleep.'

Paul opened his bedroom door. Gary and Mark stood in the doorway. They were both wearing black. Mark also had a camouflage stripe across his cheeks. It seemed unnecessary when they were going to be wearing balaclavas.

Gary's old rucksack was on the kitchen table. He usually put his sandwiches in it when he went hunt-sabbing. But now it contained a bomb.

The kitchen clock seemed loud, the second-hand clicking reluctantly around the dial towards two in the morning. The washing up had been done but the tap was dripping.

Mark swung his own backpack onto his shoulders.

'You look the part, anyway.'

Paul swallowed. His mouth had suddenly gone dry.

'I don't think we should be doing this. I'm sorry,' Paul said. They both stared at him. 'I hate Roderick Engelby as much as you do but...'

'You're scared?' Mark said. 'Of course you are. You should stick to hunt-sabbing - then you can just run round pulling girls.'

'I helped you at that chicken farm.' Paul crossed his arms, staring at Mark.

'You've not got the guts for this, Paul,' Mark said.

'What about non-violence?' Paul turned to Gary. 'Why are

we blowing something up?'

'Fuck non-violence,' Mark said.

'It's just a car,' Gary agreed. 'It's a grand gesture. But it'll wake Engelby up.'

Gary gave Paul a hug.

'It'll be fine. I promise,' he smiled. 'If you don't come, you'll be gutted.'

'He could be on the phone to the police as soon as we leave this flat. He's coming with us,' Mark growled.

'He's committed, Mark,' Gary said.

'I won't tell anyone. I'm just not sure we should be...'

Mark pushed him towards the stairs, not hard - but Paul fought the urge to turn around and punch him. Instead, he took a deep breath and put the balaclava over his head, rolling it up at the bottom so it looked like an ordinary woolly hat.

'I'm coming.'

'Pull in,' Mark said. Paul's headlights illuminated a gap in the hedge. He turned left. It was a bumpy farm track, running between a field and a wood. 'Stop here.'

Paul parked the car on the verge, against the hedge.

They left the car silently, pressing the doors shut. Paul flashed his torch over the blue Vauxhall Nova. It looked out of place parked there with fake clip-on number plates – guilty. Until Dad gave it to him, it had been the family car. Dad had bought it second-hand when Paul was twelve. He'd driven them to Mablethorpe for the day to celebrate.

'Are you deliberately advertising us?' Mark whispered.

Paul rolled his balaclava over his face and pointed the torch at the ground. Mark started walking steadily. Paul followed, trying not to stumble on the deep ruts in the track. Gary's presence behind him felt reassuring.

When the track turned a corner, Mark flashed his torch at a sign nailed to a tree at the edge of the woods. It read "Trespassers Will Be Prosecuted". He cut the barbed wire next to a fence post, where the damaged strands would be hidden by a tuft of long grass.

'Be quiet. The gamekeeper shoots first and asks questions later.' They filed into the woods. Paul was hyper-aware that last year's leaves rustled with each footstep. His nerves jumped with every snapped twig. They shone their torches on the ground, faintly revealing a path between the trees.

They passed a wire hutch full of sleeping pheasants.

'Something else he does for fun,' Gary muttered. 'Inviting a whole bunch of chinless wonders over just to...'

'Don't talk,' Mark hissed.

They reached the edge of the woods. Mark crouched, his back pressed to a tree trunk. Paul and Gary copied him.

'Switch your torches off.' The night sky glimmered, where the clouds were reflecting the moon. The white stonework of the mansion glowed faintly at the bottom of the grass slope.

'There's some cover on the way to the house but we're mostly in the open. Follow me.'

Mark crawled away from the woods on his hands and knees. He loved this, Paul could tell – all this military-style planning was like an elaborate game; playing soldiers. Gary started crawling forwards too. Paul was surrounded by darkness and silence. He felt stranded. He crawled after them, his borrowed trousers quickly soaked by the damp grass.

☆

Paul could sense the looming presence of the house. He took another step. There was a loud crunching sound - he felt gravel under his boot. Paul froze. Mark grabbed his arm.

'One more mistake and you're in deep shit.'

Paul concentrated on making every step silent, slowly lowering his boots to the ground after balancing on tiptoes. It seemed to take hours to reach the dim shape of the Rolls Royce on the drive.

Gary lay on his back. He wriggled underneath the car, near the petrol tank. Paul crouched next to him, ready to pass him everything he needed. Mark kept watch.

The paintwork of the Rolls Royce reflected the soft light of the torch as Gary shone it on the car's undercarriage. Paul got the bomb out of the bag. It was small – wires and explosives attached to a digital alarm clock bought cheap from the flea market. Paul thought about pulling a wire out. But Gary would notice straight away. He would probably be able to mend it with duct tape. And he would never trust Paul again.

'Why don't we just slash his tyres? We could put gravel in the petrol tank.'

'Don't be so pathetic,' Mark hissed.

'Come on,' Gary whispered, from underneath the car. 'Just think how good you'll feel when it blows up.'

Paul handed the bomb carefully to Gary. He passed the strips of tape he'd cut to size earlier, until the bomb was stuck firmly to the petrol tank. He still secretly hoped that it wouldn't go off.

☆

They hid inside a hollow holly bush on the edge of the woods, sitting in silence. Paul hugged himself to keep warm.

The bomb was primed to explode at six thirty-two – according to Mark, the time when Roderick Engelby opened his curtains to admire his car. Mark said that he only kept the car in a garage when the weather was bad. When Paul was hunt-sabbing, he had heard Engelby braying that having a vintage Roller on the drive completed the look of the house.

The light of Mark's torch revealed used condoms lying on the dry earth. Obviously other people also got a thrill out of dodging the gamekeeper's shotgun.

Gary nibbled a rice cake but Paul's stomach was churning. He took his balaclava off and scratched his head – it was unbearably itchy and claustrophobic. Mark ordered him to put it on again.

The dawn came earlier than Paul expected, with a riot of bird song and the strangled call of the pheasants. Paul made himself concentrate on the dawn chorus, trying to distinguish one bird from another. It was five in the morning. Time went so slowly. He peered between the holly leaves and looked towards the house, shrouded in mist. The windows were all curtained. The car was a small rectangle on the drive, like a toy. Mark pulled him back into the bush.

Paul stared at his watch but the minutes went past so slowly. Shafts of sunlight pierced through the spiky leaves. Paul's head was drenched in sweat. His lips were dry and tasted salty when he licked them.

At six-twenty, Mark handed Paul a pair of binoculars.

'Seeing as this was your idea, you can have the honour of watching it happen up close. As soon as the bomb goes off we run back to the car.'

Paul stood up and poked the lenses of the binoculars out of the bush while trying to stay hidden. He focussed on the car, looking so harmless on the drive, then up at the house. There were signs of life - most of the curtains were open now, apart from the large bay window on the first floor. Mark had discovered that this was Roderick Engelby's bedroom. It was the grandest window in this enormous house.

Paul glanced at his watch. It was six twenty-nine. His palms grew slippery with sweat. He trained the binoculars on the drive, for a final look at the car. Paul was pleased that he hadn't chickened out or sabotaged the bomb. He wanted to see the look on Engelby's face as the car exploded.

A man in a chauffeur's uniform was polishing the bonnet of the Rolls Royce. A little girl with blonde hair was sitting behind the steering wheel of the car, pretending to drive it.

Paul thrust the binoculars into Gary's hands. As he ran out of the holly bush, he felt horribly exposed on the gentle slope of cropped green turf.

He ran towards the car. Maybe he could get to them in time. He ran, waving his arms.

'Get away from the car!' he shouted. 'It's going to blow up!' But he was too far away to be heard. He kept running. Suddenly, he crashed to the ground.

'Don't fucking ruin this now.' Mark had rugby tackled him; grabbing him by the ankles.

'There's a little girl in the car.'

'You can't stop it now. Do you want us all to go to prison?' He lay low and pressed Paul into the ground. Paul struggled against him. The chauffeur was a tiny dot by the car but it was possible that he might see something moving and be alerted to the danger.

Gary ran down the hill.

'Get out! Run!' he screamed towards the car. 'We can't stop it.'

The car turned into a ball of flame. The explosion made the

ground shake, even half a mile away, followed by the sound of screams, debris hitting the ground, dogs barking frantically and horses terrified in their stables. Black smoke hung over the house.

Mark and Gary grabbed Paul and pulled him up. His legs didn't seem to work at first but then he ran, stumbling, into the woods. Everything he could see was tinged orange, as if the explosion had damaged his vision.

☆

Paul jerked awake from his recurring nightmare. He was warm, lying on something soft that seemed to be moulded around his body – the sofa bed. How had he got here? Maybe he had dreamed scribbling that note on the envelope with the newspaper cutting and going down to the river. But he remembered the shock of the cold water; the slow drift into oblivion; then Trev and Miriam's voices. He remembered lying on the grass, staring at the moon as they tried to dress him.

He sat upright. Every muscle in his body felt torn. A dim light filtered through a crack at the bottom of the van door and he could hear music and voices outside. Miriam sat at the foot of the sofa bed, wrapped in a blanket.

'You read the note?'

She nodded.

'Where's Trev?'

'I don't know.'

Paul wondered if Miriam had been awake all night. There were traces of silver make-up around her eyes but her cheeks were streaked with dirt and tear tracks.

'Did Trev read it?'

'You've been spending hours by the river. Trev worked out

that you'd be near the willow tree.'

'You know what I did?'

'You killed that girl? The chauffeur's daughter?'

'We weren't supposed to hurt anyone – just blow up the car. I ran away. Gary did the right thing – but I didn't know until Bella gave me the newspaper cutting.'

'You knew you'd killed someone and you just ran away?'

'There was another guy, Mark. He said he'd kill me if I told anyone.'

'What happened to him?'

'He could be anywhere.'

Paul saw a kitchen knife sticking out of the box where Miriam was storing food. He grabbed it. His chest hurt when he moved. Everything hurt. It would have been so easy to have done this last night. He started to cut his wrist.

'No!'

Miriam grabbed the knife and threw it to the back of the van. A thin trickle of blood dripped onto his sleeping bag. He hadn't severed the vein.

'I've got to kill myself.'

'What good would that do?' She gripped his wrist, surprisingly strongly. She covered the cut with toilet paper. 'Just tell me everything.'

'I tried to tell my mum. But Trev didn't know anything until he saw the newspaper cutting.'

☆

Sunlight shone through the edge of the van door. Miriam glanced at her watch. It was ten o'clock. Time hadn't made any sense since she and Trev had dragged Paul out of the river.

'So what are you going to do, now you know? Hand me

over to the police?' Paul wiped his eyes on his t-shirt. They filled with tears again immediately.

'It's up to you. The police don't even know there was anyone else involved.'

'I still did it, though. It was my idea.'

'They pushed you into it.'

'But Mark's still out there.'

While she had been watching over Paul, Miriam had remembered the bombing being reported on Midlands Today. The grim black and white photograph of the bomber had contrasted starkly with the sunny holiday snap of the dead girl. Her devastated parents had been interviewed holding their daughter's favourite teddy bear. Miriam remembered looking around the living room at her own family: Ruth, painting her nails alternately pink and black before a date with Mike; Dad still wearing his fluorescent cycle clips around his suit trousers; Mum finishing off the pizza that Miriam had made in her home economics lesson.

Miriam let Paul cry. She sorted through the food box for the pocket first aid kit she'd bought. She held Paul's left wrist while she unwrapped the blood-stained toilet paper. The wound was surprisingly small. He shuddered as she cleaned his wrist with an antiseptic wipe. She pressed a plaster over the cut. Paul sat passively, tear-tracks on his cheeks, as she felt his bones and his racing pulse.

Paul gave her a tentative smile. There seemed to be hope in his red-rimmed blue eyes, like a shaft of watery winter sunshine.

CHAPTER THIRTEEN
SHEEP

Miriam woke. She was curled into Paul's back, her arm wrapped tightly around his chest. She checked her watch. The glass had steamed up. It was after two in the afternoon. Paul was still sleeping. Miriam moved away from him as gently as she could and rolled up the van door. She climbed out and looked around. A few ravers were still groggily packing their cars. The field was strewn with rubbish. Miriam didn't even know where Gavin's tent had been last night. She didn't care. It seemed like a long time ago. Miriam remembered that she was supposed to be helping to clean up.

She crouched down to pee between the front of the van and the hedge. She climbed back inside and changed out of her ripped tights into her combat pants and a t-shirt. Paul opened his eyes. She couldn't leave him here. Not after what he'd tried to do with the knife.

'How are you feeling?' she asked.

He sat up, grimacing. 'Bruised.'

'Me too. But I've got to help with the clean-up. You'd better come with me.'

'You're not going to tell the others, are you? About last night?'

'Trev's still got the newspaper cutting.'

'Shit.'

Paul unzipped his sleeping bag. He put his boots on. He stood up slowly, bracing himself against the side of the van.

'Are you okay?' she asked.

'Everything's spinning.' He slid down the van wall into a crouching position, covering his eyes with his hands. 'I need to eat something.'

There was a loaf of wholemeal bread in the food box. It was going stale but she passed him a slice. Paul tore it into small pieces and started chewing.

'Water,' he said, through a mouthful of bread. She gave a half-empty bottle of mineral water and he gulped it until it was empty. He helped himself to another slice of bread.

Paul climbed out of the van stiffly but he met her gaze steadily as she swung her legs over the side and pulled the shutter down. He was pale and even more dishevelled than usual.

The stage had already been dismantled. Allie was picking up litter where people had been dancing. Tom was in his buggy, sucking the ears of his toy monkey.

'I've been out here for hours. Nice of you to turn up.'

Heather was enthusiastically stomping on a pile of empty beer cans.

'We get a penny for every can at the recycling centre. Mum's letting me keep the money,' she said. 'But you might find some other cool stuff.'

'You both look like shit,' Allie said. 'At least you're here, which is more than I can say for Lil.'

'Did she go off with that DJ?'

'I knocked on her van door and no one answered. So I walked up the lane and got a text message. She says she's gone back to Bristol.' Allie tore off several bin bags from a huge roll. 'Have these. Trev's made himself totally useless – no surprises there.'

Trev stood near the fire-pit. The embers of the fire were still smoking. He'd taped a bin bag to his plaster cast. He was staring vacantly at the ground. He picked up a whisky bottle and took a long swig, almost toppled over, then sat heavily on a log.

'Did you see him last night?' Allie asked. 'He was all blissed out. But later on, he helped himself to a load of cans from the bar. Now he's necking all the booze that people have left behind. The sooner he passes out, the better.' Allie's eyes blazed.

Paul walked straight up to Trev. Miriam started to follow him. Paul sat down next to him. Trev pushed Paul, shouting. His words were slurred. Trev pulled something out of his pocket, screwed it up and dropped it into the fire. Paul cried out but Trev staggered away from him, towards his bender, clutching the whisky bottle close to his chest. Paul stared into the ashes.

'Bloody typical,' Allie said. She picked up an empty cider bottle. 'If I had somewhere to go, I'd leave them to deal with this mess – see how it feels.'

'That's not fair. What about the skip-raids? What about all the things they built and the wood they chopped?'

'So? Anyone could do that. I've put up with them for too long.'

Miriam walked over to the fire pit with her bin bag.

☆

Paul swallowed a mouthful of baked beans. There was a burning sensation down his windpipe but he needed to eat. Allie's cupboards were full of tins and packets of food that the ravers had left behind. They had brought too much stuff in their cars, as if they needed to protect themselves from the wild.

'You're eating normally - not one bean at a time.' Heather stared at him.

Paul shrugged. Allie and Miriam stared too. He put down his

fork and pushed the plate away.

'I can eat if I want,' he said. Heather was right. He'd actually been hungry. Paul had forced himself through the pain barrier to help them clean up the field. It was almost dark outside, with a fine drizzle falling. Now there was only a big pile of bin bags and some trampled grass to prove that several thousand people had been dancing here. Every part of his body ached. He was glad of the warmth from the wood-burning stove and he'd eaten without thinking.

Trev was still flaked out in his bender. Paul had checked up on him and put a bottle of water within his reach. Trev had been breathing, at least. Paul was relieved that Trev knew his secret, even though it had ruined their friendship. He had tried to explain himself earlier when Trev had burned the newspaper cutting in front of him.

'We've worked so hard,' Miriam said. 'Especially Paul.'

Miriam smiled at him. Paul couldn't believe that he had told her everything. He'd been desperate to tell his mum and Bella but had burdened Miriam instead. He should have felt guilty about that but she was acting so calmly. She had been talking to him kindly all day. It had to be a trick.

'When you finally dragged yourselves out of bed.' Allie stretched up to the top cupboard. 'I need a brandy.'

A loud noise cut through the silence outside - an engine starting but dying away with a high-pitched grating sound. The engine tried to start several times without success.

'What the...?' Allie dumped Tom on Miriam's lap. She grabbed her torch from its hook by the door and ran outside.

Paul followed Allie. It was Lil's ambulance. Lil sat in the driver's seat, hitting the steering wheel with both hands. Allie opened the driver's door. The cab light switched on. Lil's face looked ghostly, lit from above, floating in darkness.

'You promised you'd help us,' Allie shouted. 'I should have known!'

'Allie, why won't it start?' Lil whined.

'Knowing you, you've probably just run out of diesel.'

'I had half a tank. I'm sorry I didn't help but I want to go to back to Bristol. I don't want to do this anymore.'

Paul realised that Lil wasn't wearing any make-up. He'd never seen her without thick black eye-liner before – not even when he'd slept with her. Her eyes looked tiny without it.

'I don't want to carry on either.' Allie shouted. 'I just want to find somewhere quiet for the kids. But what choice have I got? Go on, fuck off back to your trendy Bristol mates.'

Lil fixed her eyes on Paul. 'I hate you too,' she yelled at him.

She tried to start the van again but the engine died every time. She threw herself on the steering wheel, sobbing.

'What's wrong with her?' Miriam whispered. She held Tom against her chest. He looked bewildered.

'Maybe she's coming down from something she had last night. I bet she had a pill, didn't she?'

'Yeah, but…'

Paul saw headlights coming down the lane. His heart lurched. Was it the police? Had Miriam betrayed him? He sighed with relief when the farmer's tatty Land Rover drove fast through the gates and braked sharply in front of Allie.

'I should have known you lot would still be here, digging your heels in.'

'You said you'd let us stay for a few more nights if we cleaned up the field,' Allie said.

'I'm putting sheep on here first thing tomorrow morning. I want you all gone.'

'We need to fix this van first.'

'I'll get rid of you,' the farmer said. He drove off, turning in a sharp circle, smoke belching from his exhaust.

'He's running that Land Rover into the ground,' Allie said darkly, like she was muttering a curse.

'Open the bonnet,' Allie ordered Lil. She propped the lid up and peered inside. Allie passed the torch to Paul.

'Try starting the engine,' she shouted.

The engine wheezed again. Allie kept asking Lil to start the engine. She put her head under the bonnet, listening and examining the machinery.

'I think the starter motor's gone. It needs a new part.' Allie's face was shiny with drizzle. There was a smudge of oil on her forehead.

'So I'm stuck here?'

Allie nodded, her lips pressed together and her arms folded across her chest.

☆

There was a loud bang on the van door. Miriam sat bolt upright. Rain hammered on the roof.

'Police – open up!'

'I knew you'd do this,' Paul said. 'It doesn't matter. I'm ready for it.'

'What?'

'I knew you'd tell the police about me. I don't blame you.'

'But I didn't.'

'It was Trev, then.'

The banging started again. Paul pulled his trousers on and opened the shutter. He stood in the entrance of the van, silhouetted against dark storm clouds. Two policemen stood outside. A round-faced, stocky man held the harness of an excitable-looking Alsatian.

'The party's over,' said a tall, smug-looking policeman. He stared past Paul, straight at Miriam.

'But it is over,' she said. 'Everyone left yesterday. We were cleaning up.'

'We've had a complaint. You had another sound system here last night, didn't you? I bet you've got quite a few illegal substances in that van.'

'We were all in bed by ten o'clock!' Miriam said.

'So how can I help you, officers?' Paul asked politely.

'Come on, out.' the round-faced man said, yawning.

Paul jumped down from the van and held his arms out for Miriam. She scrambled out of her sleeping bag. She felt exposed in her t-shirt and knickers. Paul gave her a wide smile when he caught her. He hugged her tight. Miriam shivered – but it wasn't just the cold. She wanted to be close to him.

'Thank you,' Paul whispered.

'Enough chit-chat, love-birds,' the tall policeman said. He climbed into the van. The other policeman made his dog jump up and hauled himself after it. Miriam was frightened but Paul held her tightly. She stared at the plaster on his wrist. He had really thought that she'd betrayed him. He'd almost seemed resigned to it.

A riot van and a police dog vehicle were parked haphazardly near the gate. Two more policemen with a dog opened the door of Allie's caravan without knocking. Allie shouted at them and Tom started crying. A policeman hammered on the door of Lil's ambulance.

The wet grass froze Miriam's bare feet and her soaked t-shirt clung to her skin. Her arms were covered in goosebumps. She leaned further into Paul, desperate for warmth. Inside Paul's van, the tall policeman was ripping the sofa bed covers, prodding the foam. The dog's nose was stuck in the food box.

'Do you mind?' Miriam said. 'How would you like it if I ripped up your sofa?'

'Shh.' Paul elbowed Miriam in the ribs. He was so bony that it really hurt. The round-faced policeman emptied Miriam's rucksack onto the floor of the van.

'I'd have you arrested on the spot.' The tall policeman laughed. Miriam balled her hands into fists. Paul held her tight.

'Don't make any fuss. They'll get bored and leave us alone,' Paul whispered.

There was a crash from Lil's ambulance as the back doors were forced open. Lil screamed. Two policemen piled in. Trev ran out of his bender.

'Fuck off and leave her alone!' he roared. 'You can't do this!' Trev sprinted into the ambulance.

'Trev – don't be a hero,' Paul said, under his breath.

A large policeman ran into the ambulance. He pulled Trev out, struggling wildly.

'You can't handcuff me!' Trev said. But he was pushed to the ground with the policeman's knee pressed into his back. Trev lay gasping for breath for a few seconds until he was dragged into the riot van.

Lil came slowly down the steps of the ambulance, in front of her captors, her hands cuffed behind her back. She held her head high but looked unnaturally pale.

'Lil!' Miriam called. She tried to struggle away from Paul. He wouldn't let her go.

The two policemen and the Alsatian climbed down from Paul's van.

'I'm not going to waste my time dismantling your van,' the tall man grumbled. 'Even if we think you are hiding something.'

'Oh, thanks,' Paul replied. The dog bounded up to him. Miriam shrieked. Paul stared at it calmly until the dog handler yanked its harness. The two policemen walked away.

Miriam could see Lil and Trev through the meshed rear window of the police van as it drove through the gate. She wondered if she would see them again.

'How can they get away with doing that?' Miriam asked. 'What's going to happen to Lil and Trev?'

Paul shrugged.

'You need to get something warm on.'

'But they've had their hands on everything.'

Paul made Miriam climb back into the van. She was shivering uncontrollably. Paul put her sleeping bag around her shoulders and found dry clothes for her. She was still shivering when she'd put her army coat on top of her purple jumper. The sofa bed was tipped onto its side. Food was strewn all over the floor. She didn't want to look at the mess.

Miriam heard sheep bleating. She jumped down from the van. A flock of sheep poured through the gate. The farmer followed in his Land Rover. A collie barked madly, its head sticking out of the passenger window. The sheep spread themselves out and started grazing.

'Told you I was putting sheep on here,' the farmer said.

'How are we supposed to leave now?' Paul shouted.

'I'm coming back with my shotgun.' The farmer mimed shooting Paul's tyres through his window. He drove his Land Rover back through the gate.

CHAPTER FOURTEEN
THE ROADSIDE

Paul folded the tarpaulins from Trev's bender and put them in the back of the van. He helped Miriam to untie the string that held the willow poles together. The sheep stayed out of the way, sheltering under the trees near the river.

'Do you think he'd actually shoot at us?' Miriam asked.

Paul put on Trev's fleece and collected his meagre possessions into the holdall. He felt for the hole cut in the turf where Trev had hidden his tin. It was under the spot furthest away from the door, where he laid his head. Paul knew Trev so well, he could predict things like that. He understood Trev's anger. At least things were out in the open. Trev could see him for what he was. Maybe if Paul had told him the truth years ago? But it was too late now.

'He'd be stupid to shoot my tyres out. But it's like that sometimes. You'll have to get used to it.'

Paul helped Miriam to pull the poles out of the ground. They bundled them up and threw them into the back of the van for Trev to use again.

Miriam hugged herself for warmth. The rain dripped off her hood.

'Dodging a nutter with a shotgun isn't something I'm prepared to be doing on a regular basis,' she muttered.

Allie tied a rope onto the front of the ambulance and looped it round the tow bar of the butcher's van. She was swamped by her hi-vis waterproof jacket and trousers.

'I need to steer the ambulance while it's being towed up the hill,' she said. 'Miriam – get in the caravan with the kids and lock the door.'

Paul climbed into his van and started the engine. The

windscreen began to steam up. Allie got into the driver's seat of the ambulance and waved out of the window when she was ready. Paul's tyres slipped on the sodden grass, creating a spray of mud. He kept going and drove steadily through the gate. He gritted his teeth, keeping the van moving. The loose gravel on the lane made the wheels spin and the weight of the ambulance strained the van's engine. Rainwater rushed downhill. It was like a stream in places.

☆

Allie came back into the caravan, shaking her waterproofs outside and hanging them on the back of the door. Miriam and Heather looked up from the picture they'd been drawing in the caravan window's condensation.

'I've reconnected the gas. We all need a cup of tea,' Allie said. She lit the stove.

'How long are we staying here?' Miriam asked. Tom clung anxiously to her jumper. Not even the toy monkey could liven him up.

'We're not moving until Trev and Lil get back,' Allie said.

'Yesterday you said that Trev was useless,' Miriam said.

'I was angry.'

'And you said you didn't care if Lil went back to Bristol.'

'We stick together,' Allie said. 'Loyalty. That's what counts.'

Allie shut herself in the toilet cupboard. When she emerged, she held out a thick wad of banknotes and a handful of coins to Miriam.

'Take it,' she said. 'It's your share of the bar money – as near as I could work it out, anyway.'

'Thanks.' Miriam quickly stuffed the money into the inside pocket of her coat. Her instinct to trust Allie had been right.

She would pay the money back into her current account. If Mum or Mr Brown were spying on her transactions, they would get a surprise.

Paul stared at her with his mouth open. 'That must be thousands of pounds,' he gasped.

'It's my money. I wanted to do something with it.'

Allie laughed. 'I got fifty quid for the fridge unit from your van – so that's a hundred and forty two pounds eighty. That must be several months' worth of cider for you but Trev owes me for all those cans he stole.'

Paul took his money, barely looking at it. He didn't take his eyes off Miriam.

'But you're just a kid. How did you -?'

'Just a kid, am I? What about Saturday night?'

Paul looked ashen.

'I knew you two had been up to something.' A smirk grew wide on Allie's face. She'd got the wrong end of the stick but Miriam realised it would be convenient for Allie to think that she'd slept with Paul.

'I've got savings, Paul. Nothing much really – but enough.'

'You could have stayed in a hotel. You didn't need my help.'

'I couldn't think of anything more boring, apart from staying at home.'

'So that's all we are to you? A bit of light entertainment?'

'How can you say that – after everything?'

A red estate car stopped abruptly on the opposite side of the lane. The sticker on its side read "Porlock Taxis".

Paul and Miriam ran outside. The rain had eased off slightly. Trev got out of the taxi and slammed the door.

'We need twenty quid for the taxi,' he said. Trev's t-shirt was half ripped off his back and his right eye was turning purple.

'What happened?' Paul asked. He took Trev's fleece off and

handed it to him. Trev snatched it, without giving Paul eye-contact.

'Lil's really ill, Miriam. She fainted.'

Miriam reached inside her coat and pulled out a banknote.

'I've got some cash in my tin. I can pay you back,' Trev said.

'I've got your tin safe,' Paul told him. Trev turned his back and went to pay the taxi driver.

'I thought you were going to do a runner.' The driver stared at the creased twenty pound note in surprise.

'She can't run. You saw us get in.'

Trev opened the rear door of the car. Lil sat with her head lolling on her chest.

'What's wrong with her?' Paul asked.

Trev bent over her.

'We're back now. Take my arm,' he told her gently.

Lil mumbled something and stood up, very slowly. Her skin looked like paper. Lil's feet were bare, caked in dried mud that clashed with her pink toe-nail varnish. She smiled weakly at Trev and leaned on him heavily. He walked her into the caravan. The taxi turned round and sped back towards Minehead.

Trev glared at Paul.

'Fucking bastard,' he muttered.

☆

Lil lay on Heather's bed, wrapped in blankets. Allie had made her drink a mug of soup and Lil had spilled most of it down her t-shirt. She was sleeping now. Everyone was squeezed inside the caravan. Paul leaned against the kitchen cupboards. The air was warm and stale. Miriam felt restless.

'I wish we could go back to the old quarry.' Allie looked

exhausted. Her hair was scraped back in an unbrushed knot. 'Maybe Lil's right. She wanted to jack this in. But it would kill me, going home.'

Trev dipped a slice of bread into his soup.

'We could ditch the vans – build a bender in the woods. No one would even notice us.'

'Yeah, right – what about the kids? And even if Lil stayed with us, can you imagine her living in a bender? She'd probably need a spare one for her make-up.'

Trev nodded.

'You're right. You can't expect Lil to…'

'But I've thought of everything and there aren't any options left,' Allie said.

'What about Dave -?' Paul asked.

'He followed Flynn to Finland, didn't he? Dragged Ellie along with him.'

'Jonno?'

'Always off his head on Ketamine. I've got the kids to think of. I've not got his number, anyway.'

'Maybe we could just find somewhere quiet, even if it's just for a few days,' Paul suggested. Trev finished his soup noisily, chasing the last spoonful around the bowl.

'We're not exactly inconspicuous with a broken-down ambulance to tow around,' Allie said.

'Me and Trev can scout about in the van first,' Paul said. Trev avoided eye-contact with him.

'You'll leave us here like sitting ducks for that git with the shotgun.'

'Mum, we're off the field now. He can't do anything.' Heather put her arms around Allie. 'Something'll turn up.'

'It's hopeless even trying.' Allie sniffed. 'We think we're safe – and then something horrible happens.' She started sobbing in hiccupping gasps. Heather tried to comfort her. Miriam grabbed a handful of tissue from the toilet cupboard. Allie blew her nose and tried to breathe calmly. Trev and Paul both glanced worriedly at Allie.

She gave them a crumpled smile that dissolved into tears.

'I'm sorry. I'm supposed to be the one who's strong.'

'Why don't you let us look after you?' Trev asked.

'It was horrible, Trev. A great big police dog ran in, barking its head off. We were still asleep. Tom and Heather were terrified.'

'At least they didn't charge us with anything.'

'I just can't stand it anymore.' Allie started crying again.

Watching Allie get upset, Miriam felt useless. She knew she was still an outsider in their world. Miriam glanced at Allie's mobile phone, lying on the work surface by the sink. She stood up quietly, picked up the phone and slipped out of the caravan. Only Paul noticed her leave.

She opened the van's shutter. It looked like a tornado had struck inside. The curtain had been torn down from the metal walls and a puddle of spilt soya milk was spreading across the floor. It took Miriam several minutes to find her purse. She pulled out a rectangle of grubby white card. She sat on the floor. The mobile phone signal was good. Miriam dialled the number.

'Hello. Flying Horse Café.'

'Bella, it's Miriam.'

'Miriam! I've been so worried. Paul was in no fit state, I should never have let you go.'

'I'm fine – I'm in Paul's van. Did you get my postcard?'

'How was your rave? Have you called your mum and dad?'

'I sent them a postcard too.'

'Do they know where you are? They must be frantic.'

Miriam imagined Bella on the phone in the café's kitchen; the little wooden shelf where she scribbled orders, Alan chopping up a pile of vegetables in the background. Bella was probably right about her parents. But she didn't want to think about them now.

'I told them not to worry.'

Miriam wondered if she should tell Bella that she knew about Paul. She had given him the newspaper cutting. But what if Bella didn't know the full story? It would be too complicated and there was no time.

'The police raided us and the farmer kicked us off the field. The others are desperate. They've got nowhere to go.'

'Sounds just like the old days.' Bella sounded bitter.

'Can you think of anywhere? We're near Minehead.'

'Wait a minute.'

There was a clunk, as if Bella had put the phone down on the shelf. Miriam heard the sounds of the café in the background: the clink of a tray being put down on the counter; someone calling out because no one was serving; Alan irritably marching out of the kitchen and the whoosh of the espresso machine. Miriam hoped that Allie had enough credit on her phone.

'Still there?'

'Yeah.'

'Have you got a pen?'

Miriam found a pen in the side pocket of her rucksack and scrap of paper with a shopping list written on one side.

'There's an old friend of ours called Harold Judd. He was on the road in the old days with his wife. He bought an orchard. Makes furniture nowadays.'

'Where does he live? We need somewhere to stay, even if it's just for tonight.'

'I've got his address here. We still meet up and send each other Christmas cards. It's at Sutton Mallet. That's just off the A39 on your way to Glastonbury. Go through the village, turn left by the church – it's called Appledene Lane but there's no sign. Just as you think the lane's going to peter out, it's on your left. The apple blossom's lovely this time of year.'

'Are you sure we'll be able to find it?'

'It's easy. His name's on the gate. Give him a call first, let him know that you're coming. He's so much better at directions than me. His number's 01458 223746. Tell him I sent you.'

'Thanks, Bella – I'd better go.'

'Call me again. Let me know you're safe.'

'Bye, Bella. Thanks.' Miriam pressed the red button on Allie's phone.

She ran back to the caravan. Everyone stared at her as she flung the door open. Lil opened her eyes groggily and propped herself up on her elbows.

'Sorry, Allie, I borrowed your phone.' Miriam put the phone down on the table. 'I think I've found us somewhere to stay.'

'But who do you know?' Allie frowned.

'Bella.'

Paul looked startled, as if he was scared that Miriam would blurt out his secret.

'That café woman?' Allie asked.

'She knows a guy called Harold. He lives near Glastonbury, in an orchard.'

'And how's he going to like us turning up out of the blue?' Allie said hopelessly.

'It's only about an hour away. I think I've got enough diesel,' Paul said.

'She gave me his phone number.' Miriam punched the

number into Allie's phone. It rang for ages. She worried that Bella had given her the wrong number, or she'd written it down wrong. An answer-phone message crackled into life.

'This is Harold Judd at Orchard Woodcrafts. Please leave me a message.' It was a deep, friendly sounding voice.

'Hello. We don't know you but Bella, in Derby, said you might not mind us staying for a few nights. This is my friend's mobile.' Miriam realised she didn't know Allie's number. She put her hand over the phone. 'What's your number?'

'I can never remember it,' Allie shrugged.

'I'm sorry, I don't know the number,' Miriam said. This was the worst phone message she'd ever left. 'But it would be great if you could let us stay.' She handed the phone back to Allie.

'That's hardly going to help,' Allie said. 'We need to move, anyway. Lil – are you up to steering your van if Paul tows you?'

Lil sat up slowly.

'I'm not sure,' she croaked. 'Just leave me here. I might be able to get the ambulance started later.'

'There's no way I'm letting that happen,' Allie said. 'Miriam, can you drive?'

'I haven't even had lessons.' She shook her head.

'I'll do it.' Trev said.

'You never drive.' Paul looked at Trev like he'd gone mad. 'Are you sure? And what about your arm?'

Trev stared at Lil.

'Lil kept blacking out. What if she does it at the wheel? It's not rocket science – I won't need to change gear.'

☆

Heather had worked out the route to Sutton Mallet and written it in felt tip on a piece of old cereal packet. Paul propped it up on his dashboard. He checked his wing mirrors. Trev glared angrily through the windscreen of Lil's ambulance.

Paul waited for Allie and Miriam to help Lil into the car and strap Tom into his child seat. When he heard the sound of Allie's engine, Paul started the van and moved off. Trev looked startled but he must have taken the handbrake off because the ambulance rolled along behind the van. He stuck his tongue out to concentrate.

Trev had stolen cars for the thrill of it when he was a kid, until he'd crashed and killed his best mate. He didn't often talk about it. Trev had only been nineteen when he was released from the Young Offenders Institution. He'd disappeared into woods and derelict allotments and learned how to survive on his own. Paul couldn't remember him ever getting behind the steering wheel of a vehicle.

Paul didn't want to think about the time after the bomb but his memories of that time were mercifully vague. It had been spring again when Trev rescued him, in Bristol.

He slowed down on the tight corners so that Trev wouldn't struggle. The farmer's Land Rover was roaring up the hill in the opposite direction. When he saw them coming, the farmer screeched to a halt and leaned on his steering wheel to watch them. Paul was tempted to stick his finger up as he drove past but he didn't want the farmer chasing after them in a fit of road rage. He smiled and gave the farmer a friendly wave.

CHAPTER FIFTEEN
THE ORCHARD

Miriam noticed that Allie relaxed as she drove, singing under her breath to a cheesy eighties compilation tape. Heather followed the tattered road atlas, giving Allie directions. The A-road was busy and sunlight reflected blindingly off the wet tarmac.

Tom suddenly started crying.

'Check his nappy – see if he needs changing,' Heather shouted above Tom's bawling. Miriam tentatively felt his towelling nappy. She was sandwiched between Tom's baby seat and Lil, who was sleeping again.

'It's damp.'

'I'll pull in as soon as I can,' Allie said. Miriam tried to soothe Tom but he kept crying.

Lil's eyes snapped open. She stared in panic at Tom's frantically kicking legs. She pushed the passenger door open and tried to unclip her seatbelt, just as Allie swung into a lay-by. Allie swerved to avoid a parked lorry and slammed on the brakes. The caravan rocked alarmingly before settling back down on its wheels. Heather screamed.

'What the fuck are you doing?' Allie shouted. She parked, straightening up the caravan. Lil's chest was heaving.

Heather got out of the car and unclipped Tom from his baby seat. She rolled out his changing mat on the car's bonnet.

'I'm sorry. I don't even know.' Lil blinked and rubbed her eyes.

'What's the matter with you?' Allie craned round from the driver's seat.

'I'm pregnant,' Lil said. Tears ran down her cheeks.

Miriam's chest felt tight. She felt a prickle behind her eyes as if she was going to cry. She took a deep breath to try to stop herself. Miriam patted Lil's hand. Lil pulled it away.

'It's Paul.' Lil snapped.

Miriam froze. Really, this shouldn't affect her at all. She had only known Paul for a week and a half. After Saturday night, something had changed between them. But now Paul would want to be with Lil, for the baby's sake.

'When did you find out?' Allie asked.

'I did the pregnancy test yesterday.'

'But you slept with him in January. That makes you -?'

'Four months pregnant. I know. It took me a while to realise and then I was just in denial. You guessed, I think.'

'I suspected something. You weren't in Bristol yesterday, were you?'

Lil shook her head. 'As soon as I found out, I walked up the lane and sent you the text message. Then I went back to bed. I felt terrible.'

'And if your van had started, you would have just driven off?'

'I couldn't face everyone. I would have called you later.'

Allie groaned.

'What am I going to do?' Lil asked. 'I've not even been looking after myself. How am I going to look after a baby?'

Allie got out of the car and opened the door on Lil's side. She crouched down and took Lil's hand. Lil didn't move.

'Do you want to keep it?' Allie asked quietly.

Miriam felt excluded. She sat still and watched the traffic going past.

'I don't know,' Lil said. 'Maybe. As long as I've not damaged it already. It'll ruin my plans, though. How can I be a designer when I'm covered in baby sick?'

Allie laughed. 'Having kids hasn't stopped me from doing

crazy stuff. I was married and I already had Heather when I did my mechanics course, remember? But then I went off with Flynn. Great idea that was. But I can't go back to my old life now. Wouldn't want to.'

'It's great when the sun's shining and we're somewhere safe but what about on a day like today? I wouldn't want my kid to get hurt.'

'I've not always been the best mother but I'd protect Tom and Heather with my life.' Allie stared at her children. Heather stood on the grass bank, holding Tom. She was pointing at cars.

'Are you sure it's Paul's baby?'

'Do you think I'm a total slag?'

'It would be easier if it wasn't his.' She whispered something to Lil. Miriam guessed what she was saying. She got out of the car and slammed the door behind her as hard as she could. But there was nowhere to go. Heather stared at Miriam without saying anything. Miriam sat a few metres away, on the wet grass. She pressed the palms of her hands into her eyes.

'That one's a Vauxhall Astra,' Heather told Tom. 'It's blue. And that one's a Ford Transit – a long wheel-base. Let's wave at the man.'

☆

Heather's directions were fairly easy to follow, sticking to A-roads until they crossed the M5 and then threading through small villages. Paul had driven slowly, overtaken by a procession of impatient motorists. He couldn't see far behind the van; the ambulance blocked most of the view in his wing mirrors. Even so, Allie had fallen behind. He hoped she was alright but he had to keep going. He passed a sign that said

"Sutton Mallet welcomes careful drivers". It would be difficult not to drive carefully through the village. The road was narrow with high hedges and verges bursting with bright foliage, obscuring what was around the next corner. Occasional houses were set back from the road. The church was just ahead. Paul slowed down as he passed it. He turned into the lane on the left. There were two muddy tyre-width strips, with tall grasses growing in the middle. Cow parsley waved in the verge.

He checked that Trev was still concentrating and indicated left. The track sloped gently downhill. So far, there were just fields and a low stone wall on either side. Maybe this wasn't the right lane after all. He hoped there was somewhere to turn around. The grass got thicker, brushing against the van's bumper. There were woods on the left hand side now – no sign of an orchard. Overhanging trees made the lane dark. Suddenly, he was dazzled by a mass of white apple blossom on his left. He crawled forwards, looking for a gate. He reached the far wall of the orchard but there was a field on the other side.

Paul braked, realising that he'd completely missed the entrance to the orchard. He caught sight of Trev's panicked face and heard the blast of the ambulance's horn. The ambulance crashed into the back of the van. Paul was jolted forwards.

'Shit!' Paul muttered. He put the handbrake on.

Trev jumped out of the ambulance. He wrenched the van door open and grabbed Paul's arm. He stared at Paul with a cold fury.

'You're deliberately trying to ruin Lil's life, aren't you?'

Paul unclipped his seatbelt. He was determined to stay calm.

'Let's go and look at the damage. I'm sure Allie can get it fixed. You should have been concentrating.' Trev let him go.

'The gate was just after the woods. Are you blind?'

Paul got out of the van. The front bumper of the ambulance had a small dent and a bit of paint had flaked off where it had hit the tow-bar of the van.

'It's okay. These things are built to last. She's got more to worry about with the back door.'

'She's got more to worry about than that.' Trev glared at Paul.

'She's just tired, isn't she? A bit shocked?'

'You should know. You're the one who got her pregnant.'

'What?'

'She was sick in the police van. She told me that she was pregnant. And then she started to go all faint. I told the police that it was my baby. I told them that we were getting married. I made up a load of bullshit. Wishful thinking, wasn't it? The coppers went all remorseful then and wanted to get a doctor but Lil wouldn't let them. I said I'd look after her so they let us go and they called a taxi. Then she told me that you're the father.'

Trev jabbed Paul in the chest, pinning him against the side of the van. 'As if I didn't already know,' he said.

Paul wanted to run away but Trev had a handful of his shirt in his fist.

'It was a mistake.'

'Don't give me that. You knew exactly what you were doing. You didn't even give me a chance with Lil and now it's too late. You stole her.'

'I tried to keep my distance. I didn't want to make it worse.'

'For years you made out you were a poor little abused kid who'd run away from home. When you were really a terrorist in hiding.'

'It's not how you think. I tried to stop them.'

Trev swung back with his plastered arm. Paul shut his eyes

and braced himself. It was what he deserved but it was going to hurt. Nothing happened. Paul waited a few seconds and then opened his eyes.

A large man stood in the middle of the lane, up to his knees in wet cow parsley. He had long red hair and a grey-streaked beard. He looked like a semi-retired Viking warrior, displaced in the English countryside.

Trev stood and stared at the man. His plaster cast hung loosely by his side.

'What's going on?' the man said. He had a deep voice, with a hint of a threat to it.

'We had a little bump, that's all. I'm sorry if we disturbed you,' Paul said. There was something about the man, not just his size, which seemed to command respect.

'It looked like you were about to get beaten to a pulp.' He sounded almost amused.

Trev hunched his shoulders.

'We were looking for an orchard – a guy called Harold Judd – we left an answer-phone message,' Paul tried to explain.

'That was a girl's voice. I wasn't expecting…'

They had made the worst possible first impression on this man. Between them, they had ruined any chance of finding anywhere safe to stay. The large man, who had to be Harold, walked a few feet closer to get a better view of them. He had wood-shaving curls stuck in his beard and all over his brown jumper. Harold examined the gaffa tape holding the ambulance doors together.

'I used to work in Bella's café,' Paul said in desperation. 'And the girl who called – Miriam – she knows her as well.'

'She always was collecting waifs and strays. And now she's finally dumped some on me!'

Harold started to laugh – a rumbling roar that startled the

wood pigeons out of the trees.

☆

Lil stood in front of Miriam, looking wild.

'So what happened on Saturday night?' she asked.

Miriam was relieved to see that some of Lil's attitude had returned, even though the anger was directed at her.

Allie stood behind her, with Tom on her hip.

'Leave her alone, Lil. I wish you'd drop this obsession with Paul.'

'I'm having his baby.'

'Do you honestly think he'd be much use?' Allie said. 'So what really happened, Miriam? I thought you said…'

'It's none of your business.' Miriam felt trapped. There was no way she could tell them what had really happened. But maybe she could mix in enough of the truth to make it seem real. She stood up, facing Lil, trying to ignore the fact that her wet trousers were sticking to her bottom.

'You went off with that DJ - but then a guy started chatting me up so I let him take me down to the river. I thought he was okay at first but then he started taking it too far.'

'You didn't use your martial arts skills, then?' Lil asked. Miriam thought that she was probably being sarcastic but she decided to ignore her.

'He was too strong. But Paul was down there. He rescued me.'

'What was Paul doing by the river?'

'The crowd freaked him out. He was fed up. We spent the rest of the night talking. Why should you care? Paul thinks you're scary anyway.'

'Scary?' Lil looked shocked.

'You've been impossible for weeks,' Allie said. 'Even worse than normal.' She hugged Lil. 'You'll be okay.'

Lil sniffed, as if she was trying to fight off more tears. She looked down at her muddy feet and her dirty t-shirt with disgust.

'I can't go to that orchard place looking like this.'

'He's just some old guy that Bella knows,' Miriam said. 'Why should he care what you're wearing?'

'All my stuff's in the ambulance. I can't believe you left those two idiots in charge of it.' Lil stared at Allie. 'I don't suppose you even own any make-up.'

'Yeah, somewhere.'

'I can't even believe I'm wearing these clothes in public,' Lil said.

'That sounds more like the Lil I know.' Allie grinned.

☆

Paul reversed the van, gently nudging the ambulance back past the gateway of the orchard, while Trev tried to keep it steady. Harold opened the gate. It did seem pretty difficult to miss – the gate was hand-made, with carved leaf shapes between the bars. A wooden sign read "Harold Judd – Orchard Woodcrafts". Paul inched forwards through the gateway, checking that Trev was concentrating.

Harold beckoned him forwards onto a gravel drive that ran between ancient, twisted apple trees covered in white blossom. There were carved sculptures under the trees. The drive opened out into a courtyard in front of an old barn built of golden stone. It had an incongruous corrugated iron roof and a wind turbine.

There was a huge old furniture van parked with its back to

the woods. It looked like it hadn't moved in a long time. Barrels full of red geraniums were set out in front of it. Paul noticed a black cat basking on a round wooden table.

Paul braked and turned off the engine when Harold signalled. He stepped down from the van. Trev put his hand on Paul's shoulder. Paul flinched.

'Why didn't you trust me?' Trev asked. 'After everything we've been through together.'

'Maybe it was that kicking I got before you found me. I couldn't remember what I'd done. And when I did remember…' Paul realised that the black cat was rubbing his head against his boots. He bent down and stroked it. The cat stared at him with an inscrutable look in its green eyes but it purred deeply.

'I'm sorry,' Paul said.

'Yeah, me too,' Trev muttered. 'But you'd better mean it.'

Harold stuck his head around the side of the ambulance.

'Alright, there?' he asked. He seemed relieved that they weren't fighting again. 'I'll give you the guided tour.'

'Are you sure?' Paul wondered if Harold was a bit too trusting.

'Bella's usually been a good judge of people. Besides, it's got to be more interesting than talking to the cat.'

'Cats can be more interesting than people,' Paul said.

'He's called Arthur.' Harold walked across the courtyard. 'The woods are mine as well – four acres of mixed woodland – hazel coppice, beech, some decent old oak trees – takes a bit of managing.'

'Cool.' Trev stared at everything as if he didn't believe it was real.

Paul followed Harold into the barn. Trev seemed rooted to the spot, staring at the woods. The barn had three rows of dusty windows and a huge studded door.

The ground floor room was a workshop, with pieces of wooden furniture and sculpture in various stages of completion – several chairs and an ornate bookshelf. A large, half-finished sculpture of an owl stood near the window. The long, low room smelled of freshly cut wood and the stone flags were covered in wood shavings. There was a battered old work bench in the middle of the room. Paul stared at the ancient-looking wooden machinery at the far end of the barn.

'That's my cider press – over a century old but it still works perfectly.' Harold patted its huge oak beam. 'I've been making cider from this orchard for fifteen years.'

'Do you sell it?'

'The local pub takes a few barrels but it's mostly for friends and family – and me,' he chuckled.

A squeaking noise startled Paul. It was Trev, slowly turning the handle of the vice on the work bench. He had an awed look on his face, as if he had just walked into a cathedral.

'We work with wood a bit,' Trev said quietly. His eyes were wide. He ran his finger along the scars on the surface of the work bench.

'Really?' Harold stared at them both again.

'We knock stuff together. Benders, compost loos, shelters,' Paul explained. 'Just things we need, really.'

'I'm just a skip rat.' Trev stared at the floor, scuffing the wood shavings with his feet.

'What do you mean?'

'We get things out of skips. A load of rubbish, mostly. But it's good for firewood.'

'We find food too,' Paul added. 'And Trev's really good at making things. He can't do a lot at the moment because of his arm.'

'I've seen some really nice bits of furniture in skips, just waiting for someone to restore them. But I don't have the skills and we've only got a few basic tools – and Paul's not had the van long.'

Harold picked up a hammer and chisel. He chipped at the owl sculpture, as if he'd suddenly found inspiration. Trev watched him, totally engrossed in the instinctive way that Harold carved the feathers. His eyes were full of longing. Trev reached out to touch the top of the owl's head.

Harold stopped and stared at him.

'It's a commission for a new library in Wiltshire. It opens in a couple of weeks. And I've got to get my stock ready for the Pilton Pop festival.'

'Glastonbury, you mean?' Trev asked.

Harold nodded.

'Green Crafts field. I've had a stall there for years.' Harold smiled. 'Used to go to Stonehenge, of course, but that all got stopped in Eighty Five.'

'Were you there? At the Battle of the Beanfield?' Paul asked.

Harold nodded. 'I was in the Peace Convoy, in my removal van. It was totally trashed. I'd only just finished doing it up.'

'Bella and Alan were there too, weren't they?'

Harold nodded.

'They started the café soon after that, settled down. Believe it or not but Alan was quite chatty before the Beanfield. My kids were really young – they were terrified. That much brutality does nasty things to people. We were only trying to go to a festival.' Harold sighed. 'If it wasn't for that day, I'd probably still be married.'

'Nothing's changed. It's just on a smaller scale. We got raided by the police this morning,' Paul said.

'We really need somewhere to stay. The raid really upset the girls and the kids,' Trev said. 'If you let us stay, we'll help you. I'm not much use now, but I can hold things and sand things down and when the plaster cast comes off, I'll really...'

Harold put his chisel down. He nodded slowly.

'I can't turn you away, can I? Bella would never speak to me again. And I could do with some help. I've got to get the removal van fixed too. It hasn't moved since last summer.'

'We might be able to help you there,' Paul said.

☆

A gust of wind blew white petals onto the windscreen as they drove through the orchard.

'It looks like it's snowing!' Heather reached out of the open window to catch the blossom.

As they reached the yard, Lil's ambulance and Paul's van came into view, still tied together with the tow-rope. Paul, Trev and a large red-haired man were sitting at a round wooden table outside an enormous old removal van.

Allie parked. Miriam unclipped Tom from his baby seat. He gave her a big gummy smile as she lifted him onto her shoulder.

'You're a natural,' Lil said. 'I've always been scared of dropping him.'

'You'll be fine.'

The red-haired man walked up to them. Trev was behind him.

'Which one of you knows Bella, then?' He seemed quite stern. He was huge, built like a rugby player.

'It was me,' Miriam said, not daring to meet his eyes.

'Don't worry, it's about time something interesting happened around here.' Harold reached out to ruffle Tom's hair. Tom stared at Harold, his eyes wide as if he thought

Harold was a giant. 'Who's this, then?'

Miriam put Tom into Allie's arms.

'Tom's mine,' Allie said. 'And Heather's my daughter.'

'Please can I explore?' Heather hung back behind Allie.

'Of course you can,' Harold beamed at her. She ran towards the apple trees.

Miriam walked towards Paul. A large black cat sat comfortably on his lap, purring loudly. It glared at Miriam.

'I was a bit harsh earlier – about the money,' Paul said.

'Would you prefer it if I pretended I was skint, just so I fitted in? Allie wouldn't have been able to run the bar.'

'I'm sorry. Thanks for finding this place. It's amazing.'

Miriam looked at the photo album that was open on the table. It showed a picture of a younger, slimmer Harold, standing with two young children next to a sculpture of a bear.

'Sorry it took us so long to get here. We had a bit of a crisis on the way,' she said. She sat next to him on the bench.

'He's letting us stay, Lil,' Trev said. Lil gave him a peck on the cheek, leaving an imprint of red lipstick. He grinned, too delighted to be kissed by her to wipe away the mark of her lips.

Lil was still in her jogging pants and bare feet but she'd changed into a tight red t-shirt that belonged to Allie. Her pink and white braids were piled onto the top of her head and she'd made the most the old lipstick and eyeliner Allie had found at the back of a drawer. She sat down at the table.

Harold brought out a jug of cider and poured out glasses for everyone. He handed one to Lil but she shook her head.

'No thanks, I'm pregnant,' Lil said. 'Can I have a cup of tea?'

Paul stared at Lil. Trev spluttered on a mouthful of cider. Allie's eyebrows shot up. Lil smiled, pretending to be completely unaware of the confusion she was causing.

'Earl Grey?' Harold asked. Lil nodded.

'Lovely. Milk, no sugar, please.'

'I'll get some juice for the kids too.' Harold walked up the steps into the removal van.

'Trev told me,' Paul said. 'I didn't think you wanted anyone to know.'

'Well now I do.' Lil stared at him defiantly. 'You'd better get used to it.'

CHAPTER SIXTEEN
THE ATTIC

Paul was completely absorbed in sanding the chair, lulled into a rhythm by the Hawkwind CD on Harold's stereo. He ran his hand along the smooth grain of the wood. The chair was made from a fallen beech tree in Harold's copse. It was almost ready for the stall at Glastonbury. Harold said that he got enough orders at Glastonbury to keep the business going for the rest of the year. Paul couldn't imagine why anyone would go to a festival to buy furniture.

Trev was helping Harold to make a bookshelf. Trev's face lit up as he realised that the dovetail joints fitted together perfectly. It took time, making furniture like this – not like knocking things together from old pallet wood with reclaimed nails. Paul poured wood oil on a cloth and started rubbing it into the chair. The work stopped him from thinking about the past; tired him out so he could sleep at night.

Lil walked into the workshop, stirring up wood shavings with the bottom of her red patchwork skirt.

'I'm leaving in half an hour. You'd better be ready,' she told Trev.

Trev grinned at her. 'Look at the way this bookshelf fits together. Harold's a genius.'

Lil ran her finger along the pattern that the joints made.

'It's really good.' She looked critically at Trev. 'I hope you're getting changed. You might start an infection in the hospital, dressed like that.'

'Hospital?' Paul asked.

Trev was wearing a scruffy t-shirt and shredded combat pants as usual. But Lil had totally changed her appearance since arriving at the orchard. She had removed her pink and white braids. Her natural colour was startlingly blonde but today it was covered by a red and white spotted headscarf. She'd taken to wearing long flowing skirts and cheesecloth shirts. Paul wondered how she managed to fit so many clothes in her ambulance.

'The coppers ruined my other t-shirt. I haven't got anything else,' Trev said.

'At least have a shower.'

'Okay,' Trev nodded. He looked at her like a lost puppy.

'Don't make me late for my appointment.' Lil swept out of the barn, shaking the shavings off her skirt like a flamenco dancer.

'She's magnificent,' Harold said.

'Is this something to do with the baby?' Paul asked.

'She's going for a scan. When she went to the doctors' last week, they said she should have had one ages ago.'

'She wants you to go with her?'

Trev nodded. Lil had been paying a lot more attention to Trev since the police raid. Paul tried not to seem bitter but he felt frozen out of the whole process. Everyone seemed to be pretending that it was Trev's baby.

'I'll check on Allie. She's been doing sterling work on my van all morning.' Harold left them alone in the workshop. He understood that the situation between Paul and Trev was awkward.

'Are you and Lil getting together or something, now she thinks you're her hero?'

'I don't know. I hope so.' Trev fiddled with a bit of sandpaper.

'Why do you let her talk to you like that?'

'I don't mind,' Trev shrugged.

'Why didn't anyone tell me about the scan? You could have

told me that you were going with her.'

'She must have had a reason for not telling you. Look,' Trev put his hand on Paul's arm and spoke in a low voice, even though they were alone. Harold's stereo was still blaring away. 'When I got out of that prison place, I could have started stealing cars again but I wanted to make things right. And I want to make things right for Lil.'

'How does she feel about your past?'

'It doesn't exactly make me a great catch. She could have anyone. Why would she want me?' Trev hunched his shoulders miserably.

'Don't worry. She's got a track record of being attracted to total losers.'

'Tell me about it,' Trev laughed. 'What about Miriam? She knows what you've done.'

Paul flinched.

'We're friends. That's all we could ever be. It wouldn't be fair on her, would it?'

'She's an amazing girl. I reckon she could cope with anything, even you.'

Trev opened a drawer in Harold's work bench. He pulled out a carrier bag and a ball of string.

'Can you tie this round my arm?' he asked. Paul wrapped the bag neatly around Trev's plaster cast and tied it so it wouldn't get wet when he used the solar powered shower in Harold's removal van. 'I'm getting sick of that bloody shower. At this rate, it won't just be the plaster cast that disintegrates down the plug hole.'

'Don't let her boss you around so much.'

'I want her to like me.'

'I think you need your head examining,' Paul laughed.

⭐

Miriam wiped away the sweat that trickled down her forehead. She leaned against the neglected fence around Harold's old vegetable patch and took a swig from the water bottle. She was beginning to regret agreeing to help Paul with clearing the ground. She was only doing it because it was an excuse for them to do something together. The vegetable patch was covered with brambles and clumps of waist-high grass.

'Getting tired?' Paul grinned. He was digging steadily, bare-chested. He didn't seem to mind exposing his scarred arm any more. Paul's ribs stuck out like the framework of Trev's bender.

'This isn't a vegetable patch – it's a jungle.'

'It'll be worth it.'

Harold had showed them photos of his children standing next to wigwams of green beans and holding giant home-grown marrows and pumpkins. But the garden had been abandoned when his wife left him.

'You get all our food out of skips. I don't see why you're so bothered.'

'I want to do this to say thanks to Harold. And growing vegetables will go towards looking after the baby.'

Miriam tried to pull up a strand of bramble. The thorns stuck into her hand and she let out a shriek. Paul dropped his spade and took off her enormous gardening glove.

'You should use Trev's knife to cut the brambles. I'll dig up the roots.' He gently squeezed the splinters out of her palm. The holes they left behind oozed tiny beads of blood.

Paul carried on holding her hand. She didn't want him to let go.

'You know, I…' he said.

Lil's ambulance rattled back into the yard. Paul let Miriam's hand drop. He bent down to cut the thorn out of the way. He glanced up at the ambulance. Miriam felt a jealous twinge. Lil was the centre of attention now and loved it.

☆

Lil tipped the contents of the bin bag onto the round table. An assortment of musty-smelling clothes tumbled out like an instant jumble sale. She picked up a maroon cardigan with her fingertips.

'Bloody typical. As soon as I was having the scan, Trev went rummaging around in the bins.'

'I'd be afraid of finding something horrible,' Miriam said. She picked up a bright pink satin nightie. It looked clean.

'He said they were rejects from the charity shop but they're probably what old people were wearing when they died.'

'I'm not sure about the food he found either.' Allie blew on her tea. Her face was streaked with engine grease and her hands left black fingerprints on the mug. She had been working on Harold's removal van for hours. Tom looked pretty grubby too. 'Heather likes instant mash but it's going to take years to get through an entire catering pack.'

Miriam laughed. 'We could get Harold to build a sculpture out of it.'

'Trev must be losing his touch,' Allie said. 'I've nearly finished working on the removal van though. It wasn't too bad once I got the mice out of the engine.'

'They were sweet,' Miriam said. 'I hope you found a good home for them.'

'It might be ready for a little drive tomorrow. Fancy it?'

'It seems so permanent.' Miriam stared at the removal van. 'I

163

can't imagine it moving.'

'He's taking it to Glastonbury, remember? It might not be far but it's got to be roadworthy.'

'I wish Harold had enough tickets for all of us.' Miriam glanced at the barn. Harold had just three trader's tickets. He'd offered tickets to Paul and Trev.

'Just jump the fence,' Lil said. 'That's what I always do.'

Allie stared at Lil, fiercely.

'You're not jumping the fence in your condition.'

'So I'm meant to stay here, with a tartan blanket over my knees like an old lady?'

Allie drained her mug and picked up Tom.

'I'm going for a shower. I might cook dinner – something that'll go with mashed potato,' she said.

Miriam examined a pair of old-fashioned men's trousers. The wool felt soft and the grey material was shot through with a line of sapphire blue thread.

'You could do something interesting with this – a bag maybe.'

Lil looked at the material intently.

'Yeah. Maybe you're right. I could use that nightie as a lining – and the buttons from this cardigan.'

Lil sorted the clothes into piles, becoming increasingly absorbed.

'I'll get my sewing machine,' she grinned.

☆

Harold chipped at his owl sculpture, making the most of the early evening sunlight streaming through the window.

'Is the baby okay?' Paul asked.

'Everything's fine. She was so relieved. They gave her a little card with a picture of the scan,' Trev grinned. 'It looks like a baked bean, but Lil says she can see its nose.'

'I can't imagine you hanging around in a hospital.'

'I got bored. Lil went mad when I found her those clothes. But look. They're doing something with them.'

Lil and Miriam were sitting at the table outside Harold's removal van. The clothes were piled in a heap. Lil was making something on her little sewing machine. Miriam was talking enthusiastically, writing things down.

'Lil's being really health-conscious now. I'm going to do my skip-raiding for her in Waitrose.'

'But you're working for me.' Harold gave Trev a puzzled smile. 'You don't need to get food out of bins. I know I've not paid you yet but...'

'You're going to pay us?' Trev gasped. 'I thought you were just letting us learn stuff.'

Harold roared with laughter, stirring the sawdust on his owl sculpture into the air.

'When you two turned up, it was like something from my old biker days. I knew I had to give you a chance at least.'

Harold must have looked pretty intimidating in his youth, in black leathers, wild red hair streaming behind his motorbike. Trev just looked daft, staring, with his mouth gaping open.

'No one's given me a job before,' he said.

'You've both got talent. You understand wood. If you want to, I'll train you up properly and you'll get a cut of the profit from everything you've worked on.'

'This is amazing!' Trev's grin was so wide, it barely fitted his face.

'You've only known us for a week,' Paul said.

'And I've been working on my own for too long. I feel like I'm coming back to life again.'

Paul had an uncomfortable, panicky feeling.

Harold leaned on his workbench. It creaked with the pressure.

'Look, Paul. I know when something's right.' He folded his arms with an air of finality.

☆

Miriam wrote down her ideas in the sparkly silver notebook that Lil had given her. Lil worked intently at her sewing machine. They were going to turn this into a business. They would do more skip-raiding, scour charity shops and brave the sharp elbows of old ladies at jumble sales. Lil would use her designs but all the material would be recycled.

Miriam would be in charge of the business side of things: booking stalls at festivals, getting shops to stock the clothes, marketing the company, doing the accounts. Miriam planned to design a website. Eventually, they could do on-line sales. She felt inspired. She would be able to use her wages from the Mercia building society to invest in something she really believed in.

'I need a computer – a laptop would be best.'

'And a decent sewing machine.'

Miriam scribbled down the things that they needed to buy: thread, zips, Velcro - a small marquee for festival stalls. She marked them in order of priority. The ideas came spontaneously, like the clothes spilling out of the bin bag.

'But what are we going to call ourselves?' Lil said. 'I was going to call my stall Space Goddess but that was when I was designing crazy rave clothes. Now we're doing retro stuff…'

She finished stitching the hand-sewn rosette to the handbag and gave it to Miriam to inspect. The bag was beautifully made, although it had only taken Lil a couple of hours on her sewing machine. The pink satin lining contrasted with the suit material. Lil had cleverly plaited strips of the different material together to make a shoulder strap.

'It's brilliant,' Miriam said. 'We need a name to match - old-fashioned but glamorous.'

'Your name's quite old-fashioned. Come to think of it, so is mine.'

Miriam wrote both their names in her notebook and stared at them.

'How about Liliam? It's got both of our names in it.'

'It's just right. Let's do it.' Lil beamed. Suddenly her smile fell away. Miriam wondered if she'd changed her mind.

'But we need a studio. We need storage space – and a power supply.'

'We'll manage for now,' Miriam said.

Harold loomed over Lil.

'Curiosity got the better of us,' he said.

'And hunger,' Trev grinned. The aroma of Allie's vegetable chilli wafted out of the open door of the removal van.

'What were you making?'

Lil showed them.

'A handbag?' Harold spoke in a strange, bleating voice. 'I'm sorry, I've always wanted to say that.'

'You used the stuff I found?' Trev asked.

'It wasn't as bad as I first thought. Some of it, anyway,' Lil said.

Paul found Arthur curled up on top of an old Arran jumper. He purred loudly when Paul picked him up.

'Actually, we came up with some ideas.' Miriam hoped that Paul would be impressed.

'More than just ideas,' Lil said. 'Welcome to Liliam –

recycled fashion for the girl about town.'

'We've already got a rough business plan,' said Miriam.

'Blimey,' Harold said. 'Can I take a look?' He flicked through Miriam's notes and took a closer look at the handbag. 'This could really work.'

'You should go for it, Lil. You've got so much talent,' Trev said.

'Miriam's got the business sense – and the money to invest.' Lil smiled.

Paul stared disapprovingly.

'I'm going to help with the dinner,' he said. He walked into the removal van, with the cat on his shoulder. Miriam felt a knot of anger in her chest.

'I just wish we had somewhere to work,' Lil said.

'Have you seen the attic?' Harold pondered.

'What attic?' Lil asked.

'Come with me.' Harold led them into his workshop. Miriam hadn't really been in here since they'd arrived. The room was already full of furniture in various stages of completion. 'Could you make some cushions for these chairs?'

'Yeah. I'd like to.' Lil said.

They followed Harold up to the first floor of the barn, used for storing barrels of cider and more furniture. He stacked tables and chairs until he'd cleared a path across the room. In the corner were stairs almost as steep as a ladder. Harold climbed then and pushed up a square trapdoor. It slammed back on the floor above, stirring up a cloud of dust.

'I don't get up here much. You can't get much furniture through this hole.' His voice echoed as he disappeared into the unseen room. Miriam scrambled up the steps. Lil followed at a more dignified pace.

'And I can only stand up right in the middle of the room,' he said. Harold was almost pinned in place by the apex of the roof, his hair tangled in cobwebs. The room was like a long, low tent, with the evening light shining through windows that almost reached the floorboards. Miriam sneezed.

'It's perfect,' Lil said. She wiped away some of the grime from the window.

'Has it got power?' Miriam asked. 'We want to get an electric sewing machine and a computer.'

'I can hook the attic up to the wind turbine.'

'We'd have to get a couple of tables up here somehow though – and some clothes rails,' Miriam said.

'Can we start cleaning it tomorrow?' Lil asked.

'You're serious about this, then?' Harold said. Lil looked him in the eyes.

'This is my lifetime ambition.'

Harold picked cobwebs out of his beard and stared around the attic.

'Will you have enough clothes and handbags and things to sell by this time next month?'

'If we work really hard,' Lil said. 'Why?'

'If you really want to get this thing off the ground, you can share my pitch at Glastonbury.'

Lil squealed and hugged Miriam.

'We can do it! We can really do it!' She stood on tiptoe and kissed Harold on the cheek. He blushed. 'You don't know how much this means.'

Miriam had never seen Lil so excited.

'I'll try to wangle a couple of extra trader's tickets. They're like gold dust,' Harold said. 'But I promise I'll get you all in somehow.'

☆

There was a big saucepan of vegetable chilli and a bowl piled with instant mashed potato on the big round table. Allie had somehow managed to make it look appetizing. Harold opened the cider bottle he'd got from the barn and started pouring it into glasses.

'Harold's invited us to share his Glastonbury stall – isn't that brilliant news?' Miriam told Paul. She grabbed a plate and piled it with food.

'We'll all have to work hard,' Harold said. 'But I'm sure you'll rise to the challenge. Lil certainly seems determined.'

Everyone seemed to start talking excitedly at the same time.

Miriam realised that Paul was silently pushing the chilli around his plate.

'Are you sure about this idea with Lil?' he muttered.

'It's going to be great.'

'Are you sure Lil isn't taking you for a ride? What if she faffs about and leaves you to do all the real work? Ever since I've known her, all she's made is a few tutus and earrings.'

'Lil's drawings are great, Paul. You saw the handbag she made. I'm sure she can do this.'

Paul shrugged.

'Harold says he's going to train me and Trev properly. He's going to pay us too.'

'You should be celebrating!'

'Don't you ever worry that everything's going too well? That it's all going to start crashing down?'

'You deserve this, Paul. Just enjoy it.'

Paul gave her one of his watery smiles. He didn't really seem convinced. But he scooped up a forkful of chilli.

CHAPTER SEVENTEEN
GLASTONBURY

The removal van lurched around a corner. Miriam tried to brace her legs against the side of the shower cubicle. Paul put his arm around her but he was just trying to stop her from falling onto the chemical toilet. She shouldn't read too much into it. Miriam enjoyed being so close to him, despite the heat.

'Trev would be trying to climb out of the window by now,' Paul said. Furniture was piled against the other side of the door. Miriam started to feel trapped. She thought enviously of Trev, Lil and Harold in the front of the van, with music playing and the windows open. There was a small frosted window above the toilet but it didn't open very wide.

'I wonder where we are,' Miriam said. They'd already been in here for a long time while the furniture was being loaded.

'I reckon we might have just passed that mini-roundabout in Glastonbury town.' Paul squeezed her shoulder. 'Not too far to go. But then we've got to get through the gates.'

Miriam sighed. He'd put his scarred arm around her. It was tanned, between white lines of scar tissue. Even the most recent cuts were fading into faint red lines. But she was still shocked by the intensity of the scarring; fine lines cut with precision, millimetres apart. She traced the lines with her fingers.

He withdrew his arm. Miriam wished that she could talk to him about it but somehow she couldn't say anything. She leaned into him and held onto his knees to steady herself. She shut her eyes and tried to sleep but the van jolted around too much. The van stop-started, as if they were in a queue. Then the engine was turned off. It felt strangely peaceful after the constant juddering.

'We've arrived?' Miriam asked. She tried to stand up.

'Shh,' Paul said. 'This is just the checkpoint.' Miriam felt as if she was being smuggled across the border of a foreign country, not just a festival. She heard Harold joking with the security guard.

'That's just a house on wheels,' someone said. They slapped the side of the removal van near the shower. Miriam froze – she thought they'd been caught. But the engine started again and the removal van crawled forwards.

'We're in.' Paul said. The van pitched up and down like it was at sea. Paul wrapped both his arms around her this time. Miriam started to feel sick. She took deep breaths. She told herself that she wouldn't have to endure the movement for much longer.

The van eventually shuddered to a stop like an exhausted marathon runner. Paul helped Miriam to stand up. She leaned against the wall and gasped for air through the window. Her bottom felt printed with the non-slip pattern from the floor of the shower cubicle.

She could hear furniture being moved.

'We'll have you out soon,' Harold called.

'Still alive in there?' Trev asked.

'Only just.' Paul shouted.

It seemed like a long time before Harold wrenched open the door. Miriam stumbled out through a corridor of stacked up furniture, desperate to reach the light. She ran outside, dazzled by the blue sky. She gulped fresh air greedily. The removal van was parked next to a tall hedge in a gently sloping field, with a few other vans and large tents dotted around.

'We can leave it to the others for a while – I want to show you something.' Paul took her hand.

Miriam's legs were stiff at first but she was enthralled. Paul led her slowly uphill, past people busily setting up stalls. Miriam stopped to watch a group of people making a temporary garden with hanging baskets and pots of bright geraniums. The colours seemed miraculous after hours of being trapped in the dim light of the shower cubicle. Paul seemed to know where he was going.

'Have you been before?' Miriam asked.

'Once – properly, when I was still living at home. Trev's jumped the fence a few times.'

They walked into a quieter field, where the grass was still ankle-high. The perimeter fence was at the top of the hill. Half way up the field was a stone circle. Miriam gasped.

'It's not real, of course,' Paul said. 'It was brand new the year I came.'

'I don't believe you. It looks like it's always been there.'

The stones were about Paul's height. The grass around them was flattened. There were already a few people leaning against them.

'Turn round,' Paul said. Miriam looked in the direction she'd come from.

The opposite line of the fence glinted on the other side of the valley, miles away. The buildings just below the fence looked like a toy farm. The fields went on for miles, interspersed with marquees and trees.

'It's bigger than Derby!'

Paul laughed.

'Just wait until the punters arrive.'

☆

Bella looked slightly out of breath as she walked up the path. Alan was with her, carrying an enormous tray with steam coming from it. Alan was wearing his long green apron. It looked like they'd been teleported in from the Flying Horse Café. Miriam felt shocked to see them, even though she had expected them to arrive for Harold's party.

'Paul!' Bella ran at him like a battering ram and put her arms around him. He looked startled. She let him go and examined him at arms' length.

'You look so much better. The orchard must be doing you good.'

Miriam remembered how Paul had looked on the day she'd met him in the café. He stood up straight now – he'd lost that apologetic stoop. The starved hollows in his cheeks had filled out. His arms weren't exactly bulging with muscles but they looked strong and capable. She wondered if Ruth would have liked him like this.

'Would you like a pasty?' Alan asked.

The smell of the pastry reminded Miriam of the grease on her Mercia uniform blouse.

'Thanks – but maybe later,' Miriam said. She suddenly found herself trapped in one of Bella's hugs.

'You've blossomed,' Bella said, when she finally let go.

'You've got to see our clothes stall. And there are loads of people you know here.' She tugged at Bella's arm but she refused to move.

'Have you spoken to your parents yet?'

'I sent them another postcard. They know I'm okay.'

'That's not good enough. They must be desperate to know where you are.' Miriam stared at the ground. She felt her cheeks flush with shame. Seeing Bella had stirred up her guilt. She knew her parents would be going mad with worry.

'I just wanted to get away from them. I mean, Ruth would have loved it here but how would I ever get my mum to understand? She'd probably say it was the work of the devil or something.'

'Maybe I can help,' Bella said, softly. 'I could go and see them, explain why you felt you had to...' Miriam imagined Bella knocking on her parents' front door, wearing one of her ethnic shawls, trying to use her unique style of counselling.

'No!' Miriam shouted, without realising. The people at the edge of the party stared at her. 'I'll do it,' she said, quietly. 'But I've got to do my own way. I don't know what to say to them yet.'

'You can't go on making excuses, Miriam. Only you have the power to heal your family.' Bella drifted into the awning. She threw her arms theatrically around Harold. Alan's expression was impossible to read behind his beard. He just offered his tray of pasties around.

☆

Trev was playing his tin whistle in the awning. He'd already drunk more of Harold's special strength cider than he should have done. Paul could hear Harold laughing louder than anyone else. His friends seemed to find it amusing but Paul had escaped to the doorway of his borrowed orange tent. The sound of Trev struggling to play recognisable tunes reminded Paul of the worst winters, when he'd been too cold and depressed to move and he'd sat on the pavement while Trev had been trying to keep going, coaxing spare change out of shoppers.

Paul lit the cigarette he'd been rolling. He felt too public here, after the safe quietness of the orchard. He longed for real darkness but a string of light bulbs illuminated the path that ran through the field towards the stone circle. A steady stream of people walked up and down, casting distorted shadows on the ground. He was pleased that Harold had asked him to come to Glastonbury but tomorrow the gates opened to the ticket holders. A hundred thousand people. Paul felt his chest tighten. Tomorrow he might really feel like he was on the pavement of a city street again.

He looked up. A man had stopped outside the awning, a figure silhouetted against the light. He lingered as if he was lonely, wanting to savour the noise and life. After few seconds, he walked down the hill. Paul told himself to get over his stupid panic.

He zipped up the tent and walked back to the party. Harold was hooking up the canvas sides of the awning. Paul helped him, until only the doorway was left open. Miriam lit the old brass lanterns that hung from the roof. The awning looked like a living room, the chairs standing on pieces of patterned carpet. Harold's friends were sitting in groups. Paul had got to know most of them over the last few days. Trev poured himself another mug of cider from Harold's barrel and brought one over for Paul. Paul stared at Trev's white, skinny left arm. He wasn't used to seeing him without the plaster cast.

'This cider demands respect,' Trev said. He was already slurring his words.

Paul gulped a mouthful. It was strong and sweet, the alcohol numbing the back of his throat instantly. Harold had been saving this barrel for the party.

'Careful, Trev. We've got a big day tomorrow.'

'Yeah, selling all our furniture.'

'We've got an early start too,' Bella said. 'People are so hungry by the time they've put their tents up. We get through hundreds of pasties every year.' She stood up and brushed crumbs off her skirt. 'Still, it's good for business.'

Alan picked up his empty tray, ready to leave. Bella made a circuit of the awning, hugging everyone goodbye and telling them to come to the café. Eventually, she faced Paul.

'I can trust you, can't I?' he whispered.

'Your past's safe with me, Paul. Stick with Harold. He's offering you a future,' she said.

☆

Lil looked smug in the big armchair, sipping mint tea. Her skin looked golden. The soft lamplight accentuated the new roundness of her belly and the curves of her arms. She wore a sweep of black eye-liner and a silver bindi between her eyebrows.

The awning was quiet again now. Harold had turned the music down low. He was trading memories from the old festivals with a circle of grizzled friends. Miriam's head was spinning slightly.

Trev had dozed off in the middle of the awning, like a threadbare king in Harold's throne-like chair.

'He's just so embarrassing,' Lil complained.

'He looks happy,' Miriam said.

Lil stood up and lifted Trev's head from where it had slumped on his shoulder. He sighed but he didn't wake up. She held his head upright and inspected his straggly, sun-bleached hair. Any resemblance to a Mohican had long gone.

'The perfect opportunity,' she muttered.

'What are you doing?' Paul asked.

Lil let Trev's head gently drop. She rushed into the removal van and came out with her red skirt swirling. She held a comb and her hairdressing scissors.

'Don't you dare touch him,' Paul snapped.

He stood up and moved towards her. Lil held the scissors threateningly.

'Can't you just leave him alone?' Paul sighed.

Harold and his friends stopped talking and stared at Lil, enjoying the spectacle.

'Miriam, hold his head straight for me,' Lil commanded.

'This isn't fair,' Paul said.

Miriam stared at Lil and Paul, her loyalties divided.

'Sod you both,' Lil said. She gathered a great hank of hair from the back of Trev's head in one hand and cut straight through it. She smiled in triumph, throwing the hair onto the carpet.

'You've got no idea how his hair's been annoying me. I think he was deliberately trying to grow a bloody mullet. He's got absolutely no sense of style,' she said, as if it was a crime to look scruffy.

Lil cut more hair from the back and sides of his head.

'It's like shearing a sheep,' Harold chuckled.

'I wish I had a set of clippers,' Lil said. 'I'll just have to do the best I can.' Trev stayed blissfully asleep.

'Don't encourage her, Harold,' Paul said. He glanced at Miriam, trying to appeal to her. She shrugged. Lil knew what she was doing.

'That's nothing. One year at Stonehenge, a guy I knew fell asleep and he woke up with a cock tattooed on his forehead. At first he thought someone had drawn on him and he tried to scrub it off.'

'No way!' Miriam squealed.

'It was quite accurate, I seem to remember. A professional job. He deserved it at the time – he'd been messing around with the tattooist's girlfriend.'

'I don't believe you,' Paul said. 'Why didn't he wake up?'

'He'd taken a lot of downers. He wore a bandanna all the time after that – or he covered it up with make-up. Last thing I heard, he'd had laser surgery and was running a B&B in Exmouth.' Harold rumbled with laughter. He swayed slightly, like a tall tree in a strong wind. He had drunk a lot of his own cider.

'Shh – I don't want him to wake up,' Lil hissed. 'I want it to be a surprise.'

'You made that story up, Harold,' Miriam laughed.

Trev's new haircut was starting to take shape. It looked quite like his old Mohican so far; very short at the sides but with a fin of longer hair running down the middle of his head which Lil was attempting to de-tangle and cut.

'It's true,' Harold said. 'But you wouldn't believe the things that happened – they were wild days. It's all so tame now.'

☆

Sunlight filtered through the faded orange canvas of Harold's old tent, giving everything a warm glow. Paul didn't want to get out of his sleeping bag but his bladder felt uncomfortably full from last night's cider, even though his head felt clear. It must be the pure ingredients – just apples from the orchard, unlike the cheap white cider he used to drink, which had probably never been anywhere near an apple. The chemicals must have been gradually rotting his insides. He used to think that was a good thing.

Miriam stretched and rolled over on her air-bed. She brushed her hair away from her face and pulled her sleeping bag up to her chin. Paul wanted to put his arm around her and fall asleep again with the warmth of her breath on his face. But he couldn't tell her how he felt. She deserved so much more than him.

Paul struggled out of his sleeping bag and pulled on his trousers and a t-shirt, careful not to wake Miriam. He put his boots on without tying the laces. Outside the shelter of the tent, the breeze was cool on his arms. It felt very early. Paul walked to the long-drop toilets on the old railway track, enjoying the birdsong and the mysterious feeling of being the only person awake. The quiet wouldn't last for long.

Paul returned to the Green Crafts field. He unlaced the doorway of the awning. Trev was asleep, tangled in a nest of blankets. Paul tip-toed past him and opened the removal van door. He forgot how much it squeaked. Trev sat bolt upright. He picked up a long tuft of hair from the carpet.

'My hair's on the floor! I've gone bald, Paul. What happened last night?'

'You fell asleep,' Paul shrugged.

Trev looked horrified. He felt his head with his hands.

'Wait a minute…' He stood up and walked over to the full length mirror on Lil and Miriam's side of the stall. Paul watched Trev's reflection as a smile gradually spread across his face. Paul had been afraid that Lil would make Trev look like a fashion victim but his haircut actually looked good.

'Lil did this?'

'I tried to stop her but you know what she's like when she wants her own way.'

'She must like me.' Trev stretched and yawned. 'God, how early is it?'

'I didn't think you'd wake up. I just wanted some breakfast.'

'She likes me, Paul. How amazing is that?'

Paul stepped into the removal van. The main room almost felt like a real house, except all the furniture was bolted to the floor so that it didn't move about when the van moved. Harold had converted the van when his wife and kids were still around. There was a dining table with benches, two comfortable sofas, a wood-burning stove, shelves with records and books and a galley kitchen with a tiled worktop. Paul filled the kettle and put it on the gas hob. It was a quarter past six, according to the clock above the stove. The sound of Harold's snoring came from the bunk above the cab, which was reached by a ladder. Paul was surprised that Harold hadn't been too drunk to climb it last night.

'God, I need this,' Trev whispered, spooning coffee into a cafetiere. He got two china mugs out of a cupboard. It was still strange to watch Trev doing something so domestic. Paul was used to seeing him frying skip-raided bacon in his battered frying pan, over an open fire.

Paul cut slices of bread. It was fresh yesterday, from a bakery stall with a clay oven. He got margarine and jam out of the fridge.

'I tried sleeping in here the other night. It took me hours to get to sleep. And then I woke up and I couldn't breathe. What's wrong with me?'

'You're claustrophobic.'

'But I keep thinking of Lil – she's asleep in that double bed.' Harold had lent her the van's bedroom. 'And I can't even sleep indoors.'

'Does it matter?' Paul put the bread under the grill.

'Well, you started eating again.'

'Look, if Lil really likes you, she won't care. Maybe that's one thing about you that she can't change.'

Paul squatted down to keep an eye on the toast, while Trev poured boiling water into the cafetiere.

'I want a tattoo,' Trev said.

Paul tried to stop himself from laughing. He turned the toast over and tried to hide behind the grill pan.

'What's so funny?'

'It's just something that Harold said last night about someone having a tattoo done while they were asleep.'

'I want it on my arm here. An oak tree.' Trev pointed to the top of his right arm, just above the line where his plaster cast had been. 'The King's Oak – that big tree in the stone circle field.'

'Why?'

'Whenever I jumped the fence, I used to sleep under that tree. It protected me. I want to remember that.'

'You and your tree bollocks.' Paul smiled.

'It's not. Anyway, do you think Lil would design it for me?'

CHAPTER EIGHTEEN
BABYLON

Harold gave Paul and Trev a thumbs-up. He put on his safety goggles and ear defenders.

'You've got half an hour, starting...now!' the compere shouted through her megaphone. The crowd stood behind a rope barricade.

The sound of chainsaw motors ripped through the air. Harold stood his log on its end. There were two other contestants; a youngish man with a goatee beard and a heftily-built blonde girl who looked like she meant business.

'What's he making?' Paul asked.

'No idea!' Trev shouted in his ear. 'He's been keeping it secret.'

Harold circled his log. Suddenly, he started cutting into the top. Trev cheered, even though Harold wouldn't be able to hear him through his ear defenders and the racket of the chainsaw.

The girl chainsaw carver sent wood chips flying in an arc. The other guy whirled the chainsaw around his head and ran around the arena. The people standing at the front ducked out of his way. A few audience members squealed. Harold didn't seem to go in for showmanship. He cut a V-shape in the top of his log. He turned the log onto its side and started tapering it to a point at the other end.

'It's a crocodile!' Trev shouted. He was completely carried away. Paul realised he was actually enjoying this too. Maybe Trev's spiritual connection with wood was genuine. Before he'd met Harold, Paul had just seen the benders and shelters they'd made as survival, not as a tradition that stretched back thousands of years. There was something primal about transforming a piece of wood into something else. But while he watched Harold carve his crocodile, Paul couldn't help thinking about Miriam. They had the evening off from the stall tonight. Miriam had circled bands that she wanted to see in her programme. She was so excited about the music. Being with her was like seeing the world through fresh eyes. She was so alive and confident now. He thought of the way she'd sold furniture to people who had just come into the awning to shelter from yesterday's rain.

Harold carved jagged teeth inside the mouth of the crocodile. Paul glanced at the girl but he couldn't tell what her sculpture was yet.

A man on the opposite side of the barrier made eye contact with Paul. He kept staring. He had dark hair cut close to his skull and he was wearing a leather jacket. The man turned and disappeared. There was something strangely familiar about him.

Paul shuddered. He pushed his way out of the crowd. The man stared, then slowly turned and walked away. There was a faded "Meat is Murder" slogan on the back of his jacket. Paul ran after him. The man gathered speed, dodging down a track lined with stalls and packed with slow-moving people.

Paul kept his eyes on the jacket. He elbowed his way through groups of people and skidded on a patch of mud left over from the rain. He crashed into a girl in a green cloak selling hash cakes from a wicker basket. She shouted at him but he had to keep going. The man ran down another path, into the open space of the Green Futures field. He stumbled. Paul raced forward and grabbed the collar of his jacket.

The man turned round, gasping for breath. For a split second, Paul thought he had made a mistake. The man's eyes were red-rimmed; his skin had a grey tinge, like he didn't often see sunlight. But it was Mark. Paul's head throbbed.

'You weren't supposed to see me,' Mark wheezed.

'What are you doing here?'

'Recruitment.' Mark stared at him.

'What?'

'I'm true to the cause.' His eyes looked dead, expressionless. 'After we bombed Engelby...'

'The little girl – I only found out her name last month. And Gary...'

'Gary could have joined me. But he was weak.'

'We weren't supposed to hurt anyone.'

'He knew the risks. We could have been heroes. Even if we'd gone to prison.'

How could Mark talk calmly about the bomb – about murder - in a field where children were playing? Maybe he had killed again. The most chilling thing was that Mark was convinced that he was right.

☆

Miriam checked her watch. It had been nearly an hour since Paul and Trev had gone to the chainsaw carving competition.

'Hold still,' Lil said. Miriam fought the urge to blink while Lil applied mascara. It made her eyelashes feel sticky.

'There, that's gorgeous. Look in the mirror.'

Miriam stared at herself. She was wearing a black and red mini-dress that Lil had made out of an old blouse they'd found. It was meant to be on sale on the stall but Miriam had decided to dress up, to surprise Paul.

'Sure he won't think it's over the top? I could change.'

'You look great.' Lil gave her a wry smile. 'Paul would be mad not to appreciate you.'

'You don't mind, then?'

'God, no.' Lil rearranged the clothes on the rail, spacing them out evenly where customers had bunched the hangers together.

'You're having his baby.'

Lil shrugged.

'When I told Trev about the baby – in the back of that police van – I realised that he would care for me whatever happened. I used to think he was a prat but I realised that he loves me. I just wish…'

Trev was dragging a huge carved log down the track. Harold followed, carrying his chainsaw and a small golden trophy.

'He came first!' Trev said. 'Isn't it brilliant?'

It was a sculpture of a crocodile, with bulging eyes, scales and sharp teeth. Trev put it down proudly at the front of the awning.

'Where's Paul?' Miriam asked.

'He's not here?' Trev looked alarmed. 'He was standing next to me.'

Harold wiped the sweat from his face with a cloth handkerchief. 'I'm going to get out of these chainsaw trousers. I feel like I'm in a sauna.' He stomped into the removal van.

'This is Glastonbury, there's a million things to get distracted by,' Trev said.

'But it's our night off.'

Miriam helped Lil to tidy up the clothes rails. A girl looked through the display of earrings. Miriam helped her to pick the ones that suited her. She also sold a purple silk dress. As the light faded, customers dwindled and Miriam kept glancing at her watch. She realised that she'd already missed two of the bands she had circled in her programme.

'Where is he?'

'Paul's unstable,' Lil said. 'You should know by now. He's

fine for a while and then he'll go off on his own – drink too much, cut his arm and then pass out.'

'Shut up, Lil.'

'He'll just be moping around somewhere.'

What if Lil was right? Maybe the way he'd pulled his life together in the orchard was a temporary blip? What if Paul was going to slip down into depression again?

'He can't be.' Miriam felt a prickle behind her eyes. She rubbed them with her fists.

'You've ruined your make up. You look like a panda.' Lil lunged towards her with a tissue but Miriam pushed her away. Lil almost lost her balance. She grabbed hold of a clothes rail to steady herself. Her chest heaved – Miriam wondered if she was doing it for dramatic effect. She felt a flash of guilt. In her anger, she'd forgotten that Lil was pregnant.

'I don't care.'

'If you can't handle the truth...'

'She doesn't want to hear it, Lil.' Trev said. Miriam had never seen him talk harshly to Lil before. He put his arm around Lil's shoulders. 'You're alright though, aren't you?' he asked.

'Of course I am.' Lil's eyes widened and she smiled. She seemed impressed that Trev had taken charge. She let Trev steer her towards one of the beech-wood chairs.

'You've been on your feet all day. You need to rest,' he said.

'Yeah, whatever.'

Harold stepped back into the awning. He stretched his arms and yawned.

'Have I missed much? I felt so tired after the chainsaw carving – I hope I'm not feeling my age. Is Paul back yet?'

Trev shook his head.

'I've got to find him,' Miriam said. She stared into Trev's

eyes, trying to communicate her worries about Paul.

'Harold, what were you going to do tonight?' Trev asked. 'I know I said I'd look after the stall but...'

'I was just going to stay here and watch people admiring my crocodile,' Harold said proudly. He poured himself a cup of cider and made himself comfortable in the big chair.

'Miriam – I'll take you out tonight instead. Paul shouldn't have left you waiting here like this.' He pulled a small bundle of notes out of his trouser pocket. 'I'm rolling in it – Harold paid me. You need a proper night out.'

'I've not had that many nights out, so I'm quite easily impressed,' Miriam said.

'Fine,' Lil sulked. 'So you'd rather spend time with Miriam?'

'I'll make it up to you, Lil. I promise.'

'Thanks, Trev.' Miriam said. She got a piece of toilet roll out of her bag and wiped off the smudged mascara.

☆

Mark's eyes seemed to bore straight through Paul.

'She was a little girl,' Paul said.

'Her dad worked for Engelby. She was a legitimate target.'

'She didn't have much choice about that, did she?'

'So what have you achieved since then? Apart from a cosy little lifestyle? I've been keeping animal murderers terrified. Next time you hear about a bomb under the car of a research scientist, or there's a fire in a slaughterhouse, I'll be behind it.'

Paul shivered, feeling that Mark had him trapped. He focussed on Mark's head, noticing how his hair was receding at the temples. Paul realised that he was taller than Mark. And possibly stronger...

'Why did you run away from me, then, if you're an

international terrorist?'

'I was protecting you. I didn't want this to happen.'

'You were scared.'

'I've been watching you on that stall – that old bloke. I even saw Bella there – and that girl who's up the duff and the one with the dark red hair. Is she your girlfriend?'

Paul stared at Mark, trying to control his fear and anger. He had to have the bravery to look him in the eyes. Mark looked away. He took a crumpled packet of cigarettes out of his jacket pocket; a foreign brand that Paul didn't recognise. He lit a cigarette. He seemed to be doing everything in slow motion. Paul saw himself punching and kicking Mark until he couldn't get up but he kept his fists by his sides, clenched so hard his fingernails dug into his palms.

'They wouldn't know about what you did, would they? No. You'd be too much of a coward to tell them. You wouldn't dare to tell them about me. Because you know what would happen if you did.' Mark drew his finger slowly across his throat. His nails were bitten down to the quick; the skin around them red and raw. 'But you know too much, Paul. I should kill you anyway.' Mark blew out a cloud of smoke.

'I don't believe a word you're saying, Mark. But if you come near my friends again, I'll walk into the nearest police station and tell them everything. I'm not scared of you.'

'Of course you're not scared of me,' Mark laughed. But he seemed more uncertain now.

'This is what I did to myself, rather than betray you.' Paul pushed up the sleeve of his t-shirt, so that Mark could see his scars properly, running from shoulder to wrist. 'But you betrayed everything that we believed in.'

Paul walked away, not daring to look behind him. When he had rounded the corner, he broke into a run.

✩

Miriam stared at the paper cups and plates that littered the trampled grass in the Jazz World field. A crowd waited for the next band to come on. The field had been perfect a few days ago. She'd relaxed on the bright green grass with Lil, watching the coloured silk flags flapping against the blue sky.

'Why don't people clear up after themselves?'

'We're in Babylon now – that's just what happens.'

'What is this Babylon thing, anyway?' She'd heard people in the Green Fields say it when they were talking about the main part of the festival.

'It's kind of a reggae thing – you know – about not liking places that are trying to make money out of you. There's a fine dividing line.' Trev dodged a wheelbarrow containing two children sleeping on top of a pile of blankets. 'The Jazz stage is Babylon but it's kind of acceptable. The Pyramid stage – that's definitely Babylon. The Green Fields are okay. But now I'm not so sure. We've been selling furniture for hundreds of pounds.'

'But you worked hard to make it.'

'There's more to life than money. I don't know what I'm going to do with it.'

They passed the Flying Horse Café stall. There was a long queue of people waiting for food. Miriam stood and watched. Bella was serving customers. She seemed to take it all in her stride, chatting and laughing. Bella saw Miriam and waved.

'We could ask Bella if she's seen Paul.'

Trev put his hands on her shoulders.

'Lil's wrong – he'll be fine. It's not her fault though. She doesn't know the whole story. You're the one who changed him. He's been brilliant. I feel bad – I could only take him so far – I wasn't any better myself. If we could have talked properly…'

Trev's eyes seemed to glitter with tears. He gave her a squeeze and grinned.

'Promise me you'll forget about Paul for tonight?' he asked.

'I'll try.'

'I'll buy you a pint – that'll help.'

The DJ on the stage started playing funky Latin American music with frantic bongos. Trev grabbed Miriam around her waist and spun her around. Miriam stumbled over empty beer cups as she tried to follow Trev's steps. He whirled Miriam through the crowd, towards the pear cider bar on the other side of the field.

'I didn't know you could dance!' she shrieked.

'I'm just making it up as I go along.'

'Lil would love this.'

'Really?'

'They do dance lessons in the Lost Vagueness ballroom.'

They joined the queue. Trev stood quietly, his hands in his pockets.

'I've got it! The way to Lil's heart.' He looked stunned, as if he'd just discovered the secret of the universe.

'What is it, then?'

'I don't want you giving the game away, do I?'

Trev looked so happy that Miriam forced herself to smile and make an effort to ignore her anxieties. Trev had sacrificed his evening with Lil. The least she could do was enjoy herself.

CHAPTER NINETEEN
THE KING'S OAK

The ground-floor door slammed shut. Through a gap in the curtains, Paul watched Mark walk down the street. He still wore his "Meat is Murder" jacket. He had a small rucksack slung on one shoulder as if he was going to lectures.

'Pack all your stuff,' Gary said. 'Don't leave any trace behind.'

Alone in the box room, Paul stuffed his possessions into his holdall and a couple of bin liners. He tried to focus on what he was doing but his hands were shaking. When he had finished, he sat on the bed. A ball of flame superimposed itself in front of what he was actually seeing.

Gary came into the room. He was wearing the rubber gloves he used for cleaning the bathroom, holding a sponge and a bottle of bleach.

'I cleaned your car. There won't be any fingerprints. I'd better clean in here too.' His voice was composed but flat, as if he was trying to eliminate his emotions.

'I don't know if I can drive.'

'You've got to leave now.'

'Where should I go?'

'It doesn't matter. Have you got a passport?'

Paul shook his head. 'What about you?' he asked.

'Don't worry about me. I know what I'm going to do.' Gary took hold of one of the bin bags. 'Come on.'

They walked down the stairs. Gary opened the door but made Paul wait by the door until he was sure that they weren't being watched. The car was parked in the little yard around the back of the flat. Paul felt sick looking at it. Mark had driven the car back from Engelby Hall. He'd planned their getaway route in advance, using obscure country lanes and side streets but Paul had barely noticed.

'You'll need these.' Gary gave Paul his car keys. He pulled some crumpled banknotes from the back pocket of his trousers.

'It's not much but it'll help you to get away.'

Paul put the money in his pocket.

Gary reached out and touched Paul's face. He was still wearing the yellow rubber gloves. 'I'm sorry, Paul.'

'Thanks, Gary.' Paul managed to say. He put his hand on top of Gary's, feeling the shape of his fingers through the glove. He got in his car and drove off without looking back at Gary in the mirrors. The car smelled of bleach. Paul concentrated fiercely on the ring-road. Then he turned off towards the railway station. He left his car in the short stay car park, turned off the engine, left the keys in the ignition and walked away.

☆

'Are you alright, mate?'

Paul opened his eyes, registering darkness with pin-pricks of swimming light. His knees were drawn up to his chest. He was leaning against a rough surface. Paul put his hand out to feel it – it was the bark of an oak tree. His vision swam into focus. He was sitting in the stone circle field, under the King's oak. A young man with ginger hair stared at him, wide-eyed. He held a wax flare. Paul shielded his eyes from the flame.

'Yeah – I think so. What time is it?'

'I dunno. About half twelve. Don't tell me you missed the Chemical Brothers? They were awesome.'

Paul stood up. His legs were so stiff, he had to hang onto

the tree to stop his knees from buckling.

'Are you tripping?' he asked. Paul shook his head. He could feel himself shivering. The night was cold and clear.

'I think I just fell asleep.'

The ginger-haired lad looked concerned. He picked up a fluffy yellow blanket from the ground. He sniffed it.

'I think it's okay – just a bit of mud from yesterday.'

'Thanks,' Paul said. He wrapped the blanket around his shoulders. The lad sat down with his mates a few metres away. Paul leaned against the tree, trying to piece things together. What if Mark really was a terrorist? The worst thing was knowing that Mark had been watching all of them. The safest thing might be to run away now, through the perimeter gate and keep going. Paul started walking.

Crowds of people were making their way up to the stone circle, now the major bands of the evening had finished. As Paul made his way down through the Green Fields, he passed bands playing in cafés and people dancing to bicycle powered sound systems.

He reached Harold's awning and the familiar bulk of the removal van looming out of the darkness. The awning door was unlaced and a warm glow shone through the doorway. Paul stood outside. What if he had put everyone in danger, just by being here? The awning looked inviting, in the soft glow of Harold's candle lanterns. He could hear Harold and Lil talking. Music was playing – Pink Floyd – the Piper at the Gates of Dawn. Harold had been educating them in classic rock while they worked. It made him want to be back in the orchard. What would Gary have wanted him to do?

'It's getting cold,' he heard Lil say. She stood in the doorway before Paul had a chance to dodge away. She stared at Paul. 'How long have you been back?' she asked. 'Typical of you.

Miriam waited for ages. But she got a better offer.'

'What do you mean?' Paul stepped into the awning.

'Trev went out with her in the end. You'd better stay on the stall tomorrow night. Mind you, do I really want to have a night of rummaging around in rubbish bins?'

'I won first prize – you missed it,' Harold said.

Paul stared at the finished crocodile sculpture. It stood on the coffee table with the trophy gripped between its teeth.

'I'm sorry I wasn't there. I…'

'You alright, Paul? You look a bit peaky.' Harold reached out a steadying arm. Paul realised that he was shivering violently.

'Yeah, what happened to you?' Lil folded her arms and stared at him.

'I saw someone I used to know. It was a bit of a shock.'

'Sit down and have a pint of my special cider,' Harold said. 'You'll feel better in no time.'

☆

Miriam was mesmerised by purple lights swirling in the trees and shapes projected on the canopy. The music made her close her eyes – the bassline was like her heart thumping. She loved this place, hidden in a hollow just below the old railway track. Trev grinned at her. It was great dancing with him in the open air.

She saw Paul standing by the speakers with his back to her. He was wearing his blue shirt. Miriam raced towards him, trying not to push past people. She grabbed his arm.

'Paul!' she shouted.

He turned around. It was a man with a beefy face. He looked annoyed.

'I'm sorry. You look nothing like Paul,' she said. Not that he could hear what she was saying. She suddenly noticed the rubbish underfoot again and she realised that the decorations in the trees were only made out of cheap white material with UV lights shining on them. The music just sounded repetitive.

She took Trev's arm and steered him over to the edge of the Glade. It was quiet enough to talk without shouting.

'I want to go back. Paul might be there.'

Trev nodded.

They walked back along the old railway track; the dividing line between the Green Fields and the rest of the festival.

Stewards were holding people up at the next crossroads while an ambulance crawled across the track. What if Paul was in there? Miriam felt an urge to run after the ambulance but she made herself hang back. Trev suddenly darted into the crowd, crawling between people's feet.

He came back to Miriam with dust on his clothes, holding a large silk flower reverentially between his hands. It was bright orange under the floodlights, with dark purple spots.

'A tiger lily. It's a sign,' Trev said. He gently blew the dust off it.

'It's pretty,' Miriam said. Its petals looked slightly trampled and frayed at the edges but he looked so pleased.

Miriam felt shaky, almost guilty for enjoying herself when she should have been looking for Paul.

The Green Crafts field was quiet and dark but there was a soft glow coming from Harold's awning. Miriam though the door.

Paul was playing scrabble with Harold and Lil. He jumped up when Miriam walked in, his tray of letters scattering.

'Miriam – I'm so sorry.' he hugged her tightly. 'Something happened – I've got to tell you,' he whispered.

'You'd better be sorry,' Trev said.

'How was your big night out?' Lil asked.

'Pretty good,' he said. Trev held out the flower. 'I found this.'

Lil stared at the tiger lily critically for a second. Miriam held her breath. Was she going say something sarcastic? Lil kissed Trev on the cheek and entwined the flower into her hair.

'Are you playing this game, or what?' Lil glared at Paul.

'You can't stop now, Paul - I'm winning,' Harold said. 'Cider's good for my word power.'

Paul gathered up his letter tiles. He put down a very short word.

'Dog? Is that the best you can do?' Lil wrote down the score.

'I need to talk to Miriam – and you, Trev.'

'I was just doing Miriam a favour,' he said. 'She waited a long time for you.'

'It's not that,' Paul muttered.

Miriam exchanged a mystified look with Trev as they followed Paul out of the awning. Paul was jumpy, glancing around as if they were being followed. They followed him to the open space where the chainsaw carving competition had been held. The moon shone on the grass.

'Mark was watching the competition.'

Miriam shivered.

'Mark? How did he find you?'

'He's been watching us. He said he was still blowing things up. Mark threatened me. He thinks I betrayed him.'

'If he comes here again, I'll kill him first,' Trev said.

'I remembered him as some kind of hard man,' Paul said. 'But when I looked at him, I realised that I'm bigger than him – he looked like crap. I told him that I didn't believe him. I was so angry. I could have kicked his head in. But I just walked away.'

'You're stronger than him now,' Trev said. 'I'm proud of you, mate.'

'But then I got scared. I thought I was going to run away again.'

'I'm glad you didn't,' Miriam put her hand on his arm.

'Tell me if you see anyone watching us. Look out for a man with a skinhead and a leather jacket. But I'm not going to be frightened anymore.'

Paul's mind was still racing, trying to process what had happened. He shifted restlessly in his sleeping bag. He needed to say what he'd been too scared to before.

'Miriam.'

'What?' she muttered. Maybe this wasn't a good idea. It was late. She'd been out all night with Trev.

'I wanted to talk to you but it's okay – it can wait.'

'I'm not asleep. I was scared that something had happened to you earlier.'

'It had. But I'm alright.'

'When you didn't turn up tonight, I thought you were going to – I mean, after last time, I couldn't help worrying.'

'You changed that. You made me want to be alive.' Paul took a deep breath. 'I know sharing the van was weird at first.'

'I thought you hated me.'

'But after what happened at the river I realised I could trust you. And then – I fell in love with you.'

She was silent.

'I'm sorry. But I had to tell you. I knew you wouldn't want

me. Not in that way, anyway.'

She unzipped her sleeping bag. She was probably going to sleep on the sofa in the removal van.

'Come here,' she said.

Paul unzipped his sleeping bag and moved over towards her. He fell into the gap between the two air beds. Miriam kissed him, shyly at first but then her tongue started exploring his mouth. His body came to life as she put her arms around him; as he felt her warm skin against his.

'I wasn't expecting this,' he gasped.

'I was wondering if you'd ever notice me.'

'You looked gorgeous in that dress.'

'And how do I look now?'

'It's a bit dark. But you feel great.'

Suddenly she pulled away from him and sat up. She rummaged in her bag. 'They were giving free condoms out at one of the information points. I knew there wasn't much chance but I picked some up in case you...'

Paul put his arm around her waist. Her skin was exquisitely soft.

'We don't need to do that – not straight away, anyway.' he said. 'Are you sure you like me?'

'Isn't it obvious?'

He remembered the look on her face when she'd rushed into the awning earlier.

'I don't deserve you.'

'Shut up, Paul,' Miriam murmured. She held his face in her hands and kissed him again, softly. He felt so overwhelmed, it took his breath away. Paul started kissing her shoulders and her neck, working his way up to her lips again. He wanted to kiss every inch of her.

☆

Paul leaned on one of the awning poles. The Green Crafts field was surprisingly busy this afternoon. People looked sunburned and sweaty. They wandered under the shade of the awning, browsing listlessly, just when he needed it to be quiet. Paul kept an eye on Harold's van.

Lil tugged at the removal van's door.

'It's locked. Where are Trev and Harold?'

Paul had to think quickly. She looked determined.

'Harold isn't feeling very well. He thinks he's eaten something dodgy.'

'So why's he locked the door?'

'He doesn't want the whole field hearing him fart. It's hardly good for business.'

Lil pulled a disgusted face. 'Too much information, Paul,' she said.

Miriam was busy with two girls who'd been trying on clothes for ages, joining in with their excited chatter. She put the dresses they were buying into brown paper carrier bags and came under the awning to get change from the cashbox. She turned towards Paul, mystified.

'What are they really doing in there?' she whispered, while Lil's back was turned. Paul shrugged.

'It's a surprise.'

Paul waited. He didn't know how long it would take. They'd devised a system of secret knocks. He wished he could get rid of the customers – they would be too distracting. Just as Paul heard the knock from inside the van, a couple in their fifties started browsing the furniture. They bought a coffee table as a wedding present for their daughter. Paul processed their cheque and filled in the order form as quickly as he could without seeming rude. He glanced at Miriam and Lil's stall. It was quiet now.

Paul tapped on the van's door, letting them know that he was ready.

The door opened. Trev stepped down theatrically into the awning. Paul stared at him, open-mouthed, even though he'd been in on the plan. Trev wore a 1940s style tweed suit, complete with a waistcoat, a crisp white shirt and a tie. He was clean-shaven, smelling of aftershave. The only thing that was recognisable as Trev was his old gaffa-tape mended boots.

'Oh my god,' Miriam said.

Lil gasped. Trev kissed her hand.

'I've booked a table in the restaurant at Lost Vagueness. You'd better get into your best dress – the ballroom dancing lesson starts at six.'

'Ballroom dancing?' Lil laughed.

'You'll come, won't you?'

She threw her arms around Trev and kissed him on the lips.

'Where did you get the suit?'

'From the vintage stall round the corner. They had everything apart from shoes.'

'You did this all by yourself?'

'Harold came with me and the girl who works on the stall gave me a bit of advice.'

Lil examined Trev closely, a look of wonder on her face.

'Scrubs up well, doesn't he?' Harold chuckled.

'I'll get changed,' Lil said. 'I hope I can find something to do you justice.'

☆

Miriam watched Trev and Lil walk down the track, arm-in-arm.

Lil wore a red chiffon halter-neck dress, with a black fringed shawl. Her elegant clothes went surprisingly well with her platform boots. Miriam wished she could take a photograph of them but they soon disappeared into the crowd.

'They look good together, don't they?' Miriam said.

'I'm sorry, Miriam.' Paul put his arms around her waist. 'I wish I'd thought of a grand romantic gesture like that.'

'I don't need one,' she laughed. His eyes seemed to be a deeper shade of blue. Perhaps they were reflecting the golden late afternoon glow. She kissed him, forgetting that they were supposed to be looking after the stall. Paul held her tightly. He seemed to have forgotten too.

CHAPTER TWENTY
GOATS

The removal van crawled uphill, the engine juddering. The stack of furniture began to shake.

'I hope nothing falls on us,' Miriam said. Most of it had a red "sold" sticker – she had promised to help Harold to deliver it by courier this week.

'We wedged it in pretty well. I wish we didn't have to be stuck in here again.'

'At least we don't have to hide in the shower cubicle.'

The van lurched forwards. A chair on the top of the stack wobbled. Paul braced himself against a table and caught it. The van crawled along the steep uphill slope, until it came to a complete stop.

'Looks like Harold was wrong about the traffic,' Paul said.

The van grew hot and stuffy without fresh air flowing through it. Miriam felt a trickle of sweat run down her back. She wished she was lying under a tree. She wanted to see the view again, even though the grass was yellow and squashed and the camp-sites were strewn with litter and abandoned tents.

Paul took a tobacco pouch out of his pocket and started making a cigarette, sitting with his back to her. He seemed to be putting his barriers up again. She buried her face in his shoulder to distract him.

'Come on,' she said. 'We've got perfect privacy.' She kissed his neck.

Paul put the tobacco away. He stared into her eyes like he was trying to understand her.

'I feel like I'm seventeen again,' he said.

'What's that supposed to mean?'

'I was a different person then, before everything went

wrong.'

Miriam put her arms around him. 'I was different before Ruth died – but I was just a kid.'

'I'd got a place at uni. I believed in everything so passionately. Everything was exciting. After the bomb, my life was over. If it wasn't for Trev…' He held her gaze steadily. 'But we were just surviving. I barely knew what was happening most of the time. But now, I feel different. Bella said I had a future.'

'She's usually right about things.'

'Now I've had the guts to stand up to Mark, maybe I can do things with my life again. I want to be with you more than anything.'

Miriam pulled Paul onto the red velvet sofa cushions. She kissed him on the lips and he responded, his hands tracing her back, exploring under her t-shirt. The van's engine started and they inched up the hill another few feet. Miriam felt hungry for Paul – it was a completely new emotion. The rumbling of the engine exaggerated her urgent need for him. She undid Paul's belt buckle.

Paul suddenly put his hand on top of hers.

'I feel a bit like my head's going to explode,' he said.

'Are you okay? I'm not rushing things, am I?'

He laughed.

'It's just all a bit sudden, isn't it? Only a few days ago, we were lying on separate airbeds. I couldn't stop thinking about you but I never thought that this would happen.'

'That's exactly how I feel.' She wrapped her arms around him. Paul smelled of linseed oil and wood smoke. She wanted to melt into him until she didn't know where she ended and Paul began.

☆

The van braked sharply and veered over to the left. After the excitement of making love in the traffic jam, the hum of the engine had lulled him to sleep.

'Where are we?' Miriam said. She raised her head from his chest. Her hair tumbled about her face. He wanted to reach out and smooth it for her.

'We'd better get dressed. What if we're nearly at the orchard?'

'So? The door's bolted. They can't come in,' she said. Miriam sat up and gathered her clothes together. Paul retrieved his trousers from the floor and pulled them on. He put his t-shirt on. Miriam dressed slowly. The van was moving gradually, stop-starting as it negotiated narrow lanes. Paul squeezed past a stack of furniture and peered past the kitchen blind.

'We're in Sutton Mallet already – that was the church. We woke up just in time. I hope Allie's been watering the veg patch.'

The van turned left and started slowly bouncing down the lane.

Paul made his way back towards her, bracing himself against the furniture as the van wobbled. His head hadn't exploded but his desire for Miriam was taking over from the guilt and despair that had dominated his emotions for years. It was like this when he'd first started eating again – he'd had to ration himself to tiny portions.

The furniture van stopped and the cab door opened and slammed shut. The van rolled forwards and the tyres crunched onto gravel. After a bit of manoeuvring, the engine shuddered to a halt and the removal van seemed to sigh, as if it was relieved to be home, settling down in its usual place. Paul unbolted the door and stepped into the yard. Miriam shielded her eyes against the sun. Harold's van looked like it had never moved, apart from the tyre tracks through the gravel. Paul rolled one of the geranium tubs back in front of Harold's van. He wanted to feel like they were home to stay.

His own van looked out of place with his uncle's butcher's shop still advertised on the side. He would get round to painting over the lettering soon. Lil had designed an apple tree logo for Orchard Woodcrafts. It would look great on the side of his van.

'I've been thinking about converting our van – with a proper bed – and somewhere to sit.'

'I'd love it – I'll help.' Miriam smiled.

Arthur bounded up to Paul like a miniature panther, purring furiously. Paul picked him up, tickling his belly.

'He's relieved to see you,' Allie said. She'd appeared from the direction of the orchard, Tom balanced on her hip.

'Did anything exciting happen while we were away?' Harold asked.

'I've been quite busy.'

Allie took off her sunglasses and stared. Trev and Lil were kissing outside the removal van, oblivious to everything else.

'I never thought they would actually – obviously – oh my god.' Allie seemed lost for words. Paul saw his opportunity. He put his free arm around Miriam. She giggled.

'Not you two as well,' Allie gasped. 'What do they put in the water at that festival? Still, it had to happen eventually.'

'And it was the best year ever, business-wise. Everyone worked so hard, I can't believe they managed to fit in all that romance,' Harold said.

'People all over the country are going to be wearing our clothes,' Miriam said. 'The next stage is to get our stuff into shops.'

Heather ran into the yard. She held a tattered book with a colour picture of an animal. The cat launched himself off Paul's shoulder and fled.

'Have you told them about the goats yet?'

'Goats?' Harold asked. He sounded surprised – and not particularly pleased.

'Mum put an advert up in the pub. Some people rang her about putting a new exhaust on their old Transit van. They couldn't afford the full labour charge. But they've got goats on their farm, so they gave us a goat – and her baby - instead. You have to see them.' Heather tugged at Harold's elbow.

'I knew you wouldn't like it,' Allie said. 'I was going to tell you...'

'Was it the Uptons? Moorend Farm?' Harold let Heather lead him into the orchard. He looked stern. Paul followed them. The leaves on the apple trees were dark and glossy. Tiny apples were already growing.

'You know them?' Allie said. 'They seem really nice. They've got a little boy about Heather's age. They played in his tree house. I've already managed to milk the nanny goat. I was going to say no. They would have given me cheese instead but Heather really wanted to keep them. So I made a bargain with her.'

'If we keep the goats, I have to go to school in September,' Heather grumbled. 'But I've got a new friend now and the goats are so much fun.'

In a small clearing in the orchard was a makeshift chicken-wire enclosure. A brown and white goat was trying to trample the fence down. She stared at Paul with alien oblong eyes, as if she was challenging him to stop her. Behind the mother goat was a tiny kid, bleating with high-pitched excitement. Harold stared at the goats and the flimsy fencing. He looked grim, his eyebrows knitted together. Maybe he really would make Allie take the goats back.

'Aren't they sweet?' Heather gave the book to Paul: it was a manual about how to keep goats. She climbed into the enclosure and picked up the baby goat. It kicked its little hooves and the mother goat butted Heather's legs. 'Please can we keep them, Harold?'

'Do we get free milk?' Trev asked.

'I've already milked her this morning,' Allie said. 'I got the knack quite quickly. Of course, the baby needs some but there's loads to spare.'

'Have they got names?' Miriam asked.

'The big goat's called Toffee. I decided that her baby's called Choc-chip,' Heather said. 'Her fur's got little brown spots.'

'Goats are supposed to eat everything.' Miriam stroked the baby goat's head. 'They are cute.'

'They gave us some food mix but they keep kicking the bucket over. And they escaped yesterday.' Allie glanced at Paul and then lowered her eyes. 'We found them in the vegetable patch. I'm sorry, Paul, they ate some of your lettuces.'

'There'd better be some left,' Paul said.

Harold let out a small chuckle. His laughter grew until he was shaking silently and he wiped tears away from his eyes.

'Are you alright?' Lil touched Harold's arm, as if she was worried that he was going to keel over. Harold leaned against an apple tree until he was capable of talking.

'Six weeks ago, I only had the cat for company. And now…' Harold took deep breaths to recover. 'Of course you can keep the goats, if you can stop them from escaping. I wanted to keep chickens a while ago but I realised that I wouldn't be able to eat all the eggs by myself.'

Paul flicked through the goat keeping manual. He found a neat diagram of a goat enclosure, with a gate and a little shelter for the animals. He showed Trev the picture.

'Fancy a skip-raid in the van? I reckon it wouldn't take us long to knock something like this together.'

'What, now?' A grin spread across his face. 'Yeah, go on, why not? I've been having withdrawal symptoms.'

'I might check what's left of my vegetable patch first,' Paul said.

CHAPTER TWENTY ONE
THE PHONECALL

Miriam perched on the barn stairs with her laptop, the cable stretched from the phone socket and through the banisters. As she waited for the internet software to load, she watched Paul and Trev in the workshop, using a giant double-handled saw, cutting through a huge oak plank. Outside the window, rain fell heavily.

The software prompted her to type in her details. The disc whirred busily in her new laptop. Miriam hoped that Harold's phone line wasn't too slow for the internet. Or was she just impatient? She hadn't touched a computer since the day she'd left work.

Paul and Trev finished sawing through the plank. Paul straightened his back. He took off his safety glasses. They had made a red rim around his eyes.

'What's up?' he smiled. 'Isn't it working?' He re-tied his dreads on top of his head with a piece of blue material from Lil's scrap bag.

She sighed.

'No, it just takes time. But once I get it connected...'

'I've never even seen the internet,' he said.

'Me neither,' Trev said.

'You're both dinosaurs.'

Miriam's laptop bleeped. Finally she was getting somewhere. She started setting up an email address.

A few minutes later, she was actually connected to the internet. She felt a small sense of triumph. She opened her notebook. Miriam had done some research at Glastonbury, talking to people with independent boutiques and taking them samples of Liliam designs. Some of them already had websites.

'I made you a cup of tea,' Paul said. She hadn't noticed him coming up the stairs. Paul handed her a mug. It was lemon and ginger – her new favourite. She put it down on the step.

'Thanks.'

'You'll strain your eyes. You've been staring at that thing for hours.'

'I'm going to set up a website for Liliam.'

Paul stared at her blankly.

'Great – whatever that means,' he shrugged. He sat down next to her.

Miriam felt like laughing. Paul was young; he should understand these things. It hit her: she used to feel that she was cruelly isolated from the rest of the world. But at least she'd had Ruth's Walkman and her music magazines and she could sneak into her dad's study to use the internet. Paul had been living a Stone Age existence in a bender.

Miriam sipped her tea, although it was so hot that she burned her lips. She smiled at him patiently.

'Lots of people make websites. They put them on computers that are linked together – all over the world – so anyone with an internet connection can see them. Sometimes they're just about stuff people are interested in, like music. But now people are using them to buy and sell things. That's what I want to do – eventually.'

Paul looked blank.

Miriam turned the laptop screen towards him. It was the website of a retro shop in Bristol. Its background was bright pink with purple revolving flowers. It was difficult to read the words on the screen.

'They had that stall at Glastonbury. It's where Trev bought his suit.'

'I can't look at it – it's giving me a headache,' Paul said.

'I'll design something more subtle for our website.'

'You know how to do this stuff?'

'I got sent on an IT course when I worked at the Mercia. I've bought some special software. I'm going to teach myself from a manual.'

'You're a right little boffin, aren't you?'

'Look,' Miriam said. She clicked onto Yahoo. 'You can search for anything you want.'

'Like what?'

'When I was bored at work, I looked myself up – to see if there was anyone else with my name. There are loads for me. The weirdest one's a mayor in Australia. I'll try your name.'

'No!' Paul grasped her arm. His eyes were wide with panic. Her laptop started slipping through the banisters. She grabbed it in time.

'You nearly broke it.'

'I don't want anyone looking for me – even you,' he said. 'I don't want to be on the internet.'

Miriam felt guilty for making the bomb come to the surface of Paul's thoughts. He had seemed happy.

'I thought you weren't going to be scared.'

'I'm trying.' Paul propped his head on his hands, looking miserable.

Harold and Trev came back into the barn, carrying another oak plank between them. They were both dripping wet.

'I made tea,' Paul said. 'Looks like you need it.'

Trev pushed his wet hair out of his eyes.

'Yeah, we did the hard work while you faffed about, looking at computers,' he said.

Harold stared dubiously at the laptop. 'You say you'll be able to do my accounts on this thing?'

'Of course.'

Miriam curled her fingers around her mug. Her tea was at just the right temperature now.

'You could make a website for Orchard Woodcrafts as well, couldn't you?' Paul asked. Miriam stared at him, surprised. He smiled at her bravely.

'That would be brilliant,' Harold said. 'People have started asking if I'm online but computers are a complete mystery to me.'

'People could look at pictures of the furniture and find out how you make it – they could order furniture from the website. But I'll start with a basic design and learn all the complicated stuff as I go along.'

'Clever, isn't she?' Paul said.

'I'd be completely stuck in the past without you lot,' Harold said.

'What about your kids?' Miriam asked.

Harold snorted through his nostrils. His beard dripped on the stone flags.

'Have you ever seen them here? It's been months since either of them called. They're just not interested.' Miriam had never heard Harold sound as bitter as this. She wished she'd never asked him.

☆

The oak worktops had been cut to size and planed to follow the natural grain of the wood. Paul ran his fingers along the smooth surface. It looked even better now he was rubbing it down with linseed oil.

'How come you didn't get any kitchen design jobs before, Harold?' Paul asked.

'They would have taken too long to build. But now there are

three of us, the possibilities are really opening up.'

'And the prices people are prepared to pay for stuff like this aren't bad either,' Trev said. Paul stared at him in disbelief.

'You always said you didn't need money.'

'It's just nice for Harold, that's all. And I'm putting some money aside for the baby.'

'And now you've got a bank account, you'll be getting a mortgage next,' Paul said. Harold had helped Trev set up a bank account a few weeks ago but Paul had refused. He was keeping his earnings in an old biscuit tin, hidden in his van. The money would be safe enough there. No strangers came to the orchard, just a few customers. Paul was afraid of walking into a bank; filling in forms; the checks they would make. He knew he had to stop himself being afraid but he had to do it one step at a time.

'No way,' Trev said.

Paul knew he was being unfair. They still went on regular skip raids for food together. Trev was building up a collection of discarded furniture that he was planning to repair when this kitchen design job was finished.

'I might get another tattoo, though.' Trev studied the oak tree tattoo on his arm. It was only two weeks since he'd had it done. He was still enjoying showing it off to people. Paul had to admit that it looked good, particularly where the roots twined around Trev's biceps.

'Where?'

'On my back, I think. Something coming up my shoulder. Maybe ivy - as if it was growing there.'

'If you want to look like a walking woodland,' Paul laughed.

'What's wrong with that?' Trev frowned. 'Lil thinks I should get more tattoos. But I might wait until after the baby's born. Get something significant.'

The phone rang. They were lucky to hear it; if they were using power tools, they couldn't talk without shouting. The music that Harold played was always too loud to hear the phone. They usually picked up phone messages when they had a break. But treating the work surfaces was a quiet job and Harold was playing Fairport Convention on his stereo today anyway.

'That could be another order.' Harold ambled towards the bench where they kept the order book and the phone.

Paul dipped his cloth into the linseed oil.

'So what happens when the baby's born? Do I get a mention, or will your name go on the birth certificate?' Paul wished he didn't sound so bitter. It wasn't really any of his business.

'That's up to Lil. What do you want her to do?'

Paul shrugged. It was impossible to break the habit of being scared. He hadn't even plucked up the courage to talk to Lil about the baby.

'Paul?' Harold called. 'It's for you.'

Paul froze. The only person it could possibly be was Mark. Ever since Paul had returned to Harold's awning at Glastonbury, they hadn't been safe. Mark could have easily taken one of Harold's business cards.

'Don't look so worried, it's only Bella.'

'Bella?'

'She's got a surprise for you.' Harold smiled encouragingly.

Paul didn't feel much better. His legs wobbled as he walked across the workshop. Harold patted his back as he handed over the phone receiver. It didn't do anything to reassure him.

'Bella?'

'I've got your mum here,' she said. Paul sat down on the bench with a bump. Something dug into his backside. He grabbed it from the bench. It was a drill bit. He stared at it. It looked like a piece of twirly pasta made of metal.

'Paul? Are you still there?'

'What happened? Is she okay?'

'She came into the café about half an hour ago. Look, it's probably better if I put her on to talk to you, if that's okay?'

'Yeah.' Paul tried to imagine what was happening in the café. What was his mum doing there? He twirled the drill bit round and round in his hand.

'Paul? Is that really you?' His mum's voice. It sounded like she was trying to hold back sobs.

'Mum? How did you find me?'

She burst into tears. In the background, Paul could hear Bella comforting her. Mum blew her nose.

'Your dad's had an accident.'

Despite his old hatred for his dad, Paul's heart raced.

'He fell off a ladder – climbing up to the loft – banged his head. I had to call an ambulance. When he came to, he was talking about you.'

'Is he okay? What did he say?'

'He's got pretty bad concussion and a dislocated shoulder. They said they're going to keep him in for a few days. But he'll be alright. He'll need to be off work for a bit.'

'Yeah - but what did he say?'

'He said you had a toy polar bear – you lost it when you were about two – we were on holiday.'

'I don't remember that.'

'He's hardly mentioned you since you left but I know...'

'He wanted to get rid of me.'

'That's not true, Paul and you know it. You should have seen him in that hospital bed. He put your stuff in the loft, years ago. I think he went up there yesterday to look at it. He's sorry about falling out with you. He said he'd been wondering where you were.'

'Really?' Paul looked up. He'd pressed the drill-bit into his palm, leaving a red indentation. He realised that he was alone in the workshop. Harold had turned the music off. 'But what about – what happened – have you told him?'

'Of course not. He doesn't know anything. But Bella's been explaining.'

'She knew all along.'

'I shouldn't have run away from you when you tried to tell me – when you got the van. I was so shocked to see you – and I'd spent so long forgetting. I wondered why you'd come back after all that time. You looked terrible. I went back to the garage soon after but you'd gone. I didn't tell your dad that I'd seen you. I came into town on the bus today and I passed the café. I thought that Bella might know where you were…' Her words tumbled out. It sounded like she was crying again.

'I'm sorry, Mum. I'm sorry for everything.' Paul touched his face. It was wet. He wiped his arm across his face. The linseed oil made his eyes smart.

'You've still got the van? May was asking. She's a bit better now. I'm going out to Spain with her next month. She's getting the apartment ready to let out. There's no point in leaving it empty.'

'That's good. Tell her thanks – for the van.'

'I've got to get to the hospital before visiting time ends. Your dad might be coming home tomorrow. But I'll call again.'

'I'd like that.'

'I'm so glad I've found you, and that you're safe.'

She put the phone down. Paul imagined her in the kitchen at the café, Bella waiting nearby, thrilled that she had helped to reunite one of her lost souls with his mother. Paul stared at the dusty phone receiver in his hand, trying to take in what had just happened. Eventually, he replaced the phone on its cradle and opened the workshop door. The others were sitting around the table, staring at him. Miriam ran to Paul.

'Harold said...' she started. But Paul could only hug her tightly. He realised that he was crying, making Miriam's hair damp.

'She wants to call again. Miriam. I think I was wrong about my dad. I need to go back to see them. Not yet but...'

Miriam looked away from him. He could tell that she was thinking about her own parents.

'And if I can do it, you've got no excuse. Contact them properly. No more postcards. Promise me?'

She nodded, biting her bottom lip.

Harold had decided that the weather was too good to be making kitchen cabinets. He was getting stuck into a jug of cider with Trev at the round table. Miriam watched Paul weeding his vegetable patch. He looked totally absorbed but happy. Heather and Allie were picking windfall apples to feed the goats.

From the attic, Lil's electric sewing machine hummed. Lil sang along to the radio, slightly out of tune. She was finishing off their first wholesale order, for a boutique in Bath.

Miriam had finished the first version of the Liliam website – just a few pages, with their contact details, the address of the orchard and a few photos of herself in the orchard and at Glastonbury, modelling the clothes. She had scanned prints from Lil's camera. A digital camera would be good eventually. Miriam had also made a simple website for Orchard

218

Woodcrafts. She'd used a wood-grain pattern for the background. She'd got the idea from the web design manual she'd been using. The files uploaded slowly onto the server. Miriam was impatient to see whether everything worked.

She had been looking at the website that her dad had designed for the railway museum. It had made her feel closer to her father than she'd expected. Some of the train photographs had been taken on family holidays. Miriam and Ruth were just out of shot, eating ice creams or lounging around in boredom. Her dad had used old train livery colours as his website background. He'd used a similar colour scheme in the kitchen before Mum had realised. He was the only person who picked up emails from the website. No one else at the railway museum trusted modern technology.

The laptop bleeped. The website files had uploaded at last. Miriam sat on the stairs and checked every link and photo. She made a few minor changes but both websites looked good. She knew she had a lot to learn but felt proud that she had mastered the basics.

Miriam typed in the railway museum's email address. Hesitating, she thought about what Bella had said. She realised that she had to tell her dad the truth.

For the attention of Frank Smith, Peak Railway Museum:

Dad,

I'm sorry I haven't been in touch properly. I sent you the postcards but I realised that you and Mum really need to know that I'm okay. I didn't want to tell you where I was. I was worried about what had happened with Mr Brown in his office. I thought that Mum might make me go back there or that I was going to be in trouble for setting off the fire alarm. I was confused. But don't worry - there was someone looking after me.

I know it was stupid, running away. But I couldn't stand the things Mum was saying – I bet she's been saying things about me too. Ruth didn't do anything wrong. It's not fair that she didn't get to grow up. But it wasn't fair that I couldn't grow up either. When I ran away, I wanted to do all the things that Ruth never got the chance to do. Mum was right in some ways though – I hated working at the Mercia – but I'm using those skills to start a business with a friend. I've got my own life now.

I've designed a couple of websites: www.liliam.com and www.orchardwoodcrafts.com They're my first attempt. I'd appreciate your opinion anyway – and then you'll know what I'm doing & where I'm living. I don't think Mum will approve though.

Lots of love to you and Mum – and I really am sorry that I took so long to get in touch.

Miriam

Miriam pressed the send button. After a couple of seconds, the message appeared in the "sent" folder. It was too late to change anything now. She turned the computer off, realising that her head was throbbing. She must have been staring at the computer screen for too long. Either than, or it was the smell of wood preservative. Miriam put the laptop in its case, shoved it under Harold's workbench and ran outside.

CHAPTER TWENTY TWO
THE RANGE ROVER

Miriam carried her laptop carefully downstairs into the workshop. Harold, Trev and Paul had left at dawn. The kitchen units were finally being delivered in Paul's van and fitted today. Miriam had made herself busy in the attic with some accounts. She was wrapped in a blanket, waiting for the chill to leave the air. There was a glimmer of sunshine now. Miriam promised herself that after she checked her emails, she would relax in the hammock that Trev had strung up between the trees, then maybe do some weeding in Paul's vegetable patch.

She plugged the cable into the telephone socket and waited for the modem to connect. She pressed "send and receive" on the email programme and stared at Trev's ever-growing pile of old furniture.

The computer bleeped. There was one email in her inbox. It was from the Peak Railway Museum. Miriam's hands shook as it opened.

Dear Miriam,

You can't possibly know how much your email means to me. I'm so relieved that you're happy. The postcards barely told us you were alive.

Anything could have happened to you. You hear so many terrible things on the news. Your mother and I have been waiting for so long. We told the police that you'd gone missing but once we told them about the postcards, they seemed to lose interest. They thought it might have something to do with the incident at the building society.

I wish you'd told me that you'd been so unhappy there but I hadn't exactly made myself very approachable, had I? I've been a coward since Ruth died. Trains are much easier to deal with.

Your mother regrets the way things turned out. I printed off those pictures from your website to show her how lovely you look now. Ruth would have loved all of those unusual clothes.

Did you know that we kept Ruth's ashes after the funeral? We were going to put up a memorial to her but somehow we never did. After I got your email I remembered. The urn's at the back of our wardrobe. That's no place for Ruth. If you want to come home, even if it's just for a visit, we'll do our best not to make the same mistakes again. We're not angry at you for running away – just angry at ourselves.

Your ever loving Dad

Miriam hit the reply button.

Dad – I'll get back to you properly soon. I need time to think about things.

There's such a lot to think about.

All my love,

Miriam

She sent the email and switched the laptop off. She wandered outside, feeling dazed. It was still early. The curtains of Lil's ambulance were drawn. Miriam followed the sound of laughter coming from the edge of the orchard. Allie was milking the goat. Tom watched her, clinging onto the fence, trying to keep his balance on his sturdy little legs. Heather played with the baby goat.

'I'm teaching her to do tricks,' Heather said. 'I've almost got her to jump through a hoop.'

'I got a call this morning,' Allie said. She handed the bucket of milk to Miriam while she unfastened the goat from its milking stand. 'There's a guy who's inherited a farm and it's in a right old mess. They want to convert the farm buildings into holiday cottages but one of the barns is full of old cars – they've been in there for years – and he wants someone to get rid of them for him. He saw my advert. I said I'd take a look at them, see if there's anything worth selling.'

'Okay,' Miriam said. 'Have a nice time.'

'Why don't you come with us? You look like you need a change of scene.'

'Looking at a load of old cars in a barn?'

Heather and Allie both stared at Miriam as if they pitied her, their eyes shining.

'It's going to be brilliant,' Heather said.

☆

The man who owned the farm handed Allie an old ice-cream tub labelled "car keys".

'I don't even know if these are the right ones,' he said. He unlocked the padlock on the barn doors and left them alone. Allie dropped her matter-of-fact expression. She opened the doors a crack and peered through.

'I feel like Indiana Jones,' she said. 'Right, let's see what we've got.' She pulled the doors open, letting sunlight flood into the barn. Several large shapes were lurking under dust sheets. Straw bales were piled around the old cars and bits of old farm machinery were squeezed into the gaps. The cars had obviously not been moved or even looked at in years. Miriam sneezed. She watched from the doorway, holding Tom's hand, while Allie and Heather pulled back the dust sheets.

'Wow.' Allie had an awed look on her face. Miriam started to feel interested, despite knowing absolutely nothing about cars. There was a yellow sports car with no wheels, propped up on piles of bricks.

'That's a Triumph Spitfire.'

Miriam picked Tom up. He had grown much heavier recently. He stared around the barn. Miriam pointed at an old-fashioned car with a wooden frame at the back.

'A Morris Minor Traveller,' Heather said.

'It's heart-breaking when the wood rots.' Allie bent down to take a closer look at the car's bodywork. 'But this one seems okay. It's been kept in a nice dry barn.'

'Trev would love a wooden car,' Miriam said.

Allie shook her head. 'He hasn't got a licence.'

'But he drove Lil's ambulance to the orchard.'

'That was an emergency. I shouldn't have let him. You know he used to be a car thief?'

Miriam nodded. Trev had told her his story that first week before the rave, before she knew about Paul.

'When I first met him, Trev wouldn't even get into a car. He couldn't even sit in the back of a van. He walked everywhere.'

'But now he's sleeping in the ambulance.'

'He's doing it for Lil; he's so in love with her. But he'd rather be in his bender.'

Allie uncovered another car.

'A Ford Capri,' she gasped. 'It's like being a kid at Christmas.' She was covered in dust and cobwebs. 'You should learn to drive, Miriam. I could teach you.'

Miriam shrugged.

'Maybe. It's not something I've really thought about.'

Allie moved towards the last car that was shrouded in dust-sheets, lurking at the back of the barn. It was bulky and tall.

'I've been saving this one for last. I recognised it by the shape. I'll need your help.'

Miriam helped Allie and Heather to tug the dust sheets off the car.

It was dark red, splattered with ancient mud. One of its wing mirrors was hanging off, its front bumper was dented and all its tyres were flat, the rubber perished. Allie looked wildly excited. She switched on her pocket torch and inspected the vehicle closely.

'Mum's been looking for something like this for ages,' Heather explained. 'Can we buy it, Mum? We could name our price.'

'It'll need a lot of work. But I think I'll be able to restore it. Can you find a key that fits?'

'It's a shame I won't have much time to help you to restore it – I'll be at school,' Heather said.

'You're not getting out of going to school. You can help out with the car in the evenings and weekends.'

Miriam stared at the bonnet of the car.

'It's a Range Rover...' Miriam said.

'Yeah – a Range Rover Classic.'

'My sister was killed by a Range Rover.' Miriam touched the car. She imagined the moment of Ruth's death; Mike and Ruth, driving along, laughing in the Mini, the stereo turned up loud. Mike was cocky. Maybe he was going too fast, knowing every twist of the lane. The big car appeared from nowhere, on the wrong side of the road. What had Ruth's last thoughts been, as the Mini spun uncontrollably into the tree? Miriam leaned on the car, suddenly blinded by tears. She sobbed, hugging Tom close to her, until he began wailing too.

'I'm sorry,' she said.

'Would you rather I didn't buy it?' Allie took charge of Tom.

Miriam shook her head, waiting for her breathing to settle down. She watched the motes of dust moving in the breeze, glowing in the sunlight. This dust had been undisturbed for years.

'Are you okay?' Allie asked.

'Ruth's ashes are at the back of my parents' wardrobe. My dad emailed me.'

Allie put her hand on Miriam's shoulder.

'Do you think she's trapped in there, Allie?'

'I'm not religious but they're hanging onto the past.' Allie shrugged.

'They've been doing that for years! My mum didn't want me to grow up.' Just like the way Mum had ripped the rock-star posters off Ruth's bedroom walls, leaving the faded candy-pink wallpaper of her childhood.

'When my dad died, we had a special ceremony to scatter his ashes at the football ground. He'd put it in his Will.'

'There's a park near my parents' house. At the top of the hill, you can see for miles. Ruth always wanted to travel.' A smile grew on Miriam's face. She felt like she'd found a jigsaw piece that had been lost for a long time. 'Thanks, Allie.'

Allie attempted to brush off some of the cobwebs that were now clinging to Tom.

'Any time,' she said.

'Mum – I found the right keys for the Range Rover!' Heather shouted.

☆

'This is a piece of crap, Trev. You think you can make it into something worth selling?' Lil snorted.

Trev lovingly stroked the wooden back of the chair. Paul saw why Lil wasn't convinced. The nylon upholstery was sagging and greasy. It was covered in drips of white paint. But the frame was good, solid wood.

'Harold says it's a sixties classic.'

'I suppose he'd know.'

'It's nice pine underneath. All we need to do is strip off this horrible varnish.'

'Is it worth all that work?'

'Just look at it properly. We'll need to reupholster it, though.

I was hoping you'd make me some cushions.'

'I've got some material upstairs that might do – pale green.'

Lil moved slowly toward the stairs. A few months ago, she would have flounced. But she was too big now. She moved like she was wading through treacle. She leaned on the banisters as she plodded up the stairs, slowly bypassing Miriam who was perching on the stairs, busy with her computer.

Trev reached into his trouser pocket.

'Have you had my knife?' He stared at Paul.

'No.'

'I was sure I had it.'

'I'm not surprised you've lost it, the state of those trousers,' Lil shouted from the top of the stairs.

Trev took a Stanley knife from the workbench. He used it to rip the upholstery off the chair. Paul could tell by his movements that he was upset.

'When did you last see it?'

'I put it in my tin last night, I'm sure. I thought I had it.' Trev patted his legs, as if the knife was going to miraculously reappear.

'You must have used it today.'

Trev shrugged. He searched the workshop, opening drawers, looking in increasingly unlikely places.

'It's probably under those wood shavings,' Miriam said.

'That's a sneaky way of getting us to sweep up.' Paul grinned at her.

'You know it's a fire hazard.'

Paul and Trev tidied the wood shavings into a pile by the door. The knife didn't turn up but Paul found a pocket spirit level that hadn't been seen for weeks and an earring that Lil had been looking for.

'You don't understand,' Trev said. 'It's important.'

'Check in the bender – and what about Lil's ambulance?'

Trev dashed outside.

Paul tried using varnish remover on the arm of the chair. It started coming off quite well. He let himself get absorbed in the work and let the spacey guitar music wash over him – one of Harold's Steve Hillage CDs. Paul propped the door open so that the chemical fumes didn't get too strong.

'You've got it, haven't you? I've looked everywhere.' Trev glared at him. He was out of breath.

'I haven't got a clue where it is.'

'You used to lie to me. I knew you used to hurt yourself with it. I thought you'd stopped.'

'I swear I haven't.'

'Show me.'

'This is stupid. You saw me in a t-shirt yesterday afternoon.'

'I still had my knife then.'

Trev suddenly grabbed Paul's left wrist. Paul dropped the jam jar with the varnish remover. It shattered on the floor, the liquid splattering.

Miriam ran down the stairs. Her boots crunched on the broken glass.

'Leave him alone, Trev. He hasn't done anything like that for months.'

Trev stared at the mess in horror.

'That's nasty stuff. You didn't get any in your eyes, did you?'

'I'm okay,' Paul said. He fetched the dustpan and brush to clear up the glass. Trev got a cloth and wiped the varnish remover off the floor.

Paul rolled up his left sleeve.

'Look.' The scars were white and fading. It almost looked like a normal arm.

'I'm sorry. But it's my lucky knife. You know how much it

means to me.'

'What's lucky about it?' Paul asked. The first time he'd seen the knife, when Trev had rescued him, he'd seen it glint under the street light. Paul had seen the savage look on Trev's face. The attackers had scattered. Trev hadn't used the knife as a threat since then. They had used it to build shelters and make kindling to start fires. But when he could borrow it without Trev watching, Paul had used it to cut himself. He had been fascinated by the smooth steel handle; the sharp, precise blade and the fine lines it could etch into his skin. Trev had never understood that Paul did it to control his emotions. It was something else that he'd never spoken to Trev about. But that was over now. He didn't really care if Trev had lost his knife. It was something from the past. Trev could easily buy another one.

'I knew it was special, Trev. But why?' Miriam asked.

'I found it at the back of a drawer in the shed in the old allotment where I lived that first winter after I got out of...' Trev smiled sadly. 'I kept it sharp and polished. I used it for everything.'

'I'll look out for it. You know I will,' Paul said.

Trev shrugged.

'Lil's right though. It probably dropped through a hole in my trousers.'

CHAPTER TWENTY THREE
THE APPLE HARVEST

Miriam climbed the A-shaped ladder into the tree, making sure she had a steady footing on the highest rung that fitted both her feet. She grabbed hold of two sturdy-looking branches and shook them until all the apples showered onto the grass below. Miriam climbed down the ladder and helped Allie and Heather to collect armfuls of apples and put them in sacks. It had been Heather's idea to turn it into a competition – boys against girls.

'I've been looking forward to this all week,' Heather said. 'It makes a change from being stuck indoors in that horrible school uniform.' Her face was almost hidden by Harold's old motorcycle helmet. She wore it to protect her head from falling apples.

'Heather – you'll soon get used to it. And you said you'd made some friends,' Allie said.

'School uniforms are meant to be horrible,' Miriam said. 'And bank uniforms.' Miriam remembered the static prickle of the polyester blouse against her skin; the clammy feeling when the air conditioning wasn't working properly.

Miriam collected apples as quickly as she could. It was the sort of late September day that felt like summer was still there. But it was impossible to walk in the orchard without being bombarded by falling apples. The leaves of the orchard trees were turning brown and curling at the edges. Tom's buggy was parked well out of range.

'Air hostesses have to wear uniforms,' Heather said.

'I thought you wanted to be a trapeze artist,' Allie laughed.

'I do. But airline hostesses are cool because they look smart but they have to be experts in first aid and survival and stuff.'

'And you travel all over the world and get paid for it,' Allie said. 'But there's a height restriction. If you only grow to my height…'

'She can be whatever she wants to be,' Lil said. Bending over was almost impossible for her at this stage of her pregnancy, so she sat in a deckchair. The cat was curled around her ankles. Heather had persuaded her to keep score of how many trees Miriam and Paul each climbed.

'Stop putting the dampers on things, Mum. Get a move on, Miriam.'

Miriam moved the ladder and climbed into the next apple tree. Paul was already at the top of a tree.

'We're winning!' he shouted. He shook the tree, creating a deluge of apples. He had a wide grin on his face.

'Sod off!' she shouted. Miriam could see the next door farm from this tree. A man was standing in one of the fields, a black silhouette against the shorn meadow. His face seemed to be turned towards Miriam.

'Come on, we're waiting,' Heather moaned. Miriam started shaking the tree. She looked up. The man was still standing there. She was sure he was staring at her. She wondered if she should tell Paul. But she didn't want to worry him. The next-door farm had a B&B, and harvesting apples was the sort of traditional thing that people came to the countryside to see.

☆

Paul sat on the bed and started to undress. It was difficult to relax in the van at the moment. Everywhere he looked there was something else to do. He wondered if he would have room for a fold-down table. The next job would be to cut holes for windows. He hoped he wouldn't make a mess of it.

They'd skip-raided for the mattress and the wood for the

bed but it was a solid piece of work, with useful drawers underneath. The saggy old sofa bed sat in a corner by the door. Paul lay on the duvet, staring at the blank wall on the right-hand side, visualising cupboards, a stove, a sink, maybe even a little fridge.

Miriam lifted the shutter and climbed into the van. Cold air rushed in, making him shiver. The van needed a proper wooden door and folding steps. Miriam would love that.

'What's the matter?' she asked. 'Still sulking because the girls' team won the competition?' Her cheeks shone from the cider they'd been drinking and the glow from climbing trees all day.

'It was a fix. Lil was biased.' Trev and Harold had been playing at being sore losers all evening. It had been Paul's idea to deliberately slow down and let the girls' team win. They hadn't been too far behind, though. Heather had beamed with pride when Harold gave her his chainsaw carving trophy as the prize.

'Nimble fingers are better than brute strength any day.' Miriam jumped onto the bed and prodded his arm muscles. 'But my arms feel like they're falling out of their sockets.'

'You worked hard. For someone who spends all day at a computer.'

'What's that supposed to mean?'

'You can take the girl out of the office but you can't take the office out of the girl.' Paul grinned.

'That's not true! You're just scared of computers. Admit it. We won, fair and square.' Miriam pounced on him, slapping his cheek playfully.

'Never,' he said.

She tickled his chest and he retaliated. She was relentless, and knew exactly which places would convulse him helplessly.

'Okay, I give up.' Paul lay back on the pillows, grabbing Miriam so that she toppled on top of him. He kissed her softly. Her mouth smelled of toothpaste; her hair was scented with apple-wood smoke from their harvest fire.

Paul imagined cuddling up with Miriam in the van, in front of their own wood-burning stove.

Miriam kissed him back. He forgot all about the van. Her hands roved under his t-shirt and tugged it over his head. He was no longer aware of anything apart from her.

☆

Miriam jolted awake. In her dream, she'd heard the noise of breaking glass. Her heart thumped as she lay rigid beneath the covers. The night seemed silent. Then she heard a whoosh like a gas flame igniting. Miriam held her breath. She could hear running footsteps crunching on the gravel.

She sat up. A crackling sound came from the cab. She shook Paul awake.

'What's that noise?'

'What noise?' His voice was muffled, as if his head was under the covers.

'Listen!' The crackling noise grew louder.

Paul grabbed her wrist and dragged her out of bed. He yanked her arm. She shouted out. He ignored her. He opened the shutter and pushed her out of the van. There was a weird flickering light. Paul jumped down beside her and pulled her away from the van. The cab was on fire, flames licking out of the broken window on the passenger side towards Lil's ambulance, only a few feet away.

Miriam ran towards the ambulance. She turned the handle on the rear door. It opened. The interior was lit by a fiery orange glow. Lil slept on her side, wrapped tightly in blankets, her hands curled protectively around her bump. Where was Trev? Miriam shook Lil. She opened her eyes.

'You've got to get out of here. Our van's on fire.'

Lil stared at her. She seemed confused but the flames were getting brighter and bigger. Miriam grabbed Lil's hands and hauled her to her feet, towards the door, stumbling over the blankets.

'Where are your keys, Lil?' Paul shouted.

'Hanging up,' Lil mumbled. Paul ran into the ambulance and grabbed the keys off the hook near Lil's bed. Miriam held tightly onto Lil as she slowly stepped down onto the gravel.

Paul dodged the flames as he got into the driver's seat of the ambulance, turned on the engine and reversed it to the other side of the yard. Miriam pulled Lil out of the way, under the nearest apple tree. Flames were coming from van's body now, not just the cab. The whole thing was glowing intensely. Lil stood there like a mannequin. Demon fingers of fire reached into the sky, lighting up the whole yard and the silhouettes of the trees. Trev hurried out of the orchard, fastening his trousers. He hugged Lil tightly. Paul jumped out of the ambulance and ran to Miriam. Lil stared at them disbelievingly. Miriam's brain wasn't registering things properly. Something was strange – but everything else was wrong too. Lil started laughing.

'I'm dreaming, aren't I?' she said. 'This is too weird to be real.'

'Don't piss about, Lil. We've got to get the fire out.' Paul put his arms around Miriam. She felt his skin against hers. His hands were cold, his chest was hot, his heart racing.

'Are you okay?' he asked.

Miriam nodded.

'But you're both naked!' Lil said. 'That proves it can't be real.'

Trev shook her shoulders gently.

'This is really happening, Lil. They rescued you. I should have been with you.'

Lil blinked. Her eyes widened with horror as she stared at the fire. Miriam and Paul both pulled away from their embrace, suddenly embarrassed.

'Come on. The van could blow up,' Paul insisted.

The others were awake now. Harold ran towards them in wellies and a dressing gown that made him look like a monk. Allie and Heather stood in the doorway of their caravan, staring at the flames. Miriam began to shiver.

Lil unwound her layers of wrapping. She threw a striped blanket at Paul. He tied it around his waist and ran across the yard, towards the standpipe.

'Don't just stand there, call 999!' he yelled at Allie. 'Harold! Bring the hosepipe from the vegetable patch!'

Miriam remembered the water butts that collected the rainwater from the barn roof. There were buckets in the workshop near the cider press. She ran towards the barn.

'Miriam!' Lil shouted. She gave Miriam her pink Indian bedspread. Miriam wrapped it around herself and tied the ends in a firm knot. Lil sat down heavily on a sack of apples. She seemed to be struggling to breathe. Smoke was billowing around the yard. Trev would look after her. There was no time to waste.

Miriam raced towards the barn, grabbing handfuls of the bedspread to stop herself from tripping. She might have been better off without it. She fumbled for the door key under a flower pot behind one of the water butts. It wasn't in its hiding place. She turned the door handle. It swung open. She walked inside. Miriam remembered all the times she'd nagged Harold about security measures.

The barn smelled weird. Maybe it was varnish or wood preservative. Miriam reached for the electric light. The door slammed shut behind her. She heard the key turn in the lock. She opened her mouth to scream. A hand clamped tightly across her mouth. She felt the texture of cracked leather, a cold zip digging into her back. The smell grew stronger – the stink of petrol, with a faint whiff of stale sweat.

'Perfect,' the man hissed. His leather jacket creaked. He dropped her to the ground. He switched on a torch and shone it in her face. She shielded her eyes with her arm. But she'd seen his face, striped with camouflage paint, his eyes staring with an unnatural intensity.

'I've been looking for Paul since our little chat at Glastonbury. He wasn't very careful, was he? Everything was online. He thought I was making up stories to scare him. He didn't think I'd do it for real.'

Miriam stared, too frightened to move from her crumpled position. In the dim torchlight, she saw all the furniture piled against the stairs – anything that could be moved: the old chairs and tables that Trev had been restoring; a hand-made bookshelf that Harold was due to deliver. Allie's jerrycan lay on its side. A trail of liquid stained the flagstones dark, spreading out from under the furniture.

'Here's a test,' the man said. He seemed thrilled by his own cleverness. 'Do you know who I am? What I'm doing here?'

Miriam shivered.

'You're Mark,' she said. She'd known as soon as she'd seen him. Mark had been watching them today from the field. He was the figure she thought she'd imagined last week, almost hidden amongst the trees. 'How long have you been spying on us?'

Mark smiled slowly, like she'd given him the winning answer in a game show.

'Good. You know who I am. That means that...'

Miriam ran towards the door, kicking it and beating at it with her fists. She tried yanking the door-handle but the lock was solid iron. The door was made of ancient oak, hardened over the centuries. Mark tried to pull her away from the door. She lashed out, aiming for his face. He dropped his torch. The only light came through the window now, from the burning van. She shouted and screamed. She kicked him. He grabbed her wrists.

'Miriam!' Paul shouted. He banged on the door from the outside. She yelled back. Her voice was growing hoarse.

Mark suddenly let her go and ran towards the pile of furniture. He struck a match and dropped it onto the petrol-soaked wood. A sheet of flame flashed towards the ceiling. Mark stood and watched calmly, his hands on his hips, admiring the destruction.

A large object smashed through the window. Shards of glass flew into the room with clumps of soil and geranium plants.

Paul vaulted through the window. His face was soot-blackened. Miriam tried to run towards him. She tripped up on the bottom of the bedspread. Mark grabbed her again. He pressed something cold against her neck – a knife blade. His arm crushed her chest.

'You've made your point,' Paul said. He held his palms towards Mark. His hands were bleeding. 'Just let Miriam go.'

'Isn't this perfect justice?' Mark said. 'Isn't this what you wanted?' His hand made a swift movement and Miriam felt a sharp pain. She felt a trickle of blood run down her chest, onto the bedspread. Her eyes were streaming. Her throat burned.

She didn't dare to struggle.

'Let her go, Mark.' Paul reached forwards slowly to grab Mark's arm. Miriam heard the flames crackling up the stairs behind her.

Harold launched himself through the window. He charged towards them, an axe grasped in his fist. His eyes reflected the flames, full of rage. He bellowed as he ran, like a war cry.

Miriam screamed. Mark ducked past Harold and leaped out of the broken window.

☆

Smoke billowed through the workshop window.

'We got there just in time,' Harold said.

'Too late to stop Mark.'

Harold laid Miriam down next to the removal van. He doubled up coughing.

Paul knelt next to Miriam. The cut on her collar-bone streamed with blood. He put his hands on her to check the rise and fall of her chest. Why wasn't she waking up? His palms left more blood on that pink thing that she was wearing.

Paul could hear sirens coming down the lane. He saw flashing lights through the hedge.

Trev put his hand on Paul's shoulder.

'I saw him run into the woods.' Trev said.

'Then we'll go after him.' Paul kissed Miriam on the cheek and stood up. Something was digging into his left foot. He bent down and pulled a piece of glass out of the sole of his foot. It was a surprisingly big piece.

'Shit, Paul.' Trev's eyes widened. 'Maybe we should just tell the coppers where to find him.'

'He'll hear them a mile off. I know where he's hiding.'

'But your foot?'

'I'm okay,' he lied. There was a large gash in the sole of his left foot. He tested his foot on the ground. It left a bloody print on the gravel. But there was only a dull ache. His right foot was also trailing blood.

Paul knew that he had to face Mark. The professionals were here now, to deal with everything else.

'I'll look after Miriam,' Harold said.

Paul walked through the gap in the hedge behind the barn, into the woods. Trev followed. The flashing lights and flames became a dim flicker as the trees closed behind them. Paul's eyes struggled to adjust to the darkness. All he could see was fire. He stumbled and grabbed a tree for balance. Paul brought his breathing under control. His cut feet hurt him now but he forced the pain out of his mind. Gradually, he made out the shapes of the trees and of Trev. They had lived in darkness and firelight for years. Paul was used to walking barefoot.

'He could be anywhere.' Trev whispered.

'I saw a shelter – near that fallen beech tree – it's been there for about a week. I thought it was Heather's.'

'Let's go.'

He felt the leaf litter carefully with his toes, trying to avoid brambles. Trev followed stealthily, although twigs snapped under his boots. Paul thought he could make out a faint smell of petrol. Maybe it was just his singed senses playing tricks. But as they approached the fallen tree, the smell definitely grew stronger.

He touched Trev's arm and pointed. There was a triangular shape made from fallen branches stacked against a broken sapling. It made a small space that someone could hide in. They crept up to the shelter. Standing absolutely still, Paul heard the sound of laboured breathing coming from inside.

'Mark.' Paul said. He tried to keep his voice steady.

There was no reply. Paul could hear the creak of Mark's leather jacket.

Trev kicked the branches down. They toppled, making an oddly musical noise. Mark sprang up and lunged towards Paul.

Paul grabbed the collar of Mark's leather jacket. He tried to hold Mark at arm's length but the leather was slippery.

'The police are here.'

'I knew you'd betray me.'

'You tried to kill Miriam.'

'You know too much – and so does she.'

Mark pulled away from Paul's grasp. He reached into his jacket pocket. Paul saw the blade glimmer, reflecting the moonlight between the trees.

Trev kicked Mark sharply in the back. He grunted, hitting the scattered branches with a thump. The knife flew out of his hand.

Trev picked up the penknife. He put it carefully in the pocket in the leg of his combat pants.

'My knife,' Trev said; his voice low and dangerous. 'You stole it.'

Mark tried to raise himself, to make a run for it. But Trev kicked him in the head. Mark was on the ground again.

'You sick, murdering bastard!' Trev shouted. He booted Mark savagely in the ribs. Paul couldn't watch this. Trev had gone too far. Paul remembered cowering in his sleeping bag as he was kicked by a group of laughing men.

He grabbed the neck of Trev's t-shirt.

'Stop it!'

Trev turned and stared at Paul. He was exhilarated, panting.

'We're better than that, Trev.'

Mark was lying still, face-down. Paul kneeled down next to

him. He turned him over, carefully. Trev could have killed him. A trickle of blood ran from his lip. Mark opened his eyes and spat at Paul.

'I still believe in non-violence,' Paul said, quietly.

Mark tried to move. Paul firmly pushed him back down. He sat on Mark's legs to stop him from escaping.

'How long have you been messing with our stuff – hanging around here?' Trev hissed. They turned Mark onto his back again.

'Good job I've got this twine in my pocket,' Trev said.

Paul pinned Mark's arms back while Trev bound his wrists tightly together.

'I got sick of watching you all – so fucking smug.' Mark croaked.

'Remember what I said at Glastonbury? About telling the police?' Paul said. 'But now the police have come here. We can hand ourselves in.'

'Don't, Paul,' Trev said.

'I've got to.'

Mark tried to twist round, thrashing his arms. They each grabbed one of his elbows and dragged him into a standing position. He hung like a dead weight between them, refusing to walk. They dragged him. Paul had to steel himself to touch Mark. His leather jacket was cold and damp against Paul's bare arm.

'I always hated your jacket,' Paul said. 'Me and Gary used to laugh about it.'

'It's ironic. Not that you'd understand,' Mark mumbled.

'You really didn't stop with the Engelby bombing, did you?' Paul said.

Mark was silent.

'Walk, you bastard,' Trev shoved him from behind.

Paul and Trev dragged Mark through the gap in the hedge, in front of a group of fire fighters who barely noticed them. They were tackling the fire in the barn. There were no flames coming from the van now. It was engulfed in smoke. The noise and flashing lights confused Paul's senses. Mark tore himself away from Paul's grasp and tried to run. Trev grabbed him.

Harold was talking to a tall man in dark suit. They stood close together next to a shiny black car. There was a policeman in uniform next to them, writing in a notebook. Paul saw a police Transit van. Harold suddenly pointed at them.

'They've got him!' Harold shouted.

Mark twisted around and head-butted Paul in the chest. The policeman ran up to them and got a firm grip on Mark. Another policeman sprinted from the van, keen to be involved in the action. They got Mark on the ground again, just like Paul and Trev had done in the woods, hand-cuffing him, reeling off the police caution breathlessly.

'Paul, you don't need to tell them anything,' Trev whispered.

Mark still struggled as they put him in the back of the police van. He gave Paul a look of utter hatred. Paul stared back. Mark couldn't do anything to him now.

'Look, we're very impressed, you did a good job,' said the first policeman, locking the van doors. He looked like he should have been herding sheep, with his broad shoulders and round cheeks. 'But how did you find him in complete darkness?'

'They were both brilliant, John.' Harold spoke to the man in the suit. 'But Paul deserves some kind of bravery medal. I've never seen anything like it.' Why had Harold called the man by his first name? Harold was hardly the biggest fan of the police. He smiled at Paul. It just made it worse.

Paul caught his reflection in the car window, against a

background of flames from the barn. He barely recognised himself. He remembered that he was naked apart from a blanket tied around his hips. He was streaked in soot and blood, like a survivor from some ancient battle.

'He's been spying on us for weeks,' Trev said. He was shaking with rage. He took his knife out of his pocket. He held it between his thumb and forefinger. Trev had wrapped it in a leaf. 'He stole my knife. Keep it. It's had his hands all over it.'

'He must be a nutter,' the younger policeman said.

The suited man pulled a see-through zipper bag out of his pocket. He opened it so that Trev could drop the knife inside.

'But why? Do any of you know him?' he asked. His greying moustache gave him a world-weary air, as if he was used to getting dragged out of bed to investigate crimes in the middle of the night.

'His name's Mark McKay,' Paul said. 'I was a hunt sab in Derby. We planted a bomb under a hunt-master's car. It was my idea. We killed a little girl. I kept the secret for seven years.'

Paul couldn't look at anyone, particularly Harold. He stared at the gravel. Harold had trusted him. Paul should have walked away from everyone and gone where Mark would never find him. Instead he'd chosen to believe that Mark wasn't for real.

'So arrest me too,' Paul said. No one moved.

Allie ran towards them from the other end of the orchard.

'You can't arrest them!'

'They got the bastard, Allie,' Harold said. 'They found him in the woods. He's in the back of that meat wagon.'

'Lil's waters broke. They're getting her into an ambulance – a real one, I mean.'

'Oh my god, what do I do?' Trev said.

'They've already taken Miriam. She hasn't come round.'

'Is she breathing?' Paul asked. Allie touched his arm.

'It's the smoke, and shock. But they said she'd be okay.'

'I promised Lil I'd stay with her,' Trev said. 'But I was going back to the bender as soon as she was asleep. I just couldn't do it.'

'Go now with her now,' Allie told him. 'Take her mobile.' She stared at Paul. 'You look shocking.'

The suited policeman nodded, looking at Paul gravely.

'Go to hospital, Paul. We've got the arsonist. The last thing we need is you bleeding all over the police station. We'll need to take statements from all of you.' He sounded tired, as if nothing was going to surprise him. 'I'll come back tomorrow.'

Paul had expected to be slammed into the back of the police van with Mark. The pain in his left foot was suddenly overwhelming. He stumbled backwards. Trev caught him.

CHAPTER TWENTY FOUR
THE HOSPITAL

Paul sat on a plastic chair in the waiting room. Whatever he was waiting for, it wasn't going to be good. The nurses had fussed over him earlier but he'd been numb, his mind whirling with disjointed images. They had said he'd been lucky not to sever a tendon in his left foot. There had been smaller fragments of glass stuck into his right foot. They were astounded that he had walked through the woods with those injuries but adrenaline had kept him going. He had lost a lot of blood. Both feet were heavily bandaged and he had dressings all over his hands.

He expected that the police inspector would arrive at any moment. People were staring at him. This was worse than the bad days before Trev had found him. The nurses had given him a pair of pale green pyjamas but they were too small. The jacket didn't button up and the trousers were halfway up his calves. He wished he still had Lil's blanket. At least that had been part of his own world.

Paul hugged his knees tightly and stared at a blue floor tile in front of him that was a slightly different colour from the others. He was aware that people were coming and going but he didn't want to lift his head and look at the clock. He didn't want to know how much time was passing. All he could do was sit and stare at the floor tile until they came to get him.

Someone stood over him, blocking his view of the blue tile. What was he going to stare at in prison?

'Paul.' He looked up. It was Harold. His brown jumper still had wood shavings stuck to the front of it, from the destroyed workshop. He held one of the sacks they'd been collecting the apples in yesterday.

'I'm taking you home,' Harold said.

'But I…'

'I checked on the others. I brought clothes. I should have realised that you needed help first. They shouldn't have left you here like this.'

'Lil's lost the baby, hasn't she?' Paul asked.

'What? God, Paul. What's been going through your head? I blagged my way into the maternity ward. I said I was Lil's dad. She's knackered and Trev's a bag of nerves but that's normal. The midwife reckoned that everything was going very well. No baby yet though. Could take hours.'

'How's Miriam?'

'She's sleeping. She's okay.'

'Can I see her?' Paul tried to stand up but his legs were stiff. His foot hurt so much that he sat back down again heavily.

'You need rest first. We can come back later.'

Paul shook his head.

'The police are going to cart me off, though.'

'Not if I can help it.'

Harold rummaged in the apple sack and held out a blue checked work shirt. 'Put this on. It's a cold morning. Starting to feel like autumn,' he said.

Paul struggled into the shirt. The plasters on his fingers made his hands too clumsy to do up the buttons. The shirt was enormous but it was warm, the worn material soft and clean. Paul blinked away tears.

'I'll get you a wheelchair,' Harold said.

'I'll manage.' Paul shook his head. But Harold was already talking to the nurses on the reception desk. He returned, pushing a metal-framed wheelchair.

Paul hauled himself slowly out of the plastic chair. He grabbed Harold's arm for balance. Harold steered him erratically down the brightly lit corridors.

It was light outside, with a hint of drizzle. Paul breathed the fresh air gratefully. A pale man with a drip in his arm was sitting on a bench, smoking.

'I'd better take this thing back,' Harold said. 'Wonky wheel – bloody useless.'

'Got a spare fag?' Paul sat on the bench.

The man's hand shook as he held out the packet and offered Paul his lighter. Paul inhaled the smoke but it made his head spin, like the first time he'd tried smoking at the bottom of the school playing fields. Paul gripped Harold's arm. He limped into the car park, where Allie's car was parked diagonally across a space. The rough surface of the tarmac dug into Paul's right heel – the only part of his feet that wasn't bandaged.

'I'm no good at driving cars,' Harold unlocked the driver's door. 'I can't guarantee you a smooth drive home. I'm sure I'd be great on a motorbike though.'

Paul eased himself into the passenger seat. The clock on the dashboard showed the time as ten minutes past seven.

'Where's Allie?'

'She's asleep. It was hours before the fire brigade left. We both gave statements to the police. I had a quick nap before I came down to the hospital.' Harold's massive frame filled the car, his knee jammed against the gear lever. He started the engine and manoeuvred jerkily around the car park. Paul wound down the window to tap the ash from his cigarette but it flew out of his hand when Harold braked sharply at the junction with the main road.

'Thanks for the shirt,' Paul said. They were heading north on an A-road, driving through the outskirts of the town. 'But I've ruined everything for you. I don't see why you're doing this. Why don't you take me straight to the police station – and then I can give you your shirt back?'

Harold drove on in silence. He swerved towards the pavement, slamming the brakes on with a screech. He put the hazard lights on and cut the engine.

Harold turned to face him. His eyes blazed with anger. Paul shrank back into his seat.

'Paul, remember last night? Remember what you did? You saved lives. You fought fires; you rescued Miriam from that man.'

'You threw that barrel through the window.'

'I would have buried that axe in his head. I saw how calmly you tried to talk to him. You did the right thing.'

'If it wasn't for me, he wouldn't have come to the orchard.'

'Paul - you can't change the past.' Harold sighed heavily. 'The first time I saw you and Trev, you were fighting, remember?'

Paul nodded.

'About Lil.'

'I heard Trev say something about you being a terrorist.'

'Shit. You heard that?'

'I was wary of both of you but the cat loved you straight away – that was a good start. Actually, I had a long chat with Bella that night. Just to make sure. And she told me something about all this...'

'You knew?'

'You went missing after it had happened. She knew that you'd been mixed up in it somehow. You were just a kid. This Mark – and the other one – they had too much influence on you but she didn't realise what you were planning until it was too late. She asked me to give you a chance. So I did, and I don't regret it.'

'But I put you in danger.'

'This Mark guy – what he tried to do to Miriam...' Harold

sighed. He looked tired. Paul wondered if Harold was okay to drive. 'Paul – don't blame yourself for his actions, now or then. If I hear one more self-pitying word out of you, I'll belt you into next week. Is that clear?'

Paul nodded. Harold restarted the engine.

'You know that policeman, don't you? You called him John.'

'Yeah. It was at the Beanfield. I'd been trying to negotiate with the coppers for hours on the main road. I came back to the van and it was all smashed up. My wife and kids had disappeared. I was desperate. Then I saw a young copper standing in the middle of the field. His riot shield was on the ground. He was just staring at everything that was happening. He said he was sick of it. He didn't want to be part of the violence. So I told him to arrest me.'

'Like I did last night?'

'That shocked us both – it seemed like history repeating itself. I bumped into John again a few years later in the supermarket. We got to know each other. He's got his own smallholding on the other side of Bridgwater. His wife keeps rescued battery hens. He's like one of us, in his spare time.'

☆

Harold drove through the gates of the orchard. Paul stared at the cider barn, its windows gaping holes, the stonework blackened and the corrugated iron roof collapsed. The van was a skeleton of twisted metal. Paul wanted to look more closely, to check if he could salvage anything. But a group of people were standing in the yard, next to an unfamiliar white van marked "ITV West Country Tonight".

Harold left the car near Allie's caravan. He helped Paul out of the passenger seat. His legs and arms had stiffened up again.

Paul smelled acrid smoke as soon as the car door opened. He longed for the apple-wood smell in Miriam's hair.

'Can we interview you, about the fire?' asked a woman wearing an expensive-looking suit with long green wellies. Her eyes widened as she stared at Paul. The camera crew gathered behind her. Paul realised it would make a great news story – a dramatic fire involving a bunch of travellers; an interview with a bandaged man wearing hospital pyjamas.

'Film here if you like. I don't care – but let us sleep,' Harold barked. 'Give us some bloody privacy or bugger off.'

The woman turned to her colleagues with an extravagant shrug, tossing her immaculately straightened hair. Harold ignored her. He put his arm around Paul's shoulders and steered him towards the removal van. Harold fumbled with his keys. Paul couldn't remember him ever locking it before.

'That's all we need – bloody television crews. Cheeky bastards,' Harold muttered. He filled the kettle, lit the stove and put a Syd Barrett LP on the stereo. Harold closed his eyes and sighed as the first track started. Paul thought about all the CDs on the shelves in Harold's workshop. At least Harold kept his original vinyl records in here.

Paul leaned back on the sofa. He tried not to think about the things that had been lost in the fire. Miriam would be furious about losing her laptop. But at least she was still alive to be furious about it.

'Drink this. All of it.' Harold gave Paul a plastic tumbler, almost brim-full of whisky. Paul gulped it down. Paul's belly felt warm and his legs tingled. Harold brought him a mug of steaming tea. 'It's chamomile. My wife swore by it for getting to sleep. Lil's been drinking it.' Paul tried to pick the mug up from the table but the plasters on his fingers made them too stiff to get through the handle. The mug was scorching hot. He couldn't hold it in his hands. His thoughts were becoming less clear – the whisky must be working. Harold brought him two thick slices of toast.

'I used your margarine. I'm not trying to force animal fats down you. Just get it down your neck and go to sleep.'

☆

Paul opened his eyes and saw a ceiling clad with pine planking. He sat up, painfully. He was in the double bed in the removal van's main bedroom. Paul was sore all over but the throbbing in his left foot had subsided. The enormity of everything hit him. He was going to become a father at some point today. What if he was arrested? He had nothing to wear but these horrible pyjamas. Nothing was normal. His bladder ached.

Paul shuffled into the bathroom cubicle and used the chemical toilet. There were voices outside. He hoped it wasn't the media again. Paul hobbled outside.

Harold and Allie were unpacking the awning. A van with a fire service logo on its side was parked by the ruined barn. Two figures in protective suits and hard hats stood in the doorway, holding clipboards.

'Did you manage to sleep?' Harold asked.

'I think I passed out completely.'

'You look like a zombie.' Allie said. 'Fancy having a psychopath trying to kill you!' She stared at him. 'I knew you had a secret though. Everyone does.'

'Any news from the hospital?' Paul asked. 'What's the time?'

'It's just after two. And no one's called yet,' Harold said. 'You need to eat again.'

Paul shrugged. He looked at the people by the barn.

'What are they doing?'

'They said everything's screwed apart from the walls. They'd withstand anything apparently. But we need to get a structural engineer to check. The fire shot straight up the stairs like they were a chimney – he's an expert fire-setter, your old mate Mark.' Harold looked utterly defeated. Paul wanted to apologise but he didn't dare.

'But look what the Uptons brought round,' Allie said. 'You know - the people with the goats.'

She pointed at some old pieces of kitchen worktop, a rough wooden frame and an electric drill piled on the round table. Allie showed Paul a plastic bucket. It had a large sharp blade inside the lid. 'This is a pulpmaster. You attach the drill to the lid and it crushes apples.'

'It looks lethal.'

'The other thing is our replacement cider press. The Uptons heard about the fire and they didn't want us wasting our harvest,' Harold said. 'I usually swap them a few sacks of apples so they can make a bit of their own cider.'

'It was really sweet of them,' Allie said. 'They're sorting out some spare clothes too.'

Paul thought about the ancient oak cider press and the milling machine in the cider barn. Harold had shown them everything so proudly on that first day. They'd stood in the barn for centuries but had been destroyed in minutes. Paul couldn't bear to see his friends pretending to be cheerful about a crappy plastic bucket and an electric drill.

Suddenly, Arthur leaped onto his shoulder with a loud miaow. He nuzzled against Paul's cheek, purring like a motorbike engine. Paul stroked his back. His fur stuck up in tufts.

'I wonder where he's been hiding?' Harold said. 'I saw him before I set off for the hospital but he ran away from me.'

'He must have been terrified of the fire,' Paul said. 'I'll give him some dinner.'

'Just relax. I laid some clothes out for you in the bedroom while you were asleep. Did you notice?'

Paul shook his head.

'We'll take care of everything,' Harold said. 'Trev promised he'd call if there was any news.'

'We might give you some apples to cut up later but we're not letting you loose with this pulpmaster thing. You're not well,' Allie said.

Paul wandered back into Harold's van. Arthur was still perched on his shoulder, his tail curled under Paul's nose. He tried not to sneeze – he didn't want to alarm the cat.

'Poor old Arthur,' he said softly.

Paul caught sight of himself in the mirror above Harold's stove. His dreadlocks were so sooty, it looked like his hair was going grey. He sniffed one of them. It stank of smoke from the van fire – burning metal, fuel and plastic. It made him feel sick. Arthur glared and opened his mouth in a silent mew.

Paul got a can of cat food out of the cupboard and rinsed out Arthur's bowl. The cat jumped off his shoulder and waited expectantly on the square of lino where they always put his food. Paul got the tin opener out of the drawer. He stared at the kitchen scissors and laid them out on the work surface. He opened the tin at arm's-length and scooped out half of it into the bowl. He couldn't stand the smell of cat food. Arthur stood on his hind legs, trying to eat out of the bowl before Paul could put it on the floor.

'Bloody carnivore,' Paul laughed. Arthur liked to pretend that he was a wild cat prowling the woods, but he needed regular meals and comfortable naps. Arthur demolished the food. Paul emptied the rest of the cat food into the bowl too.

He gave him a clean bowl of water. Eventually, Arthur stretched and sat on his favourite perch on the back of the sofa, washing himself enthusiastically.

Paul took the kitchen scissors and stood in front of the mirror again. He snipped off one of his dreadlocks, letting it fall to the floor. Then he cut another one off. He wondered if he should keep some of them, so he kept cutting until he had a small clump of dreads at the top of his head.

'What do you think, Arthur?' he asked. The cat squinted at him, as if he didn't appreciate being interrupted at such an important stage of his wash. 'Okay, I look stupid.' Paul snipped again until they were all gone. He tried to get rid of the tufts that had been left behind. His head felt much lighter, like he was cutting away years of guilt and misery. He swept up his fallen hair and put it in the bin.

Paul's scalp itched. He limped into the bedroom, stripped off the hospital pyjamas and examined himself in the mirror. Bruises were blooming all over his body. The bandages on the soles of his feet were black from limping around in the hospital car park. His skin was still streaked with soot in places; white where they'd cleaned his skin with antiseptic. His arms were tanned but the rest of his body looked unnaturally pale. There was a pile of clothes laid out neatly at the end of the bed, with a threadbare towel. But a shower would ruin the bandages on his feet.

Paul wrapped the towel around his hips. He found a roll of cling-film in the kitchen cupboard. He wrapped his bandaged feet in it. The cat ignored him, tucking his paws underneath himself, his eyes shut determinedly. Paul put washing up gloves on his hands and stepped into the shower. He scrubbed himself all over with Miriam's lime fizz shower gel, getting the suds into his scalp for the first time in years.

Once he was out of the shower, he dressed in the clothes that had been left for him: one of Harold's old Hawkwind t-shirts and a pair of patched green corduroy trousers. The waistline was huge but Harold had left a belt. It was leather but Paul couldn't be fussy. He pulled it to the tightest notch. Paul carefully stretched a pair of woollen hiking socks over his bandaged feet. He put the blue shirt on again. The clothes were faded and much too big but they were soft against his skin and smelled of apple-wood smoke.

Harold had also left a huge pair of canvas shoes. Paul was easing his feet into them when he heard Allie's ringtone.

CHAPTER TWENTY FIVE
THE MATERNITY WARD

Miriam had changed out of the hospital gown into the bizarre selection of clothes that had been waiting for her when she woke up: leopard-print leggings, a bubble-gum pink Barbie t-shirt and the halter-neck dress that Lil had worn at Glastonbury. The nurse said that she was well enough to go home. She'd told Miriam that Harold had brought the clothes first thing this morning and that he was coming to collect her. So he must be alright at least. No one had told her anything else. They just told her to calm down.

She tried putting on the headphones that were hanging above her head but when she fiddled with the controls, all she got was white noise. Miriam wished she had something to do. She stared at the sleeping middle-aged woman in the only other occupied bed, trying to imagine why she was in hospital and who would come to visit her. But Miriam felt too anxious to distract herself. She kept seeing the blade of the knife reflecting the flames in the barn, Paul's face and the axe in Harold's hand. This must be how Paul felt all the time. She put her hand on her collar bone, where Mark had cut her, feeling the papery dressing under the Lycra t-shirt.

She heard a man's voice in the corridor, and heavily-striding footsteps. It sounded like someone else was shuffling along behind him. Perhaps it was an elderly patient trying to find the toilet.

Harold appeared, enormous in the low-ceilinged ward. She stood up and hugged him.

The shuffling person came around the corner – a tall man, wearing a black woolly hat and clothes that were far too big, limping unsteadily in a pair of oversize tennis shoes. He stared down at his feet, as if he was scared of falling over.

'I'll wait out here for you,' Harold said.

The man looked up and beamed a huge smile at her.

'Paul!' She threw her arms around him. He kissed her. They held onto each other so tightly, it felt like the hospital was dissolving around them. 'But you're hurt – your feet...'

'It's okay. I stood in some glass. But he stabbed you.'

'It looked worse than it actually was. Just a cut really – I only needed a couple of stitches.'

'The police have got Mark now. I'm not hiding from them anymore. I told them about the bomb.'

'What? But why?'

'Because I had to. But whatever happens, I love you,' Paul said.

He stared at her steadily. He seemed almost serene; certain of himself. He put his hands gently around her waist. His fingers were covered in plasters.

Miriam kissed him. Her nose and throat felt parched with smoke but she caught the faint scent of her lime fizz shower gel.

'Let's get out of here.'

'We can't. Not yet, anyway. We've got another visit to make.' Paul started to hobble down the corridor. She took his arm, to steady him.

'Is someone else hurt? Is it Trev?'

Paul smiled, like he'd got a secret.

'We're going to see Lil's baby.'

'But it's not due for weeks!' Miriam shrieked. She was shushed by a nurse sitting behind a desk. 'Oh my god, is she okay?'

'Trev called Allie and we came straight here. Allie's coming later. There wasn't room in the car. Lil's had a baby – that's all I know.'

'Your baby.' She hadn't meant it to sound hostile. 'But the people at the hospital must think that Trev's the father.'

They came out into a lobby. Harold pressed the button for the lift. He seemed to know where they were going.

'And Harold's pretending to be the granddad,' Paul said. He leaned against a pillar while they waited for the lift to arrive. He closed his eyes. She hoped he wasn't in a lot of pain. His temples looked clammy.

'Why are you wearing a hat? It's so hot in here.'

'It was Allie's idea. She thought I looked too much of a mess.'

'Why?' Miriam snatched the hat off his head. His hair had been unevenly cut short, sticking up in damp tufts.

'Do you like it? I thought it was time for a change. You wouldn't believe how light it feels.'

They squeezed into the lift after Harold. Its walls were lined with mirrors. Miriam stared at herself, her arm linked through Paul's. They looked far too colourful for the white and beige world of the hospital. Paul's new hairstyle suited him, even if it would take some getting used to.

'I think you'll need to get Lil to tidy it up a bit. What did you use? Garden shears?'

Miriam and Harold rubbed antiseptic gel onto their hands while they waited at the maternity unit's reception desk. They made Paul put white latex gloves on when they saw all the plasters on his hands. He felt like a complete idiot now.

The midwife beamed at Harold.

'Welcome back. Congratulations.' She smiled at Miriam and

258

Paul. 'They'll be pleased to see you. They're very tired though. It was all a bit dramatic last night!'

'You're telling me!' Paul muttered. She ushered them briskly down a corridor. Paul's foot hurt him too much to put his weight on it for long, but crutches would be no good with his hands in this state.

Miriam saw he was struggling and she offered her arm for support. He felt like he'd been hobbling around the hospital for hours.

'We weren't expecting to see Lil for a few weeks,' the midwife said. She opened the door of a small yellow-painted room with a view of sky and distant countryside. The young woman in the bed had tangled blonde hair. It was Lil. She was sleeping, propped up on pillows, with a small, blanket-wrapped bundle on her chest. Trev was asleep too, curled up on a chair. They both jerked awake as everyone came into the room.

Lil smiled unsteadily.

'Look! I still can't believe it. My baby.'

'A boy,' Trev added. 'Sorry – we didn't mean to fall asleep.'

Miriam nudged Paul. 'Go on,' she said.

Lil rearranged the baby so that he faced his visitors. He was quite red in the face. His bright blue eyes blinked. He had a grumpy expression, like a tiny old man. The baby's eyes seemed huge but his nose and mouth were tiny. He had a lick of blond hair on top of his head. Paul opened his mouth but he couldn't think of anything to say. He held his breath.

'I think he looks a bit like Billy Idol,' Trev said. Lil glared at him.

'He's perfect, Lil. He's amazing,' Miriam gasped. She sat down on the edge of the bed. 'Can I hold him? No, Paul should hold him first.'

Paul shook his head. He was mesmerised by the baby.

'He's a smashing little chap,' Harold said.

'He was determined to come out today,' Trev said. 'The midwife said he's fine, even though he's early.'

'Did it hurt?' Miriam asked. 'I didn't even know you were in labour.'

'Ten hours. But I got some amazing painkillers. I've been totally off my head. It's wearing off a bit now though.'

'The laughing gas was pretty cool too,' Trev said. 'I've had loads. I wasn't supposed to but it was great.'

'You should try it, Miriam.' Lil grinned.

'No thanks,' she said. She glanced at Paul. 'The gas sounds fun but I don't think I'll be giving birth for a few years, anyway.'

Lil gently passed the baby into Miriam's arms. Miriam was completely transfixed, gazing into the baby's eyes. Paul stood in the middle of the room, feeling like a bit of a spare part. Harold found him a plastic chair. Paul sat down, relieved to be able to rest his feet.

'I was scared I wouldn't know how to hold him or anything but it feels totally natural. I've already breastfed him.' Lil said. She sat upright and stared at Miriam. 'Why are you wearing my dress?'

'Harold just grabbed a load of things from your wardrobe.'

'What's happened to Paul's hair? It looks great. And I love all those clashing colours and textures in your clothes. I can't believe I haven't thought of wearing that dress with a t-shirt underneath. I'll use that look in my next collection.'

'You must be kidding,' Paul said.

'Trev – take a photo of them. You need to be in it too, Harold.' Paul would never get his head around Lil. She was exhausted after hours of labour. Even that couldn't stop her thinking about life as if it was a fashion shoot.

Trev took a photo with a disposable camera. Miriam stood behind Paul, holding the baby. Harold put his hand on Paul's shoulder. The flash made Paul blink.

'Are you alright though, mate?' Trev asked. 'What's with the gloves?'

'They made me wear them - because my hands are all cut.'

'You were brilliant last night,' he said.

'You should hold the baby, Paul,' Miriam said.

'He's so small. I might hurt him.'

'Go on, Paul.' Lil smiled at him. 'Support his head.' Miriam gave the baby to Paul. He kicked his arms and legs vigorously, dislodging the blanket. He was wearing a tiny nappy underneath. Paul held him in the crook of his arm, barely daring to breathe. Trev took a photo of them together. The baby stared at Paul. His mouth suddenly opened.

'He smiled! He smiled at me!' Paul whispered.

'No, he just burped, mate,' Trev grinned. 'It's wind.'

Paul stood up and gave the baby back to Lil. He was probably fed up with being passed around like a parcel.

'I think he did smile at you,' Lil said. 'That was his first smile.' Paul felt strangely pleased.

'Has the little chap got a name yet?' Harold asked.

'We've been talking about it for hours,' Lil said. 'But we've finally decided.' She paused and exchanged glances with Trev. 'His name is Jake Paul Phoenix Cooper-Cox. Jake because we both like pirates...'

'Double-barrelled, eh?' Harold laughed. 'People will think he's really posh.'

'But Paul's the most important name,' Trev said. 'You saved Lil's life – and the baby.'

'I just reversed the van,' Paul said.

'Stop being modest. You reacted so quickly,' Miriam said.

'It's a lovely name.'

'Jake's going to have two dads – me and you.' Trev's eyes shone.

'A few months ago, that would have been a recipe for disaster. But now I think it might just work,' Lil said.

'Really?' Paul was amazed. He couldn't say anything else.

CHAPTER TWENTY SIX
INSPECTOR DAVIES

The fire engines and ambulances had completely flattened the grass on Appledene Lane. The orchard gate was open, although Paul was sure that Harold had shut it earlier. The car swung into the yard.

Miriam stared at the barn as soon as she got out of the car.

'It's ruined.' She ran to the van. Her feet were bare – Harold had forgotten to bring her any shoes. Paul limped after her. He didn't want her to get hurt. Miriam touched the bent metal and stared at the soot it left on her fingertip. 'We've lost everything.'

'Nothing that can't be replaced,' Paul said. He stared at the skeleton of the mattress and the charred wood. He remembered the biscuit tin, full of his wages. The banknotes would have been completely incinerated. He'd been hiding it in the drawer under the new bed, wrapped in his Glastonbury blanket. Paul had told Miriam that he'd set up a bank account. He hadn't wanted to tell her that he'd been scared of existing officially again.

'Whose car is that?' Miriam asked. 'Has Allie got it booked in for a service?' There was a black estate car parked in the shadow of an apple tree.

'It's the police. It's that copper from last night.' Paul felt his pulse race.

'So where is he?' Miriam asked.

'I knew he was coming back. You'll visit me, won't you, if they send me to prison?'

'Don't talk rubbish.' Miriam said. She put her arms around him tightly. 'When I woke up in hospital no one would tell me if you were okay. I need you. I'm not letting them send you to prison.'

Harold was already slotting the heavy wooden awning poles together. They needed to get the awning up quickly – the sky was darkening as the wind blew strongly from the west.

Allie and Heather were coming back from the goat pen. Paul was surprised to see the policeman carrying a bucket of milk.

'I'll bring you a few chickens,' he said. 'Just enough to get you started. They get quite lively once they get used to being free. My daughter watches TV with her favourite chicken on her knee.'

Heather laughed. 'I bet it likes East-henders!'

The policeman gave the bucket of milk to Allie when he saw Miriam and Paul. He smiled gravely. There were dark shadows under his eyes. His suit was crumpled. Paul wondered if he'd had any sleep since last night.

'Is that you, Paul? You look reassuringly human.' He sounded friendly. 'I hear congratulations are in order – Allie's been filling me in.' Paul felt completely frozen, unable to do anything.

The policeman held his hand out to Miriam.

'I'm Detective Inspector John Davies. You're Miriam?' She nodded and shook his hand. 'I'm glad that you're feeling better.'

'John, do you have to talk to them today?' Harold said.

'I just want to get it over with,' Paul said.

'You should go first, Miriam.' Harold said. She nodded.

The policeman shrugged. 'That's fine by me.'

'You can use my caravan if you need somewhere private,' Allie suggested. 'We're off to the hospital. I've got some clothes for Lil's baby.'

'You'll have to get there quickly,' Harold said. 'Or they'll all be fast asleep.'

Miriam followed the Detective Inspector to Allie's caravan.

She glanced back at Paul and smiled. Allie asked John Davies more questions about chickens, as if there wasn't anything more important at stake. Miriam followed the policeman into the caravan.

Heather strapped Tom into his child-seat. Allie waved as she drove through the gate.

'I'm ready to face up to what I did,' Paul said. 'I should have gone first.'

'We need to get this awning up. We need the extra space, without the barn,' Harold said.

He gave Paul one of the awning poles to hold and pulled the canvas taut. Harold picked up a sledgehammer and knocked two giant spikes into the hard ground for the guy ropes, swinging the sledgehammer with ease. Paul held the pole in place on the other side. The first drops of rain began to fall. Paul wished he had a watch, so that he could have some idea of how long Miriam had been talking to the policeman.

Arthur came out of the rain and inspected the awning, attempting to sharpen his claws on one of the wooden poles. A rain droplet fell on his back. Harold laughed as Arthur shook himself frantically and ran into the removal van.

'He's pathetic in bad weather – but he always knows when it's coming.'

Paul started to attach the canvas sides. Harold knocked metal pegs into the ground. When they'd finished, the awning looked empty and enormous with only the round table inside it. They stood in the doorway, watching the rain. Paul wished he had some tobacco. Maybe Trev had some in his bender. He tried to dodge outside. Harold blocked him.

'I can't stand waiting,' Paul said.

'You're going to be alright.'

'I don't know that.'

'We need to start dinner,' Harold said. Paul followed him back into the removal van. He sat on the sofa, next to Arthur. His left foot was really throbbing. Paul focussed on the pain, to block everything else out.

Harold put a chopping board, a knife and several newly washed carrots in front of him. Paul had pulled them up yesterday morning; a lifetime ago.

'Get on with chopping these,' he said. 'I was just going to chuck in a couple of tins of tomatoes…'

'I'm not going to be here to eat it, though, am I?'

'I'm starting to lose my patience, Paul. You're going nowhere. I told you.'

Paul started chopping the carrots. The rain drummed on the van's roof and pooled in the skylight. Harold put on a Kinks album and whistled along loudly. He lit some kindling in the wood burning stove.

'I'll stick a few potatoes in the fire for later.'

Harold gave Paul a couple of onions to cut up. His eyes watered but it felt like a release.

Miriam walked inside. Her hair was wet. Strands of it stuck to her cheeks.

'He wants to talk to you now, Paul.'

'You were a long time. What were you telling him?'

'It's okay. He listened to me.'

Paul kissed her on the lips. He looked at her for as long as he could, making sure that her hazel eyes would stay in his mind.

'Goodbye,' he said. He walked out into the rain.

John Davies grimaced as he took a sip from his mug. His

coffee must have been cold for a long time. He continued to read out the last page of Paul's statement. Paul tried to concentrate. It was strange to hear the events of seven years ago and the details of last night read out in Inspector Davies' flat voice. He looked out of the caravan window. It was almost dark and it was still raining hard.

'Is everything I've recorded absolutely accurate and truthful?'

'Yes.' Paul hoped that the Dictaphone recording wouldn't be drowned out by the sound of the rain.

Davies gave him a copy of the statement. Paul read each page and signed and dated it at the bottom. The plaster on his index finger made it hard for him to grip the pen and his hand was shaking. He slid the statement back across the table.

'You're taking me to the police station now, right?' Paul asked.

'We charge Mark McKay with arson, manslaughter, several counts of attempted murder and - well – it's a long list.' He sounded very tired. 'So what do you think I'm going to charge you with, Paul?'

'I don't know.'

'Nothing.'

'Why?' Paul felt himself getting angry. 'I told you everything.'

'I've been interviewing Mark McKay all day. And I've got a theory about him. The Engelby bombing wasn't his first, was it?'

Paul shook his head. 'But it was smaller stuff before that – petrol bombs through butchers' windows.'

'But when he realised he'd killed someone, he had to justify it somehow.'

'He said the girl was a legitimate target…'

John Davies nodded.

'We've been trying to fit the incidents into chronological order. That tells you what sort of person Mark is. In 1996, he sent a letter bomb to the head office of a construction company building laboratories for a university. There was a girl working on reception – she was only a temp. Scarred her for life.'

'Shit.'

'And he still believes he was right to do it.' John Davies stood up and poured the rest of the coffee down the sink. 'Whereas you've been punishing yourself ever since. You're Mark's victim too. But you've helped bring him to justice.'

'So what happens now?' Paul asked.

'He goes on remand – safely locked away. There will be a trial at some point next year. The investigation's going to be a big job – different police forces, maybe even international. It looks like Mark may have spent long periods out of this country.'

'What about me?'

'You'll be asked to give evidence against Mark. Derbyshire Constabulary are going to have to reopen the Engelby case. You might be charged.'

Paul nodded. John Davies gave him a tired smile.

'But it's unlikely. There doesn't seem to be a lot of evidence against you.'

'Apart from Mark.'

'Mark's actually downplayed your role in the Engelby bombing. He said that all they did was borrow your car and drag you along as a look-out.'

Paul saw the headlights of Allie's car sweep into the yard.

'I think we've done for tonight,' John Davies said. 'I need some sleep.'

'Really? I can go – I mean stay?'

'I don't want you to be sentenced. What good would that do? Mark can't hurt you now. That's going to take a lot of getting used to. I know things look bad after the fire but you could have a great life.'

'I've got Miriam.'

'She was determined to fight your corner. But Harold's done a pretty good job of that already. And once Harold's on your side, he's with you for life.'

Paul smiled.

'And now you've got your son to worry about too.'

'Yeah.'

John Davies stood up stiffly, gathering his paperwork. His back made an audible cracking sound.

'Come on. You need food and company. I need a hot bath and a long lie down in a dark room.'

Paul followed him out of the caravan. He'd been sitting on Allie's sofa for so long that it hurt to straighten his legs. Rain blew onto him horizontally. Paul hugged himself to keep warm but it was good to breathe fresh air. John Davies unlocked his car with his electronic key fob.

'Tell Allie I'll bring the chickens round next week. My wife's collecting more ex-battery hens on Tuesday. We'll need to make room for them. You'd love the eggs.'

'I'm vegan. I don't do eggs.'

John Davies smiled.

'I know. Thanks for everything, Paul.' He got into his car and drove out of the yard. Paul stumbled into a pool of water but his feet weren't getting wet. He remembered he'd wrapped his feet in cling-film.

Miriam ran out of Harold's awning, splashing through the puddles. He ran towards her, his sodden pumps squelching. His feet didn't seem to hurt him now. He hugged her tightly.

'He's not going to arrest me.'

'I told you, didn't I? You're soaked already. Harold found some of his special reserve cider. He says he wants to wet the baby's head!'

'That sounds like a great idea,' Paul said. 'Not that Harold needs an excuse to get pissed.' He felt light, as if he'd taken off a heavy rucksack.

CHAPTER TWENTY SEVEN
THE BISCUIT TIN

A silver convertible car came through the orchard gates, driven by a man wearing mirrored sunglasses.

Paul turned off the garden shredder that Harold had borrowed as an extra apple crusher. Trev switched off the drill that powered the pulpmaster. The noise rang in Paul's ears as it died away.

Allie gasped. She scooped Tom up from the gravel where he'd been playing with his wooden toy car. His eyes were wide with amazement.

'Nice car. Mercedes SL 500. But what's it doing here?'

The car crunched to a halt near Harold's awning. The driver got out of the car. He wore an expensive-looking suit. He pushed his sunglasses to the top of his head.

'You must be lost, mate,' Trev said.

The man flashed a slick smile.

'I'm looking for the manager. Miriam Smith?'

Miriam ran out from under the awning, wiping the apple juice off her hands with a tea towel.

'Apparently you're the manager,' Paul laughed. But Miriam just glared at him. She smiled at the guy in the suit. There was a slight flicker of surprise on the man's face. He obviously hadn't been expecting a teenage girl wearing an enormous green jumper and leopard-print leggings.

The man was young, Paul realised. Not too much older than himself.

'You must be Nick Harvey.'

The man held his hand out and Miriam shook it confidently. Paul felt a twinge of jealousy. What was going on?

'Sorry. I'm still a bit sticky.' She smiled apologetically. 'We're making cider.'

'It's great that you can keep things going, despite the fire.' Nick Harvey looked at the barn with a seasoned eye. Paul suddenly remembered Miriam saying something about an insurance company person coming today but he'd been busy with the cider-making.

'We've got to. Otherwise the apples would rot,' Paul said.

'Things always seem hopeless at this stage. But we'll help you to get back into business soon.'

'Did you bring your laptop?' Miriam asked. 'I've got a full back-up of the accounts. Everything from my computer's on disc in Harold's van. And I've got loads of photos of the barn that I took for the website. Do you want to look there first?'

'So many people don't make a back-up. They just hope that nothing goes wrong. When everything goes up in flames, they're stuffed. Yes, show me the barn first. You seem very organised, Miriam.'

Harold carried a barrel of quartered apples out of the awning.

'I just scribbled on a few bits of paper that she waved at me,' he said. 'Signed a few cheques. I wasn't really listening, to be honest.'

'But I explained everything!' Miriam turned to the insurance guy with an exasperated shrug. 'Harold and the others are brilliant at making things, but...'

'We were all glad to be alive and excited about the baby and everything,' Harold said. He mopped his brow. 'But I was heartbroken really. I thought that we'd lost the business. Then Miriam explained that everything was insured. I hadn't bothered about it since my wife left.'

'Before I came along, his accounts consisted of an old box file stuffed with receipts,' Miriam said. 'He was so disorganised.

I didn't know to where to start at first.'

Nick Harvey laughed. Miriam gave the insurance assessor a conspiratorial look. They walked to the barn together. Miriam talked to him animatedly.

Paul heard Jake crying. He ducked into the awning before Trev had a chance to move away from the pulpmaster. Lil held Jake in her arms. He was red-faced; his cheeks puffed out.

'I'll change him.'

'Fine by me,' Lil smiled. She revelled in the way Trev and Paul competed to help with Jake. Paul didn't mind. He needed an excuse to retreat into the removal van. And everything that Jake did seemed miraculous.

'All my earnings were in that biscuit tin, Jake.' Paul laid his son on his changing mat. 'Miriam's going to think I'm a total idiot.'

☆

Harold didn't seem to know what to do with his hands. He held them behind his back, and then thrust them into his pockets.

'I thought it was time for a proper meeting,' he said.

A curry made with Paul's orchard-grown vegetables simmered on top of the stove, permeating the room with a mouth-watering aroma. The room was lit by candles and the red flicker from the stove. Miriam leaned her head on Paul's shoulder. The cat was curled on his lap like a black comma, purring loudly as Paul stroked him.

'I brought my new sparkly notebook,' Heather said. 'Miriam taught me how to take minutes.'

'It's going to be very important, Heather,' Harold smiled. 'Make sure you don't miss anything.' Heather sat cross-legged at the coffee table. She laid out an array of felt-tips in neat rows, positioning a candle-stick to illuminate her writing.

'I want to thank Miriam properly. I didn't take much notice of the hard work she was doing behind the scenes but we'd be done for without her.' Harold gave Miriam a long, solemn look. 'We can rebuild the barn and replace the tools.'

Miriam felt her cheeks grow hot.

'I wasn't doing anything special,' she said. 'Just what I learned at the Mercia.'

'When that insurance bloke came today, it got me thinking,' Harold said. 'I've worked here for years but it was a crappy old barn, really. Just a corrugated iron roof and bare walls.'

Miriam noticed that Heather had written "crappy old barn" in large red letters. She'd drawn a picture of the ruined barn in her notebook.

'I loved it though,' Trev said. 'As soon as I walked in, I felt right.'

'When we first found the orchard, it was totally overgrown,' Harold said. 'That's why we got it so cheap. We worked hard to get things going, but the kids were young and it wasn't working out between us…'

Harold lifted the lid of the saucepan and stirred the curry. 'Don't want it sticking to the bottom.' He tasted it with the wooden spoon, opened the kitchen cupboard and added more salt and a sprinkling of chilli powder. 'It needed a bit more of a kick. That squash is cooking beautifully, Paul.'

'Are you going to get to the point?' Lil asked. 'Jake's going to need a feed soon and…'

'Okay, Lil. I've been thinking. We could get a building firm to restore the barn, or we could do it ourselves using traditional techniques. I used to do quite a bit of building in my younger days. It'll be hard work and take a long time but, when it's finished, we can…'

'Let's do it.' Trev stood up, as if he was about to start work on the barn immediately.

'Sounds good to me,' Paul agreed.

'I'm pretty handy with a hammer,' Allie said.

'I'll help,' Lil smiled. 'Just so you can say that I'm not afraid of breaking my fingernails.'

'Can we have a thatched roof?' Heather asked. 'It would be so pretty.'

'No. It's a fire risk.' Miriam said. Then she felt stupid. Mark had been the fire risk. She'd spent too long talking to Nick Harvey this afternoon.

Harold stared at her and roared with laughter until the removal van shook. 'You're right, though. It'll have to be tiles. But the roof's south facing. I want solar panels too. And a new wind turbine.'

'Won't that cost a fortune?' Miriam asked.

Harold nodded. 'I'm going to put everything into this. But that's the other thing. I've been meaning to ask you for a while. I'm going to split the ownership of the land between us all – make the orchard into a proper cooperative. If you want to, that is.'

'You're kidding!' Trev's mouth hung open. His eyes were so wide, it looked like they were going to pop out.

'But what about your kids, Harold? Don't do this to spite them.' Paul said.

'Their step-dad's rolling in cash. They don't want the barn.'

'Are you sure about this – about inviting us all in?' Allie asked.

'Positive.' Harold said. 'Now who's with me?'

Everyone raised their hands. Miriam thought about how much money was left in her bank account.

'I'll put in the rest of my savings,' Miriam said. 'Once me and Paul have bought a new van...' She felt Paul tense up behind her. Her suspicions were confirmed. She sighed. 'I might not have that much left over but it would go towards a few solar panels.'

'Really?' Harold asked.

Miriam nodded.

'I'd like to look after the budget, especially if we're using our own time and money. I've not managed a project like this before, but...'

'I think you'll be wonderful. You know how useless I am at managing money.' Harold said. 'Right, this curry's not going to eat itself.' He ladled out bowlfuls.

Miriam dug Paul in the ribs as she sat up. She could think of someone else who was useless with money.

☆

Paul stared at the skeletal frame of his van.

'It gives me the creeps,' Miriam said.

'Yeah.' The mattress springs stuck up through the charred material. They had already gone rusty in the past week's rain. 'If you hadn't woken up, we would have died, lying there.'

'I can't wait to get rid of it.'

The recovery truck was in position. They were just waiting for Baz, the heavily tattooed driver, to finish drinking coffee with Allie. She was showing him the restoration work on her Range Rover.

'I think she fancies Baz,' Miriam said. 'Pity he's wearing a wedding ring.' She poked a blackened object just inside the van. It was a saucepan, with a melted plastic handle. 'If only I'd been able to save Ruth's tapes and her Walkman. They were the only things left that belonged to her.'

'It's a shame about my uncle's tapes too,' Paul said. 'We never even got round to Bagpipe Bonanza.'

Miriam frowned, making a tiny wrinkle between her eyebrows.

'I know about your biscuit tin,' she said.

'What?'

'Don't pretend. Harold was still paying you in cash. You didn't set up a bank account.'

'I was going to tell you.'

'When?'

'I'm not bothered about money. We're alive – that's all that matters.'

'You should have told me, Paul.'

'I didn't want you to know that I was scared.'

'Of setting up a bank account? God, even Trev managed to do it. How much money was there, anyway?'

'I don't know,' he shrugged, trying to add it up. There were the Glastonbury sales, that kitchen job, some bookshelves, an armchair... 'About two grand, maybe more.'

'You could have saved that money for your son. And now we need a van and extra money for the barn. You know, you never even paid me back for that diesel?'

'I suppose you'd rather be with that prick with the Mercedes.' Paul stared at his boots. She was right. He'd taken her money for granted, even before he knew about her savings. He'd been a total idiot to convince himself that the money didn't matter.

Miriam sighed heavily, like the air brakes on a lorry.

'What do you want me to do?' he asked.

'I want you to get the biscuit tin.'

'But the money's been burned.'

'You don't know that.' Miriam folded her arms and glared at him.

'What's this?' Baz said as he sauntered across the yard, the coffee mug in his hand. 'Hidden treasure?' Tattooed orange flames flickered from under the neck of his t-shirt. Allie stared at Paul, unable to resist any opportunities for gossip.

Paul climbed into the van. The floor creaked ominously.

'No, mate. Too dangerous!' Baz shouted. Paul ignored him. Every movement stirred up clouds of fine ash that irritated his throat. Paul took tentative steps towards the burned mattress. He shoved it onto its side. The stink of the fire overwhelmed him as the air turned black. He tried to cover his face with his hands. He coughed, making the van rock unsteadily. His eyes streamed. When the ash settled, the frame of the van groaned, as if it wouldn't be able to bear his weight for much longer.

The wooden bed frame beneath was charred but not completely burned. He tried to tug open the drawer but the front came away in his hands. He crouched down and reached inside, feeling his way past charred scraps of material. Paul reached into the back of the drawer and felt the solid shape of the biscuit tin. He pulled it out. It was still wrapped in the blanket – the material looked like melted candy-floss. He tore it apart. The tin was intact, although its red paint was blackened and blistered. He fought the urge to cough again.

'Paul? Are you okay?' Miriam called. 'I'm sorry, I shouldn't have made you...'

He grasped the tin with both hands and staggered towards the doorway, his eyes watering so much he could hardly see. The van floor suddenly buckled and he was thrown forwards. The biscuit tin flew out of his hands as he fell onto the gravel.

He sat up, his knees and elbows stinging where he'd grazed them.

'Give me the tin,' he croaked. Miriam handed it to him. His hands were black with soot. Paul prised the lid open. The tin was still full of bank notes. They looked scorched and had turned brown where they touched the sides of the tin. He picked up a twenty pound note, making a thick black smudge on it. He gave it to Miriam.

'Here's the money for that diesel, anyway.'

Miriam kissed him. When she pulled her lips away, her face was smeared with soot. Paul started laughing. He coughed instead.

'Miriam – can we buy a new van together, like you wanted to?'

'Do you know anyone with a van for sale, Allie?' Miriam laughed.

'You're both complete nutcases,' Allie said. 'Any ideas, Baz?'

The recovery driver grinned, showing a row of gold fillings.

'I'm already on it.' Baz pulled a mobile phone out of his overall pocket.

CHAPTER TWENTY EIGHT
PIGEON BOY

Miriam stared out of the window of Allie's Range Rover. The river disappeared behind a line of trees. Their leaves were already turning red and gold.

'I've got a good feeling about this one,' Allie said. 'The guy who's selling it converts the vans himself. It's a minibus. It won't be dark like that LDV we saw.'

'I think it had mushrooms growing in the corners,' Miriam agreed. The ex-Post Office van had seemed like an amazing bargain until Allie reeled off a long list of things that were wrong with it.

'You should go for the best that you can afford. This one's a Merc.'

'You'll be a prick with a Mercedes, Paul.' Miriam expected him to laugh but he had been silent since they'd hit the outskirts of Bristol.

Allie pulled into an overgrown gateway between two advertising hoardings, in front of a metal gate. "No Parking" was painted on it in white letters, under a layer of graffiti.

'Sure this is the right place?' Miriam asked.

'Unlock the gate, Paul. I wrote the combination lock number on the directions.'

Paul got out of the car. He stood on the pavement and stared across the road before he fiddled with the lock. Once the gate was open, Allie drove onto a weed-cracked tarmac track between gloomy sycamore trees.

Paul opened the car door. He seemed subdued, although he had been excited about searching for a new van.

'Trev's bender was up there in those woods,' he said.

Allie drove slowly down the track. She pulled into a narrow

yard overlooking the river. The far wall backed onto a tall old factory. Miriam saw the white minibus they had come to see. It was dwarfed by an imposing army truck. A brick shed leaned against the wall nearest to the road, surrounded by tubs of flowers and vegetables. A dog barked furiously. Tom woke up. He clung onto his toy monkey, his eyes wide with fear.

'It's okay, Tom,' Miriam said. 'It isn't a police dog.' She unclipped his child seat.

Paul opened the passenger door. He was pinned to the side of the car by a bounding white and black collie. Tom hid his face in Miriam's jumper as she carried him out of the car. The collie continued to bark. Paul laughed nervously but relaxed as the dog rolled onto her back, her feathery tail brushing the tarmac.

A woman with tanned olive skin and long, loose hair grabbed the dog's collar.

'Heidi's supposed to be a guard dog.' She smiled at Paul. 'But she's just crackers.'

A smaller dog ran around in circles behind the collie, wildly excited but unsure what to do.

'And this is Mabel,' the woman said, kindly, noticing that Tom was afraid. 'She's Heidi's puppy. She's very gentle.' She picked up the puppy and Tom tentatively reached out to touch her long silky ears.

'Puss-cat,' he whispered. The puppy licked his fingers, making Tom giggle.

'Is he your baby?' she asked Miriam. 'No - you're too young, aren't you? I'm Jill, anyway. You must be Miriam.'

'Tom's mine,' Allie laughed. 'Miriam's great with kids, though. And Paul's daft about animals; you should hear him talk to the cat.'

A tall man in a brown woolly hat slid out from under the

army truck. His face was covered in freckles. He wiped a smudge of black grease from his cheek with his sleeve.

'I'm Sandy - pleased to meet you.' He shook Paul's hand. He had a strong Australian accent.

'The nice ones are never bloody single,' Allie muttered to Miriam, with a sidelong look at Jill.

'I'll show you around the van,' Sandy said.

'Great truck,' Allie said. 'My ex had something similar.'

Sandy smiled and opened his mouth to speak.

'I don't want to sell the van,' Jill said. 'But he's fallen in love with that sodding truck. He's barely started work on it yet and he can't afford to. Look at it! A total wreck!'

Sandy shrugged.

'It's gonna be awesome.'

'We'll have to sleep in the shed until it's bearable,' Jill said. 'So I'm only selling the van to the right people.'

'Baz told me about the fire,' Sandy said. 'Sounds like you guys need a break.'

Allie studied the van's exterior, peering under the wheel arches. Miriam tried to look inside but there were blinds on the windows.

'No rust,' Allie muttered. 'Good sign.'

Sandy opened the rear doors.

'No wonder you don't want to sell it.' Miriam was surprised after the shabby vans they'd seen so far. It was spotlessly clean. The cupboards fitted perfectly and the dark blue carpet looked new. The blinds had a red gingham pattern, matching the material covering the long sofa.

Jill smiled approvingly as Miriam and Paul both removed their boots before stepping into the van.

'Can I check under the bonnet?' Allie asked.

'Go for it,' Sandy said. He tossed her the keys. He shooed

the dogs away as they tried to clamber into the van.

'I like it,' Paul whispered. 'And I can stand up – I couldn't stand up in any of the vans we saw last week.'

'The sofa folds down to make a double bed. There's heaps of storage space underneath,' Sandy said. Miriam could imagine waking up in here with Paul, with sunlight flooding through the windows.

Miriam adored the pine table, with its two fold-down chairs, next to a neat little wood burning stove. The little kitchen area had a sink and a two-ring gas burner. As she opened cupboards, she realised with a guilty twinge that they were still full of Jill and Sandy's possessions.

'It's got an electric fridge. Runs off its own battery,' Sandy explained.

Miriam opened a cupboard door.

'And a chemical loo,' she said. 'No more running across the yard in the middle of the night.'

'It doubles up as a mobile darkroom,' Jill said. 'It's got a black-out blind.'

'You're a photographer?' Miriam asked. 'Do you do fashion shoots?'

'My portfolios are in the studio. Well, the shed. I've been using it as my studio for years.'

'You can fix a surfboard up here.' Sandy pointed at a bracket attached to the ceiling.

'You could carve a surfboard, Paul,' Miriam giggled.

'Fancy a test drive?' Sandy asked.

'Yeah,' Paul said. 'I'm not very good at city traffic though.'

☆

Paul drove back into Jill and Sandy's yard. Sandy had been

patient with him as he'd learned how to handle the minibus. It was much easier to drive than the old butcher's van. He could change gear smoothly and the engine sounded good. Paul had been concentrating too hard to think about seeing these streets again. He realised how much he had changed.

He backed the van slowly into its parking space. Allie and Jill watched him, holding mugs of tea. Heidi and her puppy ran around excitedly, as if they'd never seen the van before. When he'd parked, Paul jumped out of the van. Miriam opened the passenger door.

'You drove it really well,' she said. 'Are we having it?'

He nodded.

Miriam hugged him. She bounced with anticipation. 'You've brought your chequebook, haven't you?'

Paul felt its shape in the side pocket of his new combat trousers. They had given him some strange looks at the building society with his tin of scorched banknotes but his mum had posted his old savings book and driving licence so he could prove who he was. All his old things were in his parents' loft: his identity had been waiting for him.

'We'll take it, Sandy – I mean, if you want to sell it to us,' Paul said.

'Of course I do, mate.' Sandy turned to Jill.

She smiled. 'The van's meant for you. I hope you enjoy it.'

'How much do you want for it?' Paul asked.

'We'll take it for three thousand five hundred,' Allie butted in.

Paul felt embarrassed but Allie was right to take over. She'd done some research with him, showing him the prices of vans in motor magazines and newspapers. The Mercedes van was six years old and its mileage was fairly high but it seemed to be in good condition. Sandy pressed his mouth into a straight line.

'You're having me on, Allie. It's worth at least a grand more than that. Think of all the hours of labour that went into it.'

Allie narrowed her eyes.

'Three seven fifty,' she said.

'Four grand. And that includes the toilet and the fridge and everything,' Sandy said.

'Done.' Allie said. 'As long as you're both happy with that?'

Paul nodded.

☆

Miriam was already on her new mobile phone sorting out the insurance so that Paul could drive the van straight back to the orchard. Allie had gone back to Sutton Mallet to pick Heather up from school.

Jill grabbed an armful of clothes, sighing dramatically.

'I'm sorry, I'll help,' Paul said.

'No need to apologise. Sandy had better get a move on with that truck, though.'

Paul picked up a stack of books. Miriam helped too, when she got off the phone. The van was soon empty. He realised there was something vaguely familiar about Jill.

'We need to give the van a good send-off,' Jill said. 'I've got some champagne in the shed from a wedding I did.'

'You do weddings photos too?' Miriam asked.

'Yeah, loads. I like to just wander around taking photos of things as they happen. It's great for someone as nosy as me.'

Paul sat on the steps of the truck. He stared at the new van. It hadn't sunk in yet. They actually owned it. The puppy, Mabel, bounded up the steps and stared at Paul with beseeching eyes. She lay at Paul's feet, her tail thumping. The collie dog was ignoring everyone, gnawing a branch.

'Fancy a coffee?' Sandy asked. 'Seeing as you're driving.'

'Yeah – no milk, please.'

'You should be worried, mate. Now they're on the wedding photos, you'll be stuck here for hours.'

Paul laughed. 'It's okay.'

The October sunshine was warm in the sheltered yard. Mabel relaxed and shut her eyes. Jill pulled out a couple of deckchairs. She popped the champagne and poured it into plastic wine glasses, then fetched a stack of large black folders. Sandy handed Paul a mug of coffee before disappearing underneath the truck again.

Jill and Miriam talked and slowly turned the pages. They grew increasingly giggly as they sipped the champagne. Paul drifted off, thinking about what Trev would say when he turned up at the orchard with the new van. Paul curled his fingers around the puppy's silky fur.

'Sorry – we should go. Paul's virtually asleep.'

'I should take a photo of you with the van. It's a big day.'

Jill looked at Paul and smiled. A puzzled, serious expression crept onto her face. She stood up and examined him in profile. She downed the rest of her champagne and dropped the glass on the ground.

'You're the pigeon boy.'

'What?'

Jill ran into the shed.

'What's she going on about?' Miriam asked him.

'I haven't got a clue. If we leave it much later, we'll get caught in the rush-hour.'

'I don't mind.'

Jill came back with another folder under her arm. She sat next to Paul on the step and opened it with shaking hands. On the first page was a large black and white photo of a bedraggled youth, wrapped in a grimy blanket, the mock-turrets of Bristol Temple Meads railway station in the background, under a grey sky. The boy's sunken eyes had an expression of locked away pain. He was reaching out with a skeletally thin arm to a dirty city pigeon. The pigeon ate a piece of bread from the boy's hand. The caption read "Pigeon Boy, February 1994".

A fragment of memory surfaced from his darkest days.

Miriam climbed the steps and looked at the photo. She gasped. She put her hand on his shoulder and he grasped it tightly.

'It is you, isn't it?' Jill said. 'I tried to talk to you. I felt guilty. I hadn't asked you for permission. When it was developed, I had to use it – but every time I tried to approach, you bolted.'

'I thought you might be the police.'

She turned the page. Paul was relieved that he didn't have to look at himself any longer. He found himself staring at a portrait of a younger Trev, looking straight into the camera against a background of high street shops. Trev held his tin whistle against his chest. His trademark grin didn't mask the bleak look in his eyes.

Paul laughed, despite himself. Mabel looked up at him, startled by the sudden loud noise. He stroked her ears. He scooped the puppy onto his lap.

'I asked him to keep an eye on you. Do you still know him?'

'He's making a…' Paul stopped himself in time, realising that he'd nearly ruined Miriam's birthday surprise. 'He lives in the orchard too – he's just become a dad.'

'It's Paul's baby too,' Miriam interrupted.

Jill looked confused.

'It's nearly as weird as it sounds,' Paul said. 'Trev's happier now, anyway.'

A drowsy autumn wasp flew above Mabel's head. She

snapped at it lazily.

'Mabel's really taken to you,' Jill said.

'She's lovely.'

Jill laughed.

'Just wait until she's out in the park. Any smells or noises and she wants to be off. My photos keep coming out blurred because she tugs at her lead. It's not really fair on her.'

'She doesn't look much like Heidi,' Miriam said.

'She's the result of a chance encounter with a spaniel in the park.' Jill stared at Paul. 'Would you like to keep her?'

'What do you mean?'

'We wanted to keep Mabel but it's not working out. I like the sound of your orchard and I think you'll do a good job.'

'Even though you knew me when I was - like that?'

'If you're the right people for the van, I should be able to trust you with my dog.' Paul wondered if she felt guilty for recognising him. She seemed so keen for him to have the puppy.

'How is she with cats?' Paul asked.

Miriam stroked Mabel's ears.

'Please, Paul – she can be my birthday present.' Miriam said.

Paul wondered how Miriam felt about the photo. Would she still want him now she had seen what he was like at his lowest possible point? But she looked at him steadily, smiling.

'Yes – let's keep her,' he agreed.

The traffic report on the local radio station gave a warning of a big tailback on the southbound M5. Miriam glanced at Paul. He seemed comfortable in the driver's seat but he was concentrating on driving. He hadn't said much since they left

Sandy and Jill's yard.

'It's a nice stereo. Shame we haven't got any CDs,' she said, for something to fill up the silence.

'Trev never mentioned Jill,' Paul said.

'There were so many things you didn't talk about, I'm surprised you managed any conversations.'

'I let Trev think that my dad was a total bastard. It was easier than telling him about the bomb. I was so angry that I couldn't see the truth.'

Mabel stood on Miriam's lap, looking out of the windscreen as they crawled along. She didn't seem worried about being taken away from her home.

'Mabel seems to like being in the van.'

'I've been thinking,' Paul said. 'We should drive back to Derby for a few days. Why don't we go on your birthday?'

'Really?' Miriam knew that she couldn't put it off forever.

'The demolition people will be working on the barn, so we've got some free time.'

'Yeah – maybe it's time,' she said. Now they had a van again, she could go back into her parents' world without leaving her new life.

CHAPTER TWENTY NINE
HOMECOMING

'We said we'd be there for lunch. And we'll need to keep stopping because of Mabel.' Miriam sighed. 'It looks like the others are still asleep. You'd have thought that they…'

'We've got time to give Mabel a walk around the woods.'

Mabel bounded out of her cardboard box basket and waited by the van door at the sound of her favourite word. Miriam pulled on her green jumper and wrapped a pink lacy scarf around her neck.

Paul zipped up Trev's old fleece. The cold grey mist seeped through the holes.

Mabel scampered towards the woods, stopping to chase a flurry of stray leaves around the yard. Arthur appeared in the doorway of Harold's awning and then shot back indoors again. He seemed to find Mabel's antics completely beneath his dignity.

Paul tried not to look into the skip in front of the barn. He recognised the melted plastic of Miriam's laptop and part of Harold's old chainsaw, thrown on top of a pile of charred wood. The barn was covered in scaffolding. The demolition workers were removing everything apart from the four stone walls.

They followed Mabel through the gap in the hedge behind the barn, brushing past dew-laden cobwebs. Mabel rushed ahead and barked. Paul hoped that she wouldn't give the game away too soon. He held Miriam's hand as they walked into the clearing.

'Happy birthday!' Harold shouted. The others joined in as they jumped out from behind the trees.

'What this?' Miriam smiled but she looked confused.

The large plastic tub was big enough to seat four people and it was surrounded by sanded planks. It looked good considering the hurry they'd been in. The tub was filled with balloons. There were so many balloons tied to the wooden shelter that it looked like it was going to take off.

'It's for you – for your birthday,' Paul said.

'It's a hot tub,' Trev said. 'Do you like it?' He carried Jake strapped to his chest with a long piece of stripy material. He looked like a Mexican bandit but Jake seemed warm and comfortable. Since Jake's birth, Trev appeared thoroughly contented. He had the family he'd always wanted. Trev was so devoted to Jake that Paul had come to think of himself as a sort of stand-by father. Trev held pole-position.

'We promise not to use it until you come back. Clothes are optional,' Harold said, with a wink.

'If everyone's going to be wallowing around in there, I'll bring my old swimming costume back with me,' Miriam laughed.

'Don't worry, we'll get to try it alone,' Paul whispered to Miriam. She giggled.

'Back in our day, we didn't think anything of stripping off. The youth of today…' Harold sighed.

'You heat the water up by lighting a fire under this radiator.' Allie showed Miriam a large central heating radiator suspended over a fire pit, connected to the hot tub by copper pipes. 'The hot water from the radiator goes into the tub though this pipe. When it cools down, it goes back into the radiator. It's simple, really.' Allie smiled proudly. She had spent a long time making sure the piping worked.

'It'll really work, then?' Miriam looked uncertain.

'Course it will,' Paul said. 'I know how much you missed hot baths.'

'Won't it be too cold to use in the winter?' Miriam asked.

'Just imagine,' Harold said, 'There's snow on the ground but you're relaxing in lovely hot water looking up at the stars – with a glass of cider in your hand. When we start working on the barn, it'll soothe our aching muscles.'

'The little hut's got its own fire-pit, so you can keep warm while you dry off,' Heather said.

'Why didn't I notice you were building this?'

'We kept you busy with the new van,' Paul said.

Heather gave Miriam a garland of red paper flowers.

'These are for luck.'

'And this.' Allie handed her a hand-made voucher for driving lessons.

'You don't think I'll crash the Range Rover?'

'You'd better not! We can start as soon as you've got your provisional licence.'

Lil held out a bulky package wrapped in brown paper decorated with gold stars. Miriam untied the ribbon. She gasped.

'It must have taken hours – days!'

'I'm bloody knackered, so you'd better appreciate it,' Lil said.

The coat was made of brocade material in dark red and orange. Miriam tried it on. It fitted her waist closely, flaring out towards her knees. Paul knew that Lil had started work on it long ago. She had been sewing it in her ambulance on the night of the fire.

'It's fantastic.' Miriam danced in the clearing, making her coat swirl. Mabel scurried after her.

As Miriam twirled, leaves the same colour as her coat fell from the trees. Paul wanted to remember this moment completely. A loud bang shocked him. Tom had fallen on the leaf-litter. He sat up, staring at a torn scrap of rubber in his hand, unable to work out where his shiny blue balloon had gone. His face slowly crumpled. Allie raced to pick him up and give him a new balloon.

Miriam kissed Paul on the cheek.

'Thanks,' she said.

☆

Miriam wanted to tell Paul to get off the motorway and turn around but she didn't say anything. He drove past the junction for Burnham-on-Sea. She felt increasingly tense with every mile they drove further north.

Mabel dozed next to her, her nose tucked into her tail. Miriam stared at her enviously. Her life was so simple: an exciting round of walks, play, food and sleep.

'I need something out of the glove box,' Paul said. She opened it. The glove box was full of CDs. She pulled out a handful.

'Paul!' she gasped. 'You got Screamadelica – and Nevermind – and Rage Against the Machine…'

'I went to that second-hand record shop in Bridgwater. I couldn't get the right Sonic Youth album though. But then I thought, sod it. I bought anything you might like, things that I used to like.' Paul smiled. He overtook a small purple hatchback. 'And some things that we might both have missed out on.'

Miriam rifled through the CDs. The Best of the Smiths – that was obviously one Paul had chosen for himself. Mission Control – they were one of Ruth's favourite bands. Some CDs were by bands that she'd only read about in the NME, or maybe just heard a few songs on the radio. Miriam mentally sorted the CDs. Most of the unfamiliar ones had come out after Ruth had died.

She found a copy of Definitely Maybe.

'Oasis?' she asked. 'I didn't think they were your sort of thing.'

'How do I know? We've both got a lot of catching up to do.'

Miriam slid the CD into the van's stereo, turning up the volume on the first track. Mabel opened her eyes and stared at Miriam reproachfully.

'I don't think Mabel's going to be a fan,' she laughed.

☆

Mum and Dad stood on the porch. Miriam wished that she and Paul could get back into the van and drive off but it was too late now.

'I don't know what to say to them,' she whispered. Paul stood behind her with a box of vegetables from the orchard.

Mabel tugged at her lead, keen to explore the flowerbeds.

Miriam stared at her parents. They stared back. They both looked worried.

Dad rushed forwards and hugged her.

'I don't know what I expected.' He looked just the same: thinning brown hair, eyes with deep crows' feet at the corners, steel-rimmed glasses perched on his nose. 'You look happy.' He was actually talking to her, looking her in the eyes, rather than mumbling and disappearing into his study.

'Dad – this is Paul.'

Mum came forward and put her arms around Miriam.

'You've no idea what we went through,' she said.

Dad put his hand on her arm.

'Not now, love. Just be glad that she's here.'

Miriam smiled.

'It's okay Mum, really. I'm sorry.'

Mabel jumped up at Mum's legs.

'She's adorable.' Mum stroked Mabel's head while trying to stop the puppy from laddering her tights. Her mum had changed her hair; it was shorter and blonder.

'So you're Paul, then?' Dad said. Paul was still hovering at the edge of the garden with his cardboard box. 'Miriam told me a lot about you in her emails.'

'We brought some things,' Paul mumbled. He stepped forwards, not looking at anyone.

'A pumpkin?' Dad took the box and peered inside. 'Is it going to turn into a fairy coach? And carrots, potatoes. What's this knobbly thing?'

'I grew everything myself.' Paul gave him a shy smile. 'That's a Jerusalem artichoke - and there's a bottle of cider – but leave it until Christmas at least. It needs to mature.'

'Lunch is ready. I wasn't sure when you were going to get here. But you're quite early, really.' Mum seemed keen to usher everyone indoors, as if she was embarrassed that they were talking in the garden where the neighbours could overhear. She glanced anxiously at the van. It looked out of place on the suburban street.

Miriam felt trapped when the front door was closed. It was the first time she'd been in a house for over five months. Beeswax furniture polish hung in the air, making her want to sneeze. Miriam realised that she smelled of wood smoke. She sniffed her sleeve for comfort.

Mabel's claws scratched the parquet floor. She whimpered and pressed her head against Miriam's legs.

'Have you got that ball?'

Paul pulled a half-bald grey tennis ball out of his fleece

pocket. Mabel had found it earlier in a service station car park. He tossed it gently to Mabel and she instantly forgot her strange surroundings, lying on the floor and pulling the fluff off the ball with her teeth.

'Sorry about the mess,' Paul said.

'Oh, she'll be alright,' her mum smiled indulgently. 'She seems such a nice little thing.'

The décor hadn't changed since Ruth died. Miriam was overwhelmed by the stream train memorabilia in the living room: paintings and photos were on every wall – models on every surface. Had it got worse since she'd been away? Paul hung back in the hall, taking his boots off.

Mum gave Miriam a white envelope. There was a card inside, with a picture of a cartoon elephant. Miriam opened it.

'Book tokens. Thank you.'

'Happy birthday, love,' Dad said. 'We didn't know what you liked any more - so we thought we'd better play safe.'

'Brilliant - really.' Miriam pecked them both on the cheek.

Miriam took her coat off and laid it carefully on the back of an armchair.

'That's lovely,' Mum said. 'So unusual.'

The dining table was laid with the best cutlery and Denby pottery, as if they were guests; not that they'd had many guests since Ruth died. The plates had brown bread rolls; there was houmous and a large bowl of pasta salad. When they sat down, Paul picked up the margarine tub. He smiled.

'Vegan. You did this for me?' Paul asked.

'Normally we sit down to a raw steak at every meal.'

'Dad!' Miriam was pleased that his sense of humour had returned after all these years. It was embarrassing but somehow comforting.

'We seem to have got a bit more health-conscious lately,' he said. 'How long have you been growing vegetables, Paul?'

'Only since May.'

'You've certainly got the touch.' Dad stared out of the patio window at the expanse of lawn and brown bushes in the back garden. 'I've been meaning to do something with the garden. Remember that miniature railway I was going to build?'

'No trains in the garden, Dad. Promise me?'

Mum carried bowls of soup in on a tray, carefully avoiding Mabel, who was determined to get under her feet.

'I've been doing a "healthy living" evening class. I asked the tutor and she gave me some vegan recipes. This is carrot and coriander soup,' she told Paul.

'Thanks,' he said.

The soup was delicious. Miriam buttered her roll and bit into it. It was very fresh. After Ruth had died, the food at home became dull, ready-made. No one could be bothered any more.

'You're not going to that bereavement group anymore?' Miriam asked.

'It wasn't doing me much good. Your father told me I needed to look after myself.'

'You look good, Mum.'

'We do healthy eating; we had dinner at that vegetarian place in town.'

'The Flying Horse Café? That's where I met Paul.'

'The food was good. Mind you, the lady who runs it could do with losing a few pounds.'

Paul caught Miriam's eye. She giggled.

'I'm going there later,' he said.

'Well, don't tell her I said anything. We do yoga and relaxation too.'

'My mum does yoga,' Paul said. 'I think she just uses a video.'

'Your parents live in Belper, don't they?'

Paul nodded and swallowed a mouthful of soup.

'What do they do?'

Paul stared at Miriam. There was a flash of panic in his eyes.

'My mum's a teaching assistant. My dad works at the Swarfega factory,' he said quickly, staring at his plate.

'Ah, Swarfega. We get through tons of the stuff at the railway museum. Nothing gets your hands clean like it. Lovely stuff,' Dad said.

'Any brothers or sisters?' Mum asked, in a tone of forced lightness.

The question hung in the air. Was Mum thinking about Ruth? Or was she just using the same small-talk questions she had asked Ruth's boyfriends, without realising?

'Paul's got a brother,' Miriam said. 'He's going to see his family tomorrow.'

Paul finished his soup in silence. He pushed his chair away and stood up. He seemed pale.

'I'd better take Mabel into the garden. She's well trained but I don't want any accidents.'

☆

Paul's hands shook as he rolled his cigarette. Mabel squatted down gratefully at the edge of a flowerbed. Paul hadn't been able to breathe properly in that room. He felt bad – Miriam's mum had only been making an effort. At least Mabel had given him a genuine reason for bolting outside.

'Sorry about the Spanish Inquisition in there.' Paul looked up startled. Miriam's dad stood on the patio in his slippers.

'It's okay.'

'She's out of practise. But she's trying.'

Paul lit his cigarette. He hoped it was alright to smoke in front of Miriam's dad but he didn't seem to object.

'I promise I'll take good care of Miriam.'

'When she ran away, we thought we'd lost both of our daughters. We know we've made dreadful mistakes.'

Mabel dropped the drool-covered tennis ball at Paul's feet. He picked it up and threw it to the far end of the garden. She dashed after it, her long ears flapping.

'Any ideas what I might do to the garden, Paul?'

'How about a tree at the end? And it's not too late to plant daffodil bulbs. I could help, if you want.'

'I don't know much about trees, just trains.' Miriam's dad shrugged.

'You could watch birds from your patio window. Maybe a cherry tree.' Paul couldn't help smiling. 'You could plant a miniature orchard.'

☆

'Why did you have to give him such a grilling?' Miriam asked.

'I know you're grown up now but I need him to be good enough for you. He seems a bit...'

'He's just shy,' Miriam said.

'Have I scared him off?'

Paul and her dad had their backs to the house. They were talking. Paul pointed at the gloomy laurel bush. He threw Mabel's ball and she raced down the garden to fetch it.

'It looks like he's redesigning the garden.'

'Good. One day in the summer, I came back from work and I realised the house was so dark and depressing.'

'Get it repainted. Make Dad keep all his train stuff in the shed.'

Mum smiled.

'I haven't got time. Did I tell you Dave Brown resigned, after you left?'

'I'm glad. He was such a creep.'

'I can see that now. I'm sorry. So I applied for his job.'

'You got it?'

Mum nodded. Miriam hugged her. She looked surprised.

'Treat yourself. Pay someone to do the decorating,' Miriam said. 'Or me and Paul could come up again and do it. We'll need to practice for decorating the barn.'

'You're really dedicated to this bloke's orchard, aren't you?'

'I told you over the phone, we're going to run it as a cooperative. It's going to be our orchard too.'

'You've got a good brain for business, Miriam. But these things can be a minefield. I can help you if you want.'

☆

Paul parked the van at the side of the track. The bulk of the woods loomed ahead. He'd drunk several cups of coffee in Bella and Alan's flat after dinner to put this off. He'd told them that he was going to his parents' house. Miriam thought he was staying with Bella. His lies might unravel later. But he had to do this. It was like trying to resist the temptation to pick a scab.

He picked up the torch and locked the van. The track between the field and the woods was rutted with tractor tracks. The clay mud clung to his boots. His feet felt heavy, like this was a nightmare where his legs could only move in slow motion. After about five minutes of walking, the track turned a corner. Paul flashed the torch into the woods, finding the faded "Trespassers Will Be Prosecuted" sign. He climbed carefully over the barbed wire fence.

The only sounds were the groaning of branches as they swayed in the wind and the dry leaves rustling against each other. Paul barely dared to breathe as he followed the path, keeping the beam of the torch to the ground.

He reached the edge of the woods and pressed himself against the trunk of an oak tree. The mansion hovered spectrally above the dark parkland, starkly floodlit. A large glass extension had been built onto the side of the building. The gravel drive was now a well-lit car park. Paul stared at it. He retraced his steps through the woods, back to his van.

He drove up to the front entrance of the hall and stopped. Seven years ago, the gates had been locked, operated by an electronic entry phone. Now they stood wide open.

The sign on the gatepost read "Engelby Hall Hotel and Country Club". Paul drove through the gates: there was nothing to stop him. The hall loomed into view. Paul parked the van in the darkness of the drive. His palms were sweaty on the steering wheel.

Paul walked between rows of up-market cars. He tried to find the place where the hunt master's car had stood on the gravel. It had been in front of the house, in the middle. There were too many cars here now to pin-point the exact spot. Laughter and music came from the ground floor of the hall. He didn't even know what the little girl had looked like; he'd just seen her for a split second through the binoculars.

'I'm sorry,' he said, softly. 'I wish I could change what happened.'

He got back into the van and drove until he reached Belper. He pulled into the river gardens car park and reversed into a parking space that bordered the river bank. Paul connected the gas and made himself a cup of tea. He unfolded the bed. He sat on the back step of the van, his mind soothed by the Derwent flowing swiftly in the darkness.

☆

Miriam stood in Ruth's empty room. Mabel pushed the door open with her nose and sat at her feet. There was nothing left of Ruth here now, apart from Miriam's memories.

The floorboards creaked. Mum stood in the doorway.

'Why did you get rid of all her stuff?' Miriam asked.

'At first I thought she'd walk through the door and it would be alright again. After the funeral, I realised that she was really gone. Keeping her things here was too painful but giving them away was a big mistake. I knew you'd kept some little things of hers but…'

'I want to see her ashes.'

Miriam walked into her parents' bedroom and opened the wardrobe door. Mum moved shoeboxes and dusty suitcases aside. She pulled out a black carrier bag. There was a grey plastic pot inside, flecked with black to look like marble. Ruth would have laughed at anything so tacky.

'She's in here.'

Miriam opened the lid carefully. The pot was half full of a whitish powder. She couldn't feel any connection with Ruth in here, even though she knew that the ashes were once her. Miriam replaced the lid.

'If Ruth is in here, we have to set her free.'

'What do you mean?'

'I want to scatter her ashes in the park. Today.'

Mum tried to take back the urn. Miriam wrapped her arms around it.

'I'm going to do it anyway, so if you and Dad want to come with me, that's up to you. You can't stop me.'

Mum nodded.

'If you're sure.'

☆

Paul put his box of vegetables onto the kitchen work surface. His mum had flour on her cheeks and hands. Her eyes shone. The kitchen tape player blasted out a Motown compilation.

'Miriam's coming at one, then? She's bringing the puppy? I can't wait to meet her.'

Paul nodded.

'We'll stay here tonight, in the van.'

'Penny – that's Simon's wife, remember? She's bringing the kids and picking up May on the way.' Paul began to panic. Meeting Miriam's parents had been terrifying enough. Now he had to cope with his own relatives and people he'd never met before.

Mum drained a large pan of potatoes in a colander and shook them vigorously. She darted around the kitchen at a furious speed.

'Are you sure I can't help?'

'Everything's under control. Your dad set the table.' She started rolling out pastry.

Paul opened the living room door. It looked like the table setting for Christmas dinners when his grandparents were still alive: the kitchen table and the dining table were pushed together, covered with a huge white tablecloth to disguise the different heights, a mixture of his granddad's old wooden chairs and kitchen stools. He remembered crawling under the tablecloth with Simon on Christmas Day, pretending that the table was a big cave full of spiders.

He returned to the kitchen. Mum put a loaf tin in the oven.

'I made you a cashew nut and cranberry roast. Penny gave me the recipe. She's vegetarian. Did I tell you?'

Paul shook his head.

'Dinner won't be ready for at least an hour. Simon bought the chicken. It's free-range.'

'We've got free range chickens, Mum. Allie's started selling the eggs.'

Mum shut the oven door. She stared at Paul.

'You've definitely filled out – a bit,' she said. 'Last time, it looked like you hadn't been eating.'

'I could chop some of the vegetables I brought from the orchard if you like.'

'I think we've got enough. I wish I'd known you were going to bring so much. Your dad and Simon are in the Mason's Arms.'

'That's a bit old fashioned - you staying at home and making Sunday dinner, while the men go off to the pub?'

She laughed.

'Most Sundays we go round to Simon's. He does the cooking. But today's different. This is for you. Go on – they're waiting.'

Paul opened the door of the Mason's Arms. The smell of cigarettes and stale beer enveloped him. He remembered it as an old man's pub, with its own darts team, where his dad and Uncle Ted had taken refuge for a quiet drink. It hadn't been a good pub to get served under-age. The landlord knew all the locals and how old their children were. The bar was still decorated with highly polished horse-brasses. The landlord looked up as Paul walked to the bar; the same man, just a bit balder.

'Aren't you Carl Walker's lad -?'

Paul nodded. He put his finger to his lips but they had already seen him: a broad man in his fifties, his dark hair streaked with grey. The other man was much younger, wearing an Oasis t-shirt and tracksuit bottoms.

'Paul – you're here.' Dad stood up. 'I can't believe it.'

'Alright, bruv,' Simon said. He spoke casually, as if he'd only seen Paul last week, but stared at Paul in amazement.

Paul grinned back at them.

'Three pints of bitter, please,' he told the landlord.

☆

Miriam kept Mabel on the lead. The park was full of distractions – the wind in her fur, golf balls, birds and rabbit holes. She tugged and strained to get away and explore.

Mum followed, carrying the black bag with Ruth's urn.

Dad held onto her arm. Miriam led the way to a place she remembered, facing towards the river and the Derbyshire hills. The wind blew through the valley. Ruth would really be able to fly away. Small patches of blue sky were breaking through the clouds. The skirt of Miriam's coat billowed. Miriam looped Mabel's lead around her ankle so both her hands were free.

'Are you ready?' she asked.

'Ready as I'll ever be,' her dad said.

Mum opened the urn. They each took a handful of ashes. It felt like fine sand. Miriam stretched her arm, opened her hand and the ashes were lost on the wind. She watched her parents do the same. Mabel barked and tried to jump up. Miriam managed to keep her balance. They carried on, until there was nothing left at the bottom of the jar.

'You're right. Ruth is free now,' her mum said.

She put her arm around Miriam. The wind had made her cheeks glow. She was smiling. Her dad put his hand on her shoulder. They stood together, looking down into the valley.

'We're all free,' Miriam said. 'Ruth would be proud of us.'

Miriam realised she could see the road at the bottom of the valley. The cars looked ant-sized. Paul was only a few miles away. She would see him again in a couple of hours but it felt strange to be parted from him. For a moment, she saw Mark; the knife glinting his hand. At least now Paul could begin to forget the past and get on with his life. They all could.

Mabel barked and tugged at her lead. Miriam crashed onto the damp grass.

'I think she wants to take us for a walk,' she laughed.

Hello! A note from Anne Grange.

At school, I'd get into trouble for "not listening", but I was actually lost in my imagination, fed by weekly trips to the library.

My GCSE English coursework folder was filled to bursting with enthusiastically written essays and stories.

My writing has always been inspired by my love of music. As a sixth former, I listened to 'Outside Inside' by the Levellers and Paul appeared in my head: a vegan who inherits his uncle's butcher's van.

I went to university in Sheffield to study English Literature, and I concentrated on having fun for a few years. But the characters from my novel were demanding to be written about, coming to life. Life kept intervening, but I began working hard, writing in my spare time.

In 2010, I graduated from the Writing MA at Sheffield Hallam University. I had finally finished my first novel, 'Outside Inside'. A few edits later, and here it is!

I left my full time job in 2013 to launch a freelance writing business, Wild Rosemary Writing Services, and I love helping people to tell their stories.

I still live in Sheffield, and I love it. In the summer, you'll find me at music festivals, volunteering for Oxfam.

And if you spot a mistake in 'Outside Inside', let me know, and I'll buy you a cider (if you're over eighteen), and credit you in the next edition.

3915501R00187

Printed in Germany
by Amazon Distribution
GmbH, Leipzig